THE NIGHT NURSE

COLE BAXTER

INKUBATOR
BOOKS

Published by Inkubator Books
www.inkubatorbooks.com

ISBN (eBook): 978-1-83756-054-7
ISBN (Paperback): 978-1-83756-055-4
ISBN (Hardback): 978-1-83756-056-1

1

"Shhh, don't breathe," Laura muttered as she hid under the side table in the formal living room. She sat, her knees pulled up to her chest, her eyes squeezed shut as she listened for her mother.

"Laura Marie!" her mother screeched, slamming open the kitchen door. "When I find you, you little brat, I'm going to beat you fucking stupid!"

Laura made herself as small as she could, but she was shaking from fear at her mother's words. She had only gone to play at the edge of the neighbor's yard with their dog, but her mother didn't like her doing that. No. She said it made her smell like an animal, and the last thing she could abide was a child who smelled like an animal.

But the dog was just a little thing, and she'd only been tossing a ball to her. She'd heard her mother come out the back door shouting, and Laura had quickly thrown the ball, then sprinted back to her front yard and in through the door to the living room before her mother returned to the house. However, she must have heard the dog barking and seen Laura make her way from there.

"Where the fuck are you?"

Her mother stomped through the room, and then Laura heard something metal scrape against the stone of the fireplace. What had she picked up?

Taking a chance, Laura lifted the edge of the tablecloth and peeked out. Her mother stood two feet from her, brandishing the black iron fire poker. Her heavyset body shook with each step; her fat face was flushed with either anger or exertion—Laura wasn't sure which. Her curly dark hair was a mess, but that was normal. Her mother didn't really care about her appearance.

Laura must have made some sort of sound, because her mother paused and spun back around, coming toward the table. Laura made a split-second decision to try to escape. She backed out from the table, put it between her and her mother, and then took off running behind the couch toward the front hall.

Her mother screeched again, a horrible sound, as she swung the iron poker and shattered the vase on the table. She came toward her from the other side of the couch and swung again, missing Laura by an inch. But her third swing, Laura knew she wasn't going to get away from. She saw it coming and attempted to block it with her arm, but the edge caught her temple. The next thing Laura knew, the world disappeared.

LAURA WOKE, screaming. Her whole body was shaking as it had that day. The day her mother had whacked her in the head with the fire poker. She'd woken in the hospital with a concussion, one her mother had told the doctors she'd gotten while playing outside on the front drive. Laura hadn't dared to contradict her. That would have resulted in an even worse beating. She had wondered why her mother had even bothered to bring her to the hospital in the first place. It wasn't as though she had cared about Laura. Then Laura had looked around the room and seen her father. He had actually looked somewhat worried.

Laura recalled that the doctors asked her what had happened, but she'd just shaken her head and said she didn't know. There was no way she had been going to tell them her mother had struck her with a poker, when her mother was standing right there. The doctors had then explained that she was going to have a pretty gnarly scar on her forehead after the stitches came out. They weren't wrong.

She reached a hand up and traced the scar. Thirty years had passed, and the thing was still there. Still grooved into her right temple, just above her eyebrow. If that day had taught her anything, it was to avoid being seen as much as possible. And if she was going to play with the dog, she had to do it when her mama wasn't home, and then immediately take a shower.

Laura had actually gotten pretty good at avoiding her mother's abusive hand for the most part, at least until her brother was born seven years later. Billy had been a surprise, a happy one for her and her dad, but not so much for her mother. Mama had hated being pregnant. She'd complained constantly and had made Laura wait on her like she was some ill lady of the manor.

After Billy had been born, Laura had been put in charge of him—when she wasn't in school, of course. At thirteen, it had been her job to make sure Billy was fed, changed and always clean. If he woke in the middle of the night, it was up to her to see what he needed. Mama couldn't be bothered to do it; she'd had to sleep so she could go to work in the mornings. Mama had been a teacher. None of the kids had liked her; she had been just as mean and nasty to them as she was to Laura at home.

Laura scrubbed a hand down her face and shifted her thoughts away from her now-deceased mother. There was no point in going over how terrible the woman had been to her and to her brother and... well, to everyone. Even the school had eventually asked her to retire because of some of the allegations from students and their parents. By that time, of course, Laura was already out of the house.

"Stop it," she murmured. "Stop thinking about her; she isn't worth it." Laura closed her eyes and took three steadying breaths. When she opened her eyes, she glanced at the other side of the bed where her husband, Jim, should have been, only to remember that he'd left her.

Jim Larson, the community college English teacher who liked to have students call him 'professor'. Especially if those students were nineteen, blonde, and naïve. The exact type of girl he'd left Laura for.

It had taken her a little while to even realize that he was cheating on her. He'd claimed he'd had to work late, and she'd just missed him in passing, but nope. She'd gotten suspicious and found him canoodling with the nineteen-year-old in his office. So Laura had kicked him out. Eighteen months of marriage to the man, and Laura was just now wondering what in the hell she'd been attracted to him for. It wasn't as though he was all that handsome. Or even charming. He just looked... normal. Maybe that was why she'd settled for him? Because he looked normal, quiet, non-abusive. He had a stable job.

And she'd wanted to get married.

She'd wanted that happily-ever-after that she gave all of the main characters in her romance novels. She'd gotten nothing even close to it. Instead, she had massive credit card debt, thanks to him, as well as two car loans in her name, all because his credit had been shit, and she'd been naïve. The lease on the apartment was in her name, but she could no longer afford it and all the debt she now had to pay off because of him.

Climbing out of bed, Laura moved into the bathroom. Most of it had been packed up, all except what she'd need for today. She'd finally found someone to sublet the apartment until the end of the lease, and she was moving back to the estate.

She couldn't even call it home. It had never been home. It was just the place where she'd lived until she could move out on her own. But now she didn't have a choice. She had to go back. Not just because of her finances, though that was a big part of it, but also because of her father's failing health.

She and Billy had gotten into numerous arguments over him in the last two weeks. Billy wanted nothing to do with him; he blamed their father for not saving him from their mother. He'd been just as abused by her as Laura had been. However, Laura had come to realize that their father had also been abused by her mother—he was just in denial about it. She'd seen it often as a child, and on rare occasions when she'd come back to see Billy.

Billy was her one regret over having left the family home at the age of eighteen. He'd only been five years old. She'd worried about him frequently and had made sure to get him away from there as often as she could. However, while going to school, it was hard to have him visit her as often as she'd wanted or he'd needed. Billy didn't blame her in any way for that, though she did blame herself. Maybe he wouldn't resent their father so much if she had.

Sighing, she brushed her teeth and then finished fixing her hair by pulling it up into a ponytail. She changed out of her nightgown and into a fitted T-shirt and jeans. Today was moving day, and she was not looking forward to it. She still had several boxes to pack before the movers arrived. Well, not movers exactly. More like her best friend Kelly, Kelly's husband Jack, and his friend Adam, who were going to take her furniture and things to a storage facility, because she wasn't sure which things she wanted to keep and which to sell.

She probably should sell it all, but she had hopes that staying at the estate would be temporary. That once she had her father settled and on a good routine, she'd be able to get her own place again and just visit him daily to be sure he was following the doctor's orders. However, those thoughts would have to wait until she actually spoke with his doctor and figured out what his routine should be.

Her father was being very stubborn about giving her any information. It had been Sam who'd called her and told her that he wasn't doing well. He'd also asked that she and Billy come and stay for a while to see what could be done about the old man.

The thought of Sam made her smile. Sam Willoughby was the man who took care of the house and gardens on her father's estate. He'd been there a good ten to fifteen years, so he knew her father pretty well. He'd known her mother too, unfortunately. Laura was looking forward to sitting down with him and finding out exactly what had been going on to make Sam call her and Billy.

Two hours, three loads of laundry, and forty more boxes packed later, there was a knock on the door. Laura dragged her forearm over her forehead, wiping away the sweat, and then answered the door. "Hey, Kelly, come on in. Where are the guys?" She smiled, opening the door wider.

"Jack is parking the truck. He and Adam will be up in a minute. Do you know where you want all this stuff?" Kelly asked as she hugged her.

"Diamond Storage. They have a three-month deal, so it will give me time to figure out if I'm going to be able to keep any of it."

Kelly looked around at everything. Nothing was brand new; it was all just stuff she'd collected along the way. Jim hadn't really contributed anything in the furniture department. He'd already gotten all his shit out the day she'd told him to leave. It hadn't been much. Just a TV, gaming system, and his clothes and personal items. She still had no idea where he'd gone when he'd left, and she didn't really care, except that she needed to find him to send him the divorce papers.

"Is it even worth trying to sell?" Kelly asked, interrupting Laura's thoughts.

"Hey!" Laura frowned, her hands going to her hips.

"Come on, Laura, it's like... nothing matches; you got everything from thrift stores and Goodwill."

"It's perfectly good furniture, and it's comfortable. And besides, the mattress and bed frame are new."

"Uh-huh, and you want to continue to sleep in the same bed that the sleazebag slept in?"

The thought hadn't actually crossed her mind until Kelly brought it up. "Damn it. I liked that bed," she muttered.

"Ha! You said *liked*." Kelly grinned.

"If I get rid of it all, it's going to take me that much longer to move back off the estate." Laura sighed.

"True, but you'll start fresh at least."

"Ugh. Fine. The furniture can go to Goodwill, and then the boxes can go to storage. Well, except for those. Those are going with me."

"What's in them?" Kelly asked, walking over to the group of about twenty-eight boxes.

"My books, computer, TV, clothes, personal items, that kind of stuff. Oh, and my stuff for work."

"We could get these loaded up in your car while the guys get the furniture moved out and take it to the dump... er... Goodwill."

Laura glared at her friend. "Not funny. It's all perfectly good furniture."

"And you are a grown woman who should own real furniture, not this stuff."

"Fine." Laura sighed. "Okay, let's get this stuff down to the car. Melissa is moving in tomorrow, so I have to get it all done today."

Kelly hefted a box and started toward the door. "Keys?"

"Got them," Laura said, grabbing them from the counter before picking up a box of her own and following Kelly out.

"Hey, guys," Kelly said as they ran into her husband and his friend in the hall, "just the furniture for now. Laura agreed to get rid of it, so you can take it all to Goodwill."

"For real? You're getting rid of it?"

Sighing, Laura nodded. "I guess so."

"Did Kelly talk you into it?" Jack lifted a dark blond brow, then sent Kelly a look that Laura couldn't decipher.

"Well, she made a good point."

"Oh?"

Kelly answered, "She's an adult and needs real furniture, not this college-dorm stuff."

Jack ignored his wife and looked at Laura. "You're sure you want to get rid of all of it? It's your stuff, not Kelly's."

"Yeah, I know. But yeah, she's probably right. I don't even know when I'll be moving to my own place again, so if I get rid of it, I can get a smaller storage unit."

"Okay, if you're sure."

Laura smiled. "Once you guys get back, we'll get the rest loaded up to take to the storage place."

"All right, sounds like a plan." Jack nodded, and then he and Adam—who was a handsome, muscular guy—got started carrying out the furniture while Laura and Kelly filled up her car with the boxes that she was taking with her.

Just as they were about finished with everything, Laura's phone rang. She grabbed it from the counter and accepted the call. Accepted being the operative word—it was Billy.

"I thought you weren't speaking to me," she said wearily.

"I'm speaking to you. I just don't think what you're doing is worth all the trouble you are going to."

"He's our father, Billy. Just because you blame him for what Mom did to us doesn't mean we shouldn't do what we can for him. He's our family."

"He's a bastard who still denies that Mom abused us!"

"You're right, he does, and he's probably never going to acknowledge it, but he needs help, and we can't just leave everything on Mrs. Shepard and Sam."

"Well, I don't have to be the one to do the helping, and neither should you! He's got money, just hire some more people to take care of him—hell, make him move to some old folks home and let them deal with his shit."

"You know he won't leave the estate, and full-time care is super expensive. Besides, I'm kind of in a bind and need a place to stay until I can get things back under control."

"Is the divorce final yet?"

"No, we go to court in a few months."

"What's taking so long?"

"I don't know. Do I seem like someone who can make the courts move faster?"

"No, I'm just... I'm just frustrated, Laura. You shouldn't be doing this. Jim shouldn't have left you with such a mess!"

"It's my fault. I took out the loans; I allowed him to use my credit cards. I was stupid. So I'll fix it, but first I have to have a place to stay."

"I wish you could just come here, but..."

"Yeah, I'm not moving into a college dorm with you." Laura laughed.

"Well, we could get an apartment..."

"You don't have any money either, except what's in your scholarships and grants. You don't need to be spending that money on an apartment just so I have a place to live. I can stay at the estate. It'll be fine."

"I guess, but I still think you're wrong to do this."

"I know."

"Call you later this week?"

"Sure," Laura agreed. "Love you, little brother."

"Love you too, sis."

Laura hung up the phone and shoved it in her pocket. Kelly was waiting for her at the door. "Let me take one more look around just to be sure I've got everything."

"I'll go down to the truck with the boys."

Laura nodded and watched her walk out of the apartment. She methodically opened every cabinet, drawer, and closet in the apartment, as well as the dishwasher and fridge to be sure she'd gotten everything out and that it was all clean for Melissa. Everything looked perfect. She grabbed her purse, pulled her keys from her pocket, and locked the place up before heading down to the office to drop off the keys for Melissa.

There were just two things left to do. Finish dropping off the things to the storage unit and then driving to the estate. As she climbed into her car, she felt an overwhelming bout of depression sweep over her. She began to cry.

Her life had turned to shit in the blink of an eye, and she was struggling to deal with it. When she reached the storage facility, she did what she could to wipe the tears from her face, but Kelly still noticed them.

"What's the matter?" she asked, pulling Laura into her arms.

Laura sighed. "Just everything is wrong, you know? It wasn't supposed to be like this."

Kelly nodded into her neck. "I know. Maybe you should talk with someone."

Laura snorted. "Isn't that what I'm doing with you?"

"Don't deflect. You know what I mean. A professional.

You've been through a lot, Laura, and you've never really dealt... well, with your mom, you know?"

Laura did know. And maybe Kelly was right. Maybe talking to a therapist was the way to go. She'd have to see if she could afford it once she reached the estate. "I'll see."

"Now, let's get this finished so you can get settled. Do you want me to come with?"

Laura shook her head. "No. I think it will be bad enough with me moving in. Dad won't want anyone else there too." She sighed.

"Well, you call me if you need to see a friendly face, okay?"

"Okay." Laura gave her a watery smile. "Thanks, Kelly— you guys, too. I don't know what I would have done without your help today."

"No problem. Adam suggested beer and pizza. You up for it?" Jack said, wrapping an arm around Kelly's shoulder.

"Not for me; I've got to get on the road. It's about a forty-five-minute drive." Laura gave them each a hug; then Jack handed her the key to the storage unit. She climbed back in her car, gave them a wave, and set off for her father's place.

2

Radcliffe estate was set on four acres of land, with the house taking up one and a half of it. The rolling front lawn was a half-acre, and then the backyard consisted of the other two. Of course, Samuel's small three-bedroom caretaker cottage sat toward the back of the property, so those two acres weren't just lawn. There was also a pool, cabana, gym and hot tub, a large back garden, and a pond.

After the incident with the neighbor's dog, her mother had insisted that her father put in a fence around the property, so now there was a large stone wall with a gate at the front, and iron fencing along the property lines as well.

Laura pushed the button at the gate and waited.

"May I help you?" a voice came through the call box.

"Hi, Sam, it's Laura."

"Hey, Laura, I'm so glad you're here. Let me get the gate open for you, and I'll be over to help you move stuff in."

"Oh, thanks, Sam, you know you don't—" Laura started.

"It's my pleasure, darlin'," he said before she could finish.

"All right, then." Laura shook her head. Sam had always

been very kind to her... and, if she was honest, she'd had a major crush on him for a long time.

True to his word, the gate opened and then closed behind her car once she'd driven through, and then he met her on the front drive. Laura took a final sip of her soda from the drive-thru she'd stopped at and tossed the empty cup in the bag of trash from her on-the-go dinner.

"It's so good to see you," Sam said as she climbed out of the driver's seat.

"It's good to see you, too." Laura smiled and popped the hatchback on her car.

"Your old man is sleeping, so best we go as quietly as possible. Where do you want these?"

"My old room, I guess." She jogged over to the garbage can by the large six-car garage and tossed her trash away, then returned to the car.

"I'll get started, then." Sam grabbed two of the boxes from the back of the car as if they weighed nothing.

It took them thirty minutes to get everything up to her old room, which was still just as sterile as it had been when she'd been growing up. There was nothing to distinguish that a little girl had once lived in it. It held a double bed with a cherrywood frame, a matching nightstand, desk, and dresser. There was a lamp with a green shade on the nightstand along with an alarm clock. The green shade of the lamp matched the striped comforter on the bed and the curtains over the windows.

"Do you want me to move your car to the garage?" Sam asked. "You look worn out."

Laura sank down on the bed. "Yeah, would you mind?"

"Not at all. I think there's some stuff for sandwiches in the fridge, and the cook put leftovers of chicken curry in there, too."

"Chicken curry?" Laura couldn't recall if that was something her father should be eating or not.

"I know, the spice isn't good for him. But he insists, and with no one here to tell him no…"

Laura sighed. "He gets his way."

"Yes."

"I'll talk to Mrs. Shepard."

"Oh, I guess you haven't heard, then. Mrs. Shepard quit. He hired someone new. Um, I think her name is Mya Bakshi."

"Great. Let me guess: Dad said something offensive to Mrs. Shepard?"

"He threw his plate of food at her."

Laura groaned. "Okay, I'll send her an apology, along with the offer of a reference, and a gift basket."

"I think she's aware there is something wrong with the old man, but she wasn't going to put up with that. Mya has been here for less than a week, but she only comes in to cook dinner for him. She doesn't do the other housework."

"Please tell me you aren't doing it."

Sam chuckled. "No, the cleaning service still comes in twice a week. Mrs. Shepard just took care of the day-to-day stuff."

Laura nodded. "Any trouble yet, as far as this Mya is concerned?"

Sam shrugged. "Not that I know of, but give it time. He's pushing everyone away."

"When we spoke on the phone, you said he's throwing tantrums, yelling and stuff, but also gets confused and forgets things. Do you know what the doctors have said?"

"He won't tell me, but I've picked up some of his meds, and I know they're for dementia. Which doesn't surprise me, based on his behavior."

"He's not going to get better, is he?" Laura said softly, half to herself and half to him.

"Not many do." Sam put his hand on her shoulder and

rubbed it. "I'm sorry, darlin'."

"It's okay, Sam. Thanks for doing what you can for him around here. You're staying on, right? You're not planning to quit?"

"No, of course not." Sam smiled at her. "I should go now and let you get settled in. Don't forget, if you're hungry, there's sandwich fixings in the fridge."

"I'll be fine. I ate while I drove." Laura couldn't stop the yawn that took over her a moment later as she pulled her keys from her purse.

"I'll leave your keys in the kitchen on the rack." He took them from her and then paused and pulled a paper from his shirt pocket. "Here, thought you might want this. It's the Wi-Fi password."

"Oh, thanks, Sam."

"Have a good night, Laura. I'm glad you're home."

Laura took the paper from him and smiled. "Thanks, Sam. Can't say I'm glad to be back, but it is good to see you."

He chuckled as she closed the door behind him.

She stared at all the boxes, the couple of bags and her suitcase. She didn't even know where to begin with unpacking all of it, or even if she wanted to. She wasn't sure what she wanted to do, but she wasn't hungry, and despite the yawn, she wasn't tired.

Her thoughts returned to her mother and then to Jim, the asshole cheater. She recalled Kelly's suggestion of a therapist. It was a valid idea. She just wasn't sure she could swing it. As a romance novelist, she made pretty good money. She wasn't rolling in it like J. K. Rowling, or Nora Roberts, but she did pretty well. Well, decent. About equal to what she'd make if she were teaching again.

It had been enough when she'd lived on her own, and enough to have a nice wedding. But not enough to cover all of the debt Jim brought to the marriage, let alone the debt he'd incurred after they were married. In less than two years, he'd racked up over seventy thousand dollars in debt. How that was even possible, she didn't know, because they had nothing to show for it. Well, except for his car, which he'd insisted be a top-of-the-line Mercedes. He'd sworn he'd cover the bill, but she had yet to see even one cent from him toward it.

"There's no going back now, Laura. It's done; all you can do is deal with it," she told herself.

Expelling a breath, she dug through a box labeled *work* and pulled out her laptop. She'd bubble-wrapped it just to be on the safe side because she couldn't afford for it to be damaged at all. After booting it up, she put in the Wi-Fi password that Sam had given her and went through her email. She answered a few fan questions and sent her publicist her new address, along with a sample of her newest manuscript for marketing.

There was so much more than just writing when you were a romance novelist. When she'd first started out, she'd had to do everything on her own, because she hadn't gone the traditional route, but had instead self-published. Now she had an entire team: a publicist, an editor, beta readers, and a virtual assistant who helped her keep things on track. The team helped her market and reach more readers. That didn't mean there wasn't still a ton of work she had to do nearly daily. There were blog posts to write, fan mail to answer, author interviews... and she still had to find time to actually write.

She'd taken three days off to pack and move and get settled, but that didn't really mean three days off. It meant *mostly* three days off, during which she still had to make sure her blog entries that she'd written beforehand were posted; that her editor, Erin, had updates on where she was on her latest project, and her publicist, Jacklyn, too; and that her fan mail was answered.

So once she finished all of that, she cleaned the computer and was about to close it down when Kelly's idea drifted through her mind again. She decided to look at her finances and see what she could afford now that she wasn't paying rent and utilities, nor having to buy food. After about fifteen minutes of doing some calculations, she figured she had enough to start seeing a therapist if they weren't too expensive. With that in mind, she began looking them up on the internet.

An hour later, she had it narrowed down to three. She decided she'd call the one closest to her father's place tomorrow and set up an appointment. She wrote down the name and number to the office, and then closed everything down.

Setting her computer aside, she opened her suitcase, grabbed her nightgown and toiletries, and left her room for the bathroom across the hall. The room still held the blue towels she and Billy had used as kids. Even the blue rug was in place. Nothing had changed in at least twenty years.

She quickly changed into her nightgown, went through her evening routine and then headed back to her old bedroom and closed the door. She climbed into bed and turned off the light, but it was another hour before she fell asleep.

THE NEXT MORNING, Laura woke at six a.m., dressed and headed down to the kitchen. She was surprised that her father wasn't awake yet but knew that he'd be down any moment to find something to eat. After checking the fridge, she pulled out eggs, cheese, mushrooms, peppers, and spinach, and then a package of bacon. She turned on the stove and began scrambling the eggs and chopping the veggies to go with them.

A noise at the entrance to the kitchen drew her attention, and she noticed her father coming into the room, shuffling his feet in his slippers.

"What are you doing here?" he demanded.

"It's good to see you too, Dad. Would you like some breakfast?"

"I want waffles."

"I'm not making waffles. I'm making scrambled eggs with veggies and bacon."

"I want waffles!" He stomped his foot, picked up a kitchen chair and slammed it back down again.

Laura took a deep breath, counted to ten and then calmly said, "I'll make you scrambled eggs with veggies and bacon, and you're going to eat them."

He threw himself into the chair and sulked. "Can I at least have some coffee and the paper?"

"Of course. I'll pour you a cup as soon as it's ready." Laura switched the coffee maker on and got it started. "The paper is on the counter."

Grumbling, he got up and moved to the counter, grabbed the paper and then shuffled back to his seat. "Don't know why you're even here," he muttered.

Laura poured the egg mix into the skillet. She laid the bacon in a second pan and put it on the stove, too. "I'm here to help you. I understand Mrs. Shepard quit."

"Nosy old woman," he muttered. "Wouldn't fix me the dinner I wanted."

"So you hired someone who would, I take it?"

He smirked. "I did. Best curry I've had in years."

"And you shouldn't be eating it."

"You mind your own business!" He glared at her.

Laura turned back to the food and finished scrambling the eggs. She decided to placate him for a while until she could figure out what was going on with him. Once everything was ready, she set his coffee and plate in front of him, then sat down with her own.

They ate in silence. Then without even a "thank you", he dropped the paper on the table and walked out of the room.

Laura rolled her eyes and sighed. "This is going to be so much fun," she muttered under her breath.

She finished eating and then pulled out her phone, finding the name and number of the therapist she planned to call. Taking a breath, she dialed the number and waited. She hoped it wasn't too early, glancing at the clock to check the time. It was just going on eight.

"Dr. Fischer's office, this is Amanda. How may I help you today?"

"Good morning, Amanda, my name's Laura Radcliffe. I'd like to make an appointment with Dr. Fischer."

"Yes, ma'am. Are you a regular patient?"

"No, I, well, I've never seen a therapist before."

"I see. Is it urgent that you speak with her? Is it an emergency situation?"

"Well, I don't know about an emergency, but yeah, the sooner I can see her, the better."

"Okay, well, she does have an open window from ten to ten thirty for a call-in session, would that work for you?"

"Oh, yes, that would be great. Um, I hate to ask, but... how do the, uh, the payments work?"

"The initial consultation is free, which is what you'll do over the phone this morning. After that, it depends. Some insurance will cover the cost; some won't. I'll have to run yours to find out what's covered."

Laura hadn't even thought to see if her insurance would cover it, and she really hoped that it would. She gave Amanda her information and waited.

"Lovely, you are covered with a small co-pay."

"That's amazing, thank you so much. Do I just call back at ten, then?"

"No, ma'am, Dr. Fischer will be calling you right at ten, so be sure to have a quiet place you can speak to her."

"That sounds perfect, thank you." Laura hung up the phone and started to clear the table.

"What do you need a shrink for?" her father asked, sounding suspicious.

Laura jumped and bit her cheek. She hadn't noticed her father lingering in the doorway. Obviously, he'd heard way more than she'd intended for him to hear. "I'm just going through some stuff right now and need to speak to a professional, that's all."

"You're going to complain about your mother! That woman does everything around here, and you're going to go bad-mouthing her to this shrink!"

Laura frowned. It sounded as though her father thought Mom was still alive. "Dad, you know Mama is gone, right?"

"Of course she's gone; she's at work, isn't she! Teaching those damn brats some manners!"

"No, Dad. Mom died three years ago. Remember?"

"What? I don't..." he started and looked confused, then stubborn. "Of course I know she died. I'm not stupid." He turned and shuffled out of the room.

She could hear him moving through the living room as something glass hit the floor. "Dad!" She set the plate down and ran toward the living room. "Dad, are you okay?"

"Who put that blasted table here? Whoever did it is fired! Can't even walk in my own damn house!"

"Come on, Dad, why don't you go in your study and watch the business report. It should be on about now." She guided him away from the mess and toward his study.

He grumbled but allowed himself to be pulled away.

· · ·

LAURA SPENT the next hour cleaning both the kitchen and the mess from the broken glass lamp that had been on the table. She carried the pieces out to the garbage and ran into Sam.

"What happened?"

"He ran into the table, knocked it over." She wiped her hands on her jeans.

"Did he have his meds this morning?"

Laura blinked; had he? She had no idea. "Where does he keep them?"

"Kitchen cabinet next to the sink."

"Then no, he didn't." She sighed. "Is he supposed to have them before he eats?"

"Doesn't matter, I think. He just needs to take them."

"Okay, I'll give them to him. Thanks for letting me know."

"No problem. I usually check on him since Mrs. Shepard's not here anymore, but I'll leave him in your hands now that you're here."

"Thanks, Sam." Laura waved to him as she went back into the house.

She headed to the kitchen, found her father's medicine and read all the bottles and noted when they were supposed to be taken. She gathered them up and then filled a small glass with water and took them to her father in the study.

"Here, Dad, you need to take these."

"No."

"Come on, Dad. You have to."

"I'm busy."

"It will take less than twenty seconds."

He sighed, took the glass and the pills and swallowed them, drinking down the water. "Happy?"

"Ecstatic." She grabbed the glass and left him on his own. As she headed out the door, she said, "I'll be in my old room if you need me, but I'm going to be on the phone from ten to ten thirty, and I need quiet, okay?"

He just waved a hand at her as she left the room.

Laura headed upstairs and closed the bedroom door. She still had time before her call, so she did a bit of work, wrote out a new blog post about one of her characters, and answered some more fan mail. At ten minutes till ten, she pulled her phone out and set it next to her as she worked.

When it rang, she immediately answered. "Hello? This is Laura Radcliffe."

"Ms. Radcliffe, this is Dr. Vera Fischer. I understand that you need to speak to a therapist?"

"Yes, yes I do." Laura closed her laptop so she wouldn't be distracted.

"Well, why don't we start with some basic information? How about you tell me a little bit about yourself and the situation that is causing you problems?"

Laura nodded and then shook her head, realizing the doctor couldn't see her. "Okay, yes. Well, I'm not even sure where to begin."

"Wherever you like. I usually suggest at the beginning."

Laura gave her a half-laugh. "I don't know that we have that much time, but, well... you see, I grew up in an abusive household, but that's not really my main problem right now. I got married about two years ago, and I thought Jim was a good man, but, well, it turns out he wasn't. I caught him cheating on me."

"Okay, that's a lot to unpack in just a thirty-minute call."

"I know." Laura sighed. A noise made her look up. She saw her door cracked open. "Would you excuse me for just a minute?" She got up off the bed and opened the door to find her father in the hall listening in on her conversation. "Dad, what are you doing? I told you I was making this call."

He glared at her. "Just don't want you saying anything about your mother, God rest her saintly soul."

Laura reined in her temper. "Dad, go back downstairs. I'll

be down soon, and we can talk."

He glared again, but Laura closed the door in his face and locked the handle. "I'm sorry, Dr. Fischer. That is the other issue I'm having right now. I filed for divorce from my husband and had to give up my apartment to move back to my parents' place, because, well, my husband left me in a huge amount of debt, and because my father has dementia and needs help."

"So you've moved back to a household where you were abused as a child?" She sounded gravely concerned.

Laura's eyes strayed to the door as she softly answered, "Yes, but the one who did that is no longer living, and it wasn't just me who endured it..."

"Laura, can you not speak freely?"

"About that subject, at the moment, no. Might we revisit it at our next session?"

"Of course. So you've mentioned your husband left you in great debt?"

"Yes, I was stupid and allowed him to use my credit cards, and I took out loans for him. I was naïve to think that he would pay them."

"Why did you take out the loans for him, or let him use your cards?"

"Well, his credit was bad. He told me that his former wife had done exactly what he's done to me. I didn't even find out until recently that the whole thing was a lie. He'd never been married before. He'd just gambled away all his money and declared bankruptcy, and that was why he couldn't get any credit."

"Is that what he did with the loan and your cards?"

"Well, one was for a car that was really out of my price range, but I did it anyway, because I thought... I don't know what I thought. I guess I just wanted to make him happy. I wanted him to love me."

"Is that why you let him use your cards? Because you wanted him to love you?"

Tears slid down Laura's cheeks. "Yeah, I guess so. I mean... I really wanted to be happy, you know? I wanted that happily-ever-after..." She sniffled into the phone.

"I see." Dr. Fischer paused for a moment. "Laura, what do you do for a living?"

"I'm an author. I write romance novels," she answered.

"Ah. So you've been looking for the kind of love you write about. I tell you what, our time is nearly up, but I want to delve into things a little more deeply on our next session. Let's set it up for an hour, twice a week. Can you come into the office?"

"I can try, but as I said, I'm here to take care of my dad, so I'm not sure I can leave him alone just yet."

"Alright then, why don't we plan for you to come in, but if that won't work, just give Amanda a call the morning of, and we'll do another phone session. Right now, let's look at Tuesdays and Thursdays at ten. Does that suit you?"

"Yes, that would be fine."

"Then we will talk next week on Tuesday. If you get overwhelmed, you call me." Dr. Fischer gave her a private cell number for emergency use. "I mean it. You've moved back into a home that you were abused in; it's possible you might experience some night terrors or have some extra anxiety."

"Okay. Thank you, Dr. Fischer."

Laura hung up the phone and put it in her back pocket and then opened the door. The hallway was thankfully empty, so she rushed across to the bathroom and cleaned up her face. Now that she had someone to talk to for herself, she needed to see about what she could do for her dad. And that meant finding out exactly what the doctors had told him.

With that in mind, she headed down to confront him in the study.

3

"D ad?" Laura called as she hit the bottom step.

He didn't answer, but she could hear drawers slamming in the kitchen. Laura hurried toward the sound. "Dad, what are you doing?"

"Can't find my damn keys!"

"Your keys for what?"

"For the car! For the car, what do you think? For the henhouse?"

Laura shook her head at that. They didn't even have a henhouse. "Dad, you can't drive, remember?"

"Of course I can drive! Don't tell me what I can't do! I have to go to work; I've got business to discuss with Williams—"

"Dad, you're retired."

"I'm not! I'm..." He looked befuddled for a moment. "Where are my keys?"

Laura sighed. She tried a little white lie to get him to stop thinking about work. "Oh, um, Williams called to say that he has everything under control, and to enjoy your vacation..."

He looked taken aback for a moment, then nodded. "Vacation?"

"Yes, remember you took some time off to spend relaxing?"

"Well, I needed the break, didn't I? I worked my ass off for years, providing for your mother and you and Billy." He seemed unsure and slightly grumpy.

"You did. And you deserve this break. Now why don't you sit down, and I'll make us some lunch. Whatever kind of sandwiches you want."

"I want turkey and mayo."

"That sounds great. How about some iced tea to go with it?"

He nodded as he sank into a chair, still looking a bit out of sorts.

As she worked, she could hear him grumbling about ungrateful kids who didn't appreciate everything he and their mother had done for them. Laura nearly snorted at his description of the happy family he'd deluded himself into believing they'd had.

A few minutes later, she set the plate down in front of him and waited until he was about halfway finished before handing him his afternoon pills. "Dad, what's the name of your doctor?"

He looked at her suspiciously. "Why?"

Laura didn't want to tell him that she wanted to go over his diagnosis, so she gave him another little white lie. "I just want to make sure I'm giving you the right pills at the right time."

"You just want to be nosy, that's what you want!"

She sighed with frustration. "I just want to be a help to you. I can't do that if I don't know what I'm doing."

"Fine, it's Dr. Temple. Number's in the phone book on my desk, but don't go bugging him."

"Of course not, Dad. I just want to be sure I know what I'm doing."

He grumbled some more, but he finished his meal and then yawned.

"Maybe you should take a nap, Dad. You've had a busy morning."

"Maybe I will." He nodded.

"Why don't I walk upstairs with you to your room?"

"I don't need a babysitter. I'm not a child!"

"I know that. I'm just worried about you."

"Don't need anybody fussing over me. Your mother doesn't fuss. She's too busy to fuss, just like you should be! Why are you here?"

"Mom's not here, Dad; she died. I'm here to help you."

He completely ignored the first part of what she'd said, but she'd seen the flicker of confusion just before he answered, "I don't need any help."

"Fine, Dad. You don't need any help."

"That's right." He nodded as he kicked off his slippers and climbed into bed.

Laura pulled the blanket up to his chin and said, "Get some rest, Dad." She quietly backed out of the room as he closed his eyes. She pulled the door closed and returned downstairs to clean up the lunch mess. Once that was finished, she headed for the study and flipped through her father's phone book to find Dr. Temple's number.

"Dr. Temple's office, how may I help you?"

"Good afternoon. My name is Laura Radcliffe. I'm Michael Radcliffe's daughter; I believe he's a patient of Dr. Temple's?"

Laura heard some keyboard clicking, and the receptionist said, "Oh, yes, ma'am. You aren't listed as someone we can speak to about your father's health."

"I'm sure I'm not; he doesn't want any help. However, I think I still need to speak to Dr. Temple, if that's at all possible?"

"I will check with the doctor. One moment, please."

Laura heard the phone switch to hold, and some kind of elevator music played on the line. She stayed like that for ten minutes; then finally the nurse came back on the line. "Hello?"

"Yes, Ms. Radcliffe? Dr. Temple has agreed to speak with you. Hold just one moment while I transfer you."

"Ms. Radcliffe? Dr. Declan Temple, I understand you need some information about your father?"

"Yes. You see, I've moved back to the estate to help out because, well, the staff has either quit or is threatening to quit, and Sam—he's the caretaker of the property—he called to say Dad has been having extreme temper tantrums and throwing things. I felt I needed to step in, but he, of course, won't tell me anything. I know from what Sam has told me that Dad has dementia, but... well, I need more details."

"I see. Well, yes. I did explain to your father that he'd probably need full-time care as the disease progressed. That was about six months ago. If he takes his pills on a regular schedule, the rages and tantrums should be minimal. However, this disease is progressive. Over time, he'll need more and more care. It's a daunting task, Ms. Radcliffe. Are you capable of being there full-time to care for him?"

"Yes, I, well, I work for myself, so I can be here to do that. I just need to know what he's allowed and what he isn't. Is there a diet he should be following? Is there something he should avoid eating or drinking?"

"As the dementia progresses, you might want to stick to finger-style foods, fruits, bite-size things like chicken nuggets, french fries, carrot sticks, berries. Not eating can be an issue, but we've noticed that if you offer a variety of colors, dementia patients tend to eat more. He should avoid alcohol and caffeine as much as possible."

"I did notice that the coffee was decaffeinated—at least,

I'm pretty sure it is. I'll double-check that. Why the finger-style foods though?"

"As this disease progresses, patients tend to lose motor skills and have trouble holding utensils. They also have trouble with multitasking, so it's best to let them eat in quiet and not converse with them, because they'll forget to eat."

"Okay. Is there anything else I should know?"

"Yes, dealing with dementia patients can be tough. There are a few things you should avoid if you can. Things like reminding him your mother has passed away. Or asking him what he wants to eat. It would be best to just allow him to continue to think she's alive somewhere, but not home. I know that sounds, well, cruel, but it only upsets them when they don't remember and you remind them that they don't remember."

"I see. We've done that a few times already." Laura sighed. "I'm not sure what to do about the food thing, though. His regular housekeeper quit, and he hired this woman I've not met yet to cook him spicy food. I didn't think he was supposed to be having that."

"He's not. You'll have to have a talk with her. No spicy foods. They should be mostly bland. Salt and pepper are fine, but the spices will give him heartburn and can lead to an irritable bowel."

"Okay, thank you. Can I call again if I have questions?"

"Of course. I might not be able to answer right away, but if you leave a message, I'll get back with you as soon as I can."

"Thank you, Dr. Temple."

Feeling much better about what she was in for with her father, Laura logged his office number into her phone right under Dr. Fischer's. With that finished, she headed back up to her room to grab her computer. She wanted to get some writing in before Mya showed up to make dinner and her father woke from his nap.

She brought the laptop down to the kitchen and sat down at the table where she could look out the windows to the backyard. She could see Sam out there weeding in the garden. It made her smile.

She spent the next two hours working on her latest manuscript, getting three chapters finished before the kitchen door opened and a small Indian woman came into the room.

"Hello," Laura said.

"Oh, miss, you startled me."

"I'm sorry. I'm Laura, Mr. Radcliffe's daughter. I understand my dad hired you?"

"Yes, just last week. He said he wanted to have spice, and that I can do." She smiled.

"Yes, I'm sure you can—except he's not allowed to have spice, per his doctor's orders."

The woman's face fell. "But what will I fix, then?"

"The doctor said basic simple foods. Grilled chicken, mashed potatoes, that kind of thing would be fine. Salads…"

"No, Mr. Radcliffe, he ask me to do spicy, so that is what I will do."

"Right, and I'm telling you no."

"Then I cannot work here." She took the key off her key ring and handed it over to Laura. "I'm sorry."

"I'm sorry, too. I'll make sure you get paid and a nice reference."

The woman merely frowned, then left through the kitchen door without another word.

"Damn it. Now what?" Laura muttered. She hadn't pulled anything out to fix for dinner and knew she had to think of something quickly. "Grocery delivery!" She sat back down at the computer, pulled up the online grocery service and placed an order for things that fit the menu that Dr. Temple had suggested.

She knew her father wasn't quite to the point of having to eat finger foods yet; she'd seen him use a fork just fine this morning. However, she still wanted to make sure it was good but bland food. She didn't have her father's credit card number, so she used her own debit card to place the order, then headed to the study to see if she could track down his financial records. That was something else she'd have to make sure was in order.

With her story forgotten for the moment, Laura spent the next hour going through his finances to make sure everything was good. She even put in a call to his accountant, Mr. Pippen, and he agreed to issue her a card for household and food expenses, once she explained what was going on. By then the groceries had arrived. Laura put them all away except for what she planned to use for dinner.

She decided on baked chicken, mashed potatoes and a leafy green salad with berries. It would be fairly simple to make and wouldn't take too long. As she set those things in the fridge, her father came downstairs.

"Did you sleep well?" she asked.

He nodded, looking confused.

"We're having baked chicken and potatoes for dinner. Mom's recipe."

"Where is your mother?"

Laura cursed herself; she shouldn't have said anything about Mom. "Um, I guess still gone?"

"What time is it?"

Laura glanced at the clock. "Just gone on three."

"She'll still be at the school, then. You'd better have the kitchen cleaned up before she gets home. You know she doesn't like a mess."

"I know." Laura bit her cheek in frustration. "Why don't you go sit on the deck and get some sun, Dad?"

"That's a good idea. I'll read the paper out there."

"But you—" Laura stopped herself. She'd been about to remind him that he'd already read the paper, but then thought better of it. "I mean, would you like a glass of tea?"

He nodded.

Laura poured him a glass and followed him outside.

4

"Dad, dinner's ready," Laura said as she stepped out to the back patio. "Come inside and eat."

"No. I'm not hungry," he muttered as he continued to hold the paper up in front of his face.

Laura sighed in frustration. Dinner prep had taken her a bit longer than she'd imagined it would, as she wasn't used to the oven, which was old and temperamental. It really needed to be replaced; in fact, the entire kitchen needed to be updated, because everything in it was at least thirty years old. She'd have to call the accountant, Mr. Pippen, to see if there were funds for that.

"Dad, I made Mom's chicken. It's getting cold."

"Is your mother home yet?"

"Um, no, Mom is working late."

"Oh?"

"Yeah, she said for us to go ahead and eat." Laura hated lying to him, but Dr. Temple had said not to remind him that she'd died, so she didn't feel like it left her with much of a choice but to lie.

"Then we'd better go eat it before it gets cold. Why didn't

you just say that?" he grumbled as he folded up the paper and set it on the table next to his chair before coming into the house.

Laura wanted to remind him that she did say exactly that, but it would just lead to an argument. Instead, she followed him to the dining room table and sat down in the seat that had always been hers while growing up.

"Where's your brother? Why isn't he here?" he demanded.

"Billy is at school."

"This late?" He looked surprised.

"Yes, he had some after-school event to go to."

Her father gave a nod, accepting her reply, then dug into his food.

They continued to eat in silence until he was nearly finished, and then Laura got up and went to the kitchen to get his evening pills. When she returned, he was pushing away from the table.

"Where are you going, Dad?"

"I want an after-dinner drink."

Laura started to panic. He couldn't have alcohol anymore. "Um, don't you want dessert? I, um, I have your favorite, mint chocolate chip ice cream." She'd tossed it into the online cart at the last minute, thinking maybe it would help to settle him down some.

He stopped at that and looked at her. "Ice cream would be good."

Laura smiled. "I'll go fix you a bowl while you take these." She handed him his pills and waited until he swallowed them before taking their plates to the kitchen and fixing him a small bowl of the green mint chocolate chip ice cream. "Here you go, Dad, just as I promised."

His eyes started to droop as he ate, and he began to yawn.

"It's been a long day," Laura murmured. "We should head up to bed."

"Need to wait up for your mother," he mumbled, sounding extremely tired.

"Oh, Dad." Laura softly sighed. "Mom had to go to a teacher's conference, said she wouldn't be home until really late."

Her dad's brow furrowed, but then he nodded.

Laura started to clear the table, but he stopped her.

"Leave it. Mrs. Shepard can deal with it. Help me up the stairs. These damn pills make me stumble."

"Okay, Dad." She set the bowls back down on the table and gently took his arm. She walked with him up the grand staircase to his room in the central section of the house. While he took a shower, she pulled out a set of pajamas for him and then left the room. She returned and knocked on the door about ten minutes later.

"What!" he called out.

"Um, I just wanted to come in and say good night?" She gently opened the door.

Her dad was dressed in the pajama bottoms with the top in his hands, as if he was trying to figure out how to get it on. "Can't find the damn sleeves!"

"Maybe let me look?" she said calmly.

He shoved the shirt at her with a glare.

Laura quickly unbuttoned the shirt and held it open for him. "Here's the sleeves."

"Blasted thing," he grumbled as he slid his arms in and then buttoned some of the buttons, but they weren't quite right. "Where's your mother? She always knows how to deal with this thing."

Laura didn't say a word as he climbed into bed. She pulled the covers up over him, kissed his forehead and turned out the light. "Night, Dad. Get some rest."

He didn't say anything, as he'd already fallen asleep.

Laura felt extremely depleted as she quietly left his room

and headed down the stairs. It was just going on six thirty, not even dark out yet. She quickly cleaned up the dining room and did the dishes, shoving them in the ancient dishwasher and setting it.

Through the window, she noticed Sam outside near one of the garden beds with the hose pointed at some roses. Smiling, she finished up and decided to go for a walk in the garden to clear her head. And if Sam wanted to talk, well, she wasn't going to say no to that. Seeing him was the brightest spot of her day. She moved through the patio door and down to the yard, following the stone path through the yard to the garden.

She walked up next to him quietly and murmured, "Hi, Sam."

Sam looked over at her, his brown eyes lighting up as he smiled at her. "I see you made it through the first day."

Laura sighed, feeling every bone in her body aching with fatigue. "Yeah, but at what price? I'm so exhausted. I don't know how I'm going to do this every day and make my writing goals, you know?"

Sam's smile faded, and he looked at her with concern as he shut off the hose that he was using to water the flowerbeds. "Maybe you should hire some help? Like a nurse or a health aide? Someone to take the burden of the daily medical stuff from you."

Laura shrugged. "I just don't know if Dad would work with a nurse; he's pretty stubborn. He doesn't even want me here, from what I can tell. But since now I have to watch him and take care of the house—Mya is no longer going to be coming in to cook, so I'll have to do that too—and I still have my work... I might have to actually hire someone. I don't know. I'm just... overwhelmed, you know?"

Sam reached out and stroked her arm. "You shouldn't have to be dealing with all of this on your own. You deserve better than that. You deserve to have someone taking care of you."

Laura gave him a smile. His hand on her arm was so comforting and sweet; it sent a secret thrill through her. She felt a wave of disappointment when he took his hand away. "Well, I have you here to listen to me when I need to chill, so maybe it'll be okay."

Sam looked at her gently, but seriously, as if trying to make her understand something that he wasn't saying. "I will always be here for you, darlin'. That still doesn't mean you shouldn't hire some help. No one can do it all, darlin'. Even I have a teenager who comes to help with the yard a few days a week."

"You do?"

Chuckling, Sam nodded. "I'm not getting any younger, and in case you haven't noticed, this estate is pretty big. Takes a lot of work to keep it looking good."

Laura smiled as she looked out into the evening light across the estate. "I suppose it does. Thanks, Sam. I'll keep the idea in mind and speak to Mr. Pippen about getting some extra help. I need to call him anyway, about updating the kitchen. I think the oven is about to go out, and the dishwasher sounds like—well, I don't know what, but it's loud."

"I don't think your dad bothered replacing anything after your mama passed on. She'd been planning an update before she died, from what I recall."

"I'm surprised she didn't do it years ago, honestly."

"She didn't do much kitchen work. She left it all up to Mrs. Shepard."

"Yes, I'm sure she did. She always did like playing lady of the manor." Laura rolled her eyes.

"She was very good at ordering people around," Sam agreed.

"I'm definitely aware of that." She shook her head, trying

to rid her mind of thoughts of her mother and how she'd acted like she was better than everyone else. "Enough about her. I don't want to think about her anymore."

"Tell me about your latest project," Sam said.

"Oh, it wouldn't interest you." Laura laughed. "It's just another silly romance."

"I've enjoyed reading all the stories you've written, and I didn't find any of them silly."

Laura was startled. "You've read my books?"

Sam nodded. "Of course. I even read your blog."

Blushing, Laura looked down at the ground. "I... I didn't know that. Oh God, you must think I'm a sex-starved lunatic!"

He laughed. "Not at all. Why would you say that?"

"Well, they aren't exactly close-the-bedroom-door romances..."

"No, but they are very sexy." He winked at her.

Laura felt her cheeks heat. She didn't know what to say. "Um, I think... I think I'd better call it a night." Her heart was racing at the thought of Sam reading her words.

The light in Sam's eyes dimmed slightly, but he smiled. "Sweet dreams, darlin'. I'm sure I'll see you tomorrow."

Laura nodded, then practically ran back up to the house. Her heart was beating extremely fast, and she was finding it hard to breathe properly over the fact that he'd read some pretty racy scenes that she'd written. Sam, the man she'd had a crush on for years, had read her work. Hell, a couple of the scenes she'd written with him in mind. That thought alone had her sprinting up the stairs to splash water on her very hot face. She couldn't even fathom facing him again. How would she look at him now, knowing that he'd read those scenes? It was so embarrassing!

Slowly, her heart decelerated, and she began to breathe properly again. He couldn't know that she'd written some of them with him in mind. No one knew that, so he couldn't.

That made her feel a little bit better. She decided she could either be happy that he'd read her work and enjoyed it, or be embarrassed about it... and she wasn't going to be embarrassed. Hell, she worked hard at her craft, and she was damn good at it. She didn't have anything to be embarrassed about.

That thought made her feel even better. So, smiling, she headed across the hall, sank down on her bed and opened up her laptop. She still had more work to do to stay on track to meet her publishing deadline.

At midnight, Laura shut down her computer and headed downstairs to make sure the house was locked up. She probably should have done that prior to running upstairs, but she'd had other things on her mind at the time. Now she checked the doors and windows, then headed into the kitchen to make sure there was enough fixings to make her dad some waffles in the morning. She set everything out on the counter so it'd be ready for her when she woke up.

She went back upstairs to get ready for bed, making a mental list of everything she needed to remember to do the next day. That was something she'd need to start writing down, because she felt sure that she'd forget something important.

She was still listing things she needed to do as she drifted off to sleep.

5

"Hey, Sam?" Laura called, waving to him in the garden. It was Monday evening, and Laura had just realized that she was supposed to have her first actual in-office therapist appointment in the morning, and she wasn't sure if she'd be able to leave her dad on his own.

"Hey, darlin', how ya doin'?" he asked as she approached.

Laura wasn't quite sure how to answer. She was very overwhelmed, she was behind on her writing, and her father had been giving her fits. Having mini-temper tantrums that were leaving her at her wit's end. She shrugged. "Okay, I guess. Mostly just hanging by a thread, I think." She sighed.

"Anything I can do?"

"Actually, that is why I came out here. Um, I need a favor."

"Of course, whatever I can do, you know I'll help," he replied.

"Um, well, I have an appointment tomorrow with my therapist, and I'd... well, I'd like to go to her office for it? It's just in town, and it's only, like, an hour long, so I wouldn't be gone too long..."

"Sure, no problem. I can keep an eye on the old man for a couple of hours. My assistant will be here, so I can just get him busy on the back section and then come up to the house to watch over your dad."

Laura felt a wave of relief wash over her. "Oh, thank you! I don't know what I would have done if you'd said no. I just can't do another phone appointment with Dad lurking about and listening in."

"He did that?"

"Yeah, with my first one. It was so distracting; I felt like I couldn't talk about the stuff I needed to talk about." She sighed and looked out over the nearby pond at the ducklings splashing about in the water.

"They're cute, aren't they?" Sam smiled as he, too, looked at the water.

"They're so tiny and fuzzy." Laura grinned. She turned her gaze back to him. "I'm supposed to be there at ten, so I'll leave around nine thirty, okay?"

"Sure, no problem."

She reached a hand out and gripped his arm. "Thank you, Sam. You have no idea how much I appreciate this."

"It's no trouble at all, darlin'. You've got the code for the gate, right?"

Laura nodded. "Yes, thank you. How often do you change it?"

"About once a month. Probably should change it again, since Mya is gone now."

"Oh, yeah, that's probably a good idea. How do I take care of that?"

"I'll take care of it after you get back tomorrow. You don't need to worry about it."

Laura blushed. "Okay, well, thank you. I appreciate it."

The next morning, Laura took a quick shower and then headed down to make breakfast for her and her father. She filled a mug with decaf for him and fixed herself some instant caffeinated coffee. Her father joined her a few minutes later at the table and, without saying a word, sipped his coffee and read the paper.

Laura set his plate of eggs and bacon with a side of toast down in front of him and then joined him at the table. "Dad, you need to eat."

"When I'm done with the paper."

"Your eggs will be cold."

Grumbling, he folded the paper and set it aside. He picked up his fork and immediately dropped it. He started swearing, and Laura quickly hopped up and grabbed him another. "Here, a nice clean one. That one must have had some grease on it or something."

He swiped it from her hand and held it firmly as he took a bite of his food.

Laura sank back down into her chair and began to eat as she watched him out of the corner of her eye. He seemed to be doing okay, so when she finished, she got up and got his pills ready. She brought them over to the table and handed them to him. "Here you go."

He took them without fussing and then picked up the paper again and began to read.

Laura cleared the table as he grumbled, "Where's Shepard? She should be doing that."

"It's Mrs. Shepard's day off." Laura had gotten used to explaining away the people who were missing in her father's life. She had to stop looking at it as lying to him and just think of it as making his life easier. It made hers easier, too. "Sam is going to come visit with you today."

"What for?"

"I think he has some estate things to talk about with you."

Her father nodded. "What time? Did he schedule an appointment?"

"He did. Nine thirty." Laura loaded the last dish in the dishwasher. "I have some errands to run, so you'll have a quiet house to speak to him in."

"Good." He stood up, then looked as if he wasn't sure why he'd just done that.

"Your business report should be starting in a few minutes. I don't want to keep you if you want to go to your study and watch it."

"I do. I'll be in my study." He shuffled out of the kitchen through the living room.

Laura moved to the doorway to watch and make sure he made it in there without any trouble. She made another mental note to have the maids rearrange the living room so that he could make it through the room without running into anything anymore. Just one more thing added to the list of the many things that needed doing. She still hadn't managed to call the accountant to ask about upgrading the kitchen, something that really needed to happen.

She decided to do that now, while she was thinking about it. Once she got Mr. Pippen on the phone, she explained what was going on with the oven and dishwasher and asked if the household funds would cover that.

"Yes, I recall your mother had planned to do that before she passed. There are funds to cover those sorts of expenses. I'll shift it to the household account, and you can make the purchases."

"Thank you," Laura said, then decided to ask another question. "Also, I was wondering... I've been considering hiring some staff to help with Dad, a nurse and caregiver. Is that possible?"

"Allow me to go over the estate accounts, and I'll get back with you on that, alright?"

"Of course. It's just I think he really needs full-time care that I can't do on my own, and I know he doesn't want to leave the estate..."

"I know he has been adamant about staying in his home. I'll do some calculating and call you this afternoon, Ms. Radcliffe."

"Thank you again." Laura hung up.

She still had an hour before she needed to leave, so she ran upstairs and got her laptop. She decided to make a list of daily chores and then went into her calendar app and put in everything that she had scheduled to do for each day. She set reminders for giving her father his medicine, and then even started planning meals.

By nine twenty-five, she had two weeks planned out. Glancing up, she noticed Sam coming up onto the patio, and she got up to let him in. "Hi, Sam, thanks for doing this."

"No problem, darlin'. Where's the old man?"

"In his study. I told him you had some estate business you needed to go over. I hope that's all right?"

"That's fine. I'm sure I can think of plenty of things to discuss with him. You don't have to worry."

"I'll be back in time to make lunch; I hope you'll stay."

Sam smiled. "I'd like nothing more."

"Great. I'd better get going if I don't want to be late." Laura shut down her computer and moved it to a shelf out of the way. She grabbed her keys from the rack and headed down the hallway to the laundry room and out through the garage door.

It took her fifteen minutes to get to Dr. Fischer's office in town. Nervous, Laura headed into the small building and found the receptionist.

"Good morning, how may I help you?"

"Hi, I, um, have an appointment with Dr. Fischer? I'm Laura Radcliffe."

"Yes, of course, Ms. Radcliffe. Dr. Fischer will be right with you."

A few minutes later, she was directed to go back to the office, and she spent the next hour talking to Dr. Fischer about her childhood. She told her about the verbal and mental abuse, as well as the physical things that her mother had done to her.

"And CPS was never called?" Dr. Fischer asked.

"No, my mother never marked me where anyone would see it, well, except for the one time with the fire poker, which she blamed on me falling on the front drive."

"I see." She nodded. "Have you had trouble sleeping? Since being back at the estate, I mean?"

"Some, but I haven't had any nightmares. I think by the time I actually go to bed, I'm too exhausted to even dream."

"Yes, I imagine taking care of someone with dementia can be quite a tiring task. However, you do need to be making sure you're getting plenty of good sleep. I want you to try going to bed an hour earlier than you have been, all right?"

"I can try," Laura agreed.

"Now, back to the childhood trauma. How do you think you've coped all these years? Your honest opinion."

Laura thought about it. "Well, I didn't blame myself for the abuse, if that's what you mean. I knew Mama's reasoning for it was wrong. She'd gaslight me, but I knew what she was doing. I mean, I didn't know that's what it was, but I knew it was just how she was. I learned how to avoid her ire, for the most part, after the poker incident. I learned to be a ghost of sorts, at least, until Billy came along. It got harder after that. And then, of course, I got out of there as soon as I could. I wish I could have taken Billy with me. I know he suffered from her abuse, and I feel guilty that I wasn't there to protect him from it. I think that's where most of my trauma comes from."

"You realize it wasn't your job to protect him? You were a child yourself, Laura."

"I know that, but it still doesn't change the way I feel."

"Does your brother blame you for leaving him there?"

Laura shook her head. "No. He blames Dad for not standing up to Mom and defending him, telling her to stop."

"He's not wrong, you know. Your father was the other adult in the home. It was his job to protect the two of you from her abuse."

"She wasn't any better to him, you know. She'd belittle him, talk down to him... she wasn't nice to anyone, really."

"I understand. That still doesn't take away from the fact that he should have done something about her abuse when she first started behaving in an abusive manner."

Laura sighed. "I am aware, but isn't it all beside the point now? I mean, Mom's dead. It's not as if she's coming back to continue to abuse us."

"True, and I am glad that it doesn't seem to be causing you too much trouble in your daily life. I do, however, think it is why you chose to marry a man who also treated you badly."

Laura knew what she was getting at. "I think you're probably right. I mean, I didn't go looking for a man who would treat me badly. I don't think I deserve to be treated badly or anything like that. I just got taken in by him. Maybe I'm a bad judge of character?"

"Maybe. I want you to make a list of all the things that attracted you to him in the first place, and we'll discuss it at your appointment on Thursday."

"Okay."

"Then that's it for today. I'm glad you were able to make the trip to the office. It is less of a distraction for you when you don't have to worry about anyone overhearing what you have to say."

"I'm glad, too. Thank you, Dr. Fischer." Laura left the office and headed back to the estate.

A FEW DAYS LATER, Laura startled awake. A loud crashing sound from downstairs had made her jump awake in a panic. Her first thought was that someone had broken in. With her heart hammering in her chest, she grabbed her robe and pulled open her bedroom door. She hurried down the hall, down the stairs and toward the sound of something metallic hitting the kitchen floor. She ran in and hit the lights, then gasped. "Dad! What are you doing?"

He was standing in the middle of the kitchen with the utensil drawer in his hand and all the silverware spilled on the floor. There was also a scattering of pots and pans, as if he'd swept them out of the cabinet to the floor. That must have been the initial crashing sound she'd heard.

"Can't find a damn thing around here!" he screamed and slammed the drawer to the ground as he reached for another drawer.

"Dad, stop! I'll find it! Whatever you need, I'll find it for you! Please!" She rushed over to him, stepping on a fork and wincing as the tines dug into her bare foot. "Ow, Dad, please stop." She grabbed his hand and pushed the drawer back into place before he could drag it out. "What are you looking for?"

"Batteries! Can't find the blasted things so I can watch my report!" He jerked his arm from her, and his elbow slammed into her face.

"Ow!" Laura cried out. She gasped at the pain radiating from her nose. She grabbed it with one hand, rubbing it.

Her dad looked at her in confusion and then murmured, "I'm... I'm... sorry... I don't..."

Laura took a breath and then said, "Okay, batteries?" She nodded, still holding her nose and trying not to cry. "Okay, I know where they are... come on... just sit down, and I'll get them for you." She guided him over to the kitchen table and chairs. "Here, sit down."

Once he was seated, she went to the fridge, pulled open the freezer and took out the batteries he'd need for the TV remote. As she headed back to him, avoiding the utensils scattered over the floor, she glanced at the clock. It wasn't even six a.m. yet. "Dad, your report doesn't come on for two hours."

He looked at her, confused, and then looked at the mess all over the floor. "Wh... what happened in here?"

Laura stared at him in exasperation. She wanted to scream at him, but instead she took a deep breath and counted to ten. "A raccoon got in. It's gone now."

"But how?"

Laura shook her head. "Who knows? Maybe they can open doors now."

"Don't be ridiculous, Laura."

"Look, why don't you go have a shower, and I'll get this cleaned up and start breakfast. Okay?"

He stood up and looked around, then down at his pajamas. "How did I get down here in my pajamas?"

Laura rolled her eyes. "The raccoon must have woken you."

He nodded slowly but looked utterly confused again.

"Just go, Dad. Unless you need me to help you up the stairs?"

"I can do it myself," he muttered, waving a hand at her to back off.

Frowning, he left the room, and Laura sank down into a kitchen chair and started crying. This was too much. She couldn't take much more without having a complete mental breakdown. She needed to get some help. The sooner the better.

6

The bridge of her nose throbbed. Laura was pretty sure it was slightly swollen, but she didn't have time to go look in the mirror. She was too busy fixing her dad's breakfast. Yawning, she plated the waffles and set the plate on the table, then grabbed the syrup, adding it to the table as well. She fixed their coffees and then made up her own plate, taking it to the table, but her father hadn't returned yet.

Sighing, she went to the stairs and looked up. "Dad?"

He didn't answer.

Frowning, she climbed the stairs, crossed the hall and knocked on his door. "Dad? Breakfast is ready. Are you dressed?"

The room on the other side of the door was silent. Taking a chance, she opened the door and poked her head in. Her father was seated on the edge of the bed, staring at the floor.

"Dad?" She moved into the room and noticed he was dressed in a pair of slacks and a button-down shirt, only the buttons weren't done right, and his feet were bare. He held a mismatched pair of socks in his hands. "Dad, let me help you."

He looked up and asked, "Laura? What are you doing here? Where's your mother?"

Biting the inside of her cheek, Laura answered, "Mom left for work fifteen minutes ago." She moved to the dresser, pulled out a matching pair of socks, and then bent down to his feet, sliding them on for him. "Oh, I think one of your buttons are off. Let me fix that." Before he could reply, she had his shirt unbuttoned and rebuttoned quickly.

"If your mother's already left, I'm going to be late to the office."

"Mom left early. She had a meeting with the teaching staff. Plenty of time. Let me grab your slippers." She went over to the side of the bed and picked up his slippers, then returned to him. "Here you go."

He looked at them in confusion. "Where's my dress shoes? I need to go to the office."

"You have more time on your vacation. You don't have to go to the office. Williams is calling later to give you an update."

He silently put his slippers on. "Laura, I'm hungry."

"I know, Dad. I've got waffles waiting for you in the kitchen. Let's go eat."

She walked with him down the stairs and to the table, where they ate in silence. She gathered his pills and handed them to him once he was finished eating, and then sent him off to his study to watch his business report, even though it was still too early for it to come on. She was so exhausted she didn't know how she was going to make it through the entire day. She wished she could go back to bed, but that wasn't going to happen. There was just too much to do.

All of the things she needed to do passed through her mind. The new appliances were arriving later that afternoon, so she needed to be available for that. She still had numerous chapters to write, and she hadn't answered any fan mail in a week, so that was on her to-do list. She had another project to take care of for Dr. Fischer, and she wanted to talk to Sam again. Not to mention all the things she had to do for her dad.

And her nose still hurt.

Once the kitchen was clean and the dishwasher was running—for the last time, she hoped—she grabbed an ibuprofen and swallowed it with a glass of water and then went upstairs to dress for the day. A look in the mirror told her she was right, her nose was swollen and red, and there were dark circles underneath her eyes. She dabbed on a little bit of concealer, but it didn't do much to disguise the swelling or the darkness above her cheekbones.

Sighing, she headed downstairs and outside for a few minutes of fresh air. She had just stepped onto the back deck when Sam looked up from weeding the garden. "Hi, Sam." She waved, hoping he couldn't see the swelling or dark circles.

Sam grinned and stood up, pulling off his gloves. He joined her on the deck, and his smile slowly faded. "What happened, darlin'?" he asked, gripping her chin and looking at her face.

"Dad had an episode this morning. I got in the way, I guess. His elbow caught me in the nose." She gestured to her face with a rueful smile.

"You should put some ice on that." He had a concerned look in his eyes. "Sit down; let me get you an ice pack." He drew her over to the chair and sat her down. "I won't be a minute."

Laura sighed. She liked how he took care of her, and wished that he'd been the one she'd married, not Jim. But, of course, she and Sam had never dated. She didn't even think he looked at her in that way. Sure, he called her *darlin',* but that was just Sam's way. She was sure he called the checkout girls at the supermarket *darlin'* too. It wasn't anything special.

Sam returned and put the ice-filled plastic bag on the bridge of her nose. "There. Now hold that there for at least fifteen minutes, and hopefully the swellin' will go down."

"Thanks, Sam."

"My pleasure, darlin'. How's the old man doin' now? Is he better?"

"I don't know about better, but he's calm for now. He's watching his business program." She sighed. "Sam, I think... I think I'm going to hire a nurse or two. I can't keep this up. I'm so tired." Laura's voice was small and defeated. She looked down, and tears shimmered in her eyes.

Sam knelt down in front of her and tipped her chin up. "Laura, there is nothin' wrong with hirin' more help. Your father can afford it, and you shouldn't be runnin' yourself ragged trying to do everythin'. His accountant got back to you, didn't he? Said there was plenty to cover a couple of full-time nurses, so do it."

Laura nodded. "Mr. Pippen said there was plenty of savings readily available to hire someone. I just... I don't want to feel like I failed my dad," she said meekly.

"You're not failin' anyone, darlin'. You're doin' what's necessary."

Laura gave him a small smile. "Thanks, Sam. You always seem to know what to say to make me feel better."

"You make it easy." He winked. "The new appliances arrive today, don't they? That should help with the meals, I should think."

"Yes, they should be here after lunch. Will you make sure they get in the gate?"

"Of course. I'd best go get the weedin' done, so I can help get them in later. You'll be alright?"

"Yes, thank you, Sam." Laura nodded.

"I'll see you later." He winked again and headed back down to the garden.

Laura stayed where she was for a few more minutes, holding the icy bag to her nose. Talking to Sam had her making up her mind, and she decided to give Billy a call and let him know what her plans were. She headed back inside, dumped the ice in the sink and threw the plastic bag away, then went upstairs to grab her phone.

A glance at the clock told her that it was still early enough to catch Billy before he went off to his first class. The phone rang a few times before he finally answered.

"Hey," he said when he picked up.

"Hi, Billy."

"Okay, what's the matter?" he questioned.

"Nothing. Everything's fine except…"

"What's he done now?" Billy demanded.

Laura sighed. "He hasn't done anything—well, not that he can control anyway. It's just… this is a lot more work than I first imagined. Dad's dementia is getting worse."

"I told you not to move out there, didn't I? Let him figure it out for himself! It's not like he'd help us if we needed it!"

"Billy, that's not true—"

"That is true, and you know it! He's proved it, hasn't he? He never lifted a finger to help us when Mom was beating the shit out of us! Or screaming at us! Not one word did he say in our defense!"

"I know, but—"

"But nothing! I can't believe you are actually there and helping him! He doesn't deserve it! He doesn't deserve to have anyone help him! He's an evil old man, and I hope his brain rots!"

"Billy! That's enough! He's our family, and he's not evil! He was just as abused as we were by Mom! You think she didn't beat him or scream at him? She did! I saw it!"

"Whatever. If all you called to do is defend him, then I'm getting off the phone!"

"Wait! No... that isn't why I called! I need to talk to you!"

"Fine. You have three minutes."

Laura sighed. "Thank you. Look, I called because, well, I can't do this all on my own, and—"

"Don't even think about it! I'm not coming home! I can't believe you'd even ask!"

"Would you stop? I'm not asking you to come home! Geez! I'm just trying to tell you that I'm going to hire a couple of nurses, or a nurse and a caregiver. People who are trained to deal with dementia patients!"

"Oh. Well, good, then you can get the fuck out of there, away from the bastard."

"I'm not leaving the estate!" Laura cried out in frustration as she tugged on her ponytail. "I'm just going to hire some help. I can't do everything that needs to be done and still work on my novels. There just isn't enough time in the day. I'm not sleeping well, and I'm so tired I can't even get two chapters written in a day right now!"

"I don't know why you're staying! There's no point in being a martyr, Laura! He doesn't care about us! He doesn't care about you! Or me! You should leave him alone!"

"Billy, I can't do that. That would be cruel and make me like Mom."

"Whatever, I've gotta go."

Laura felt defeated. "Okay... well... I love you, Billy."

"Yeah, yeah, love you too." He hung up.

Laura sat staring at her phone, tears rolling down her cheeks. His attitude hurt her heart, even if she did understand how he felt. She just wished that he could see her point too. Dashing the tears from her cheeks, she tossed her phone on the bed and went downstairs to unload the dishwasher and prepare lunch.

The afternoon passed in a flurry of activity. While her father took his afternoon nap, the delivery guys and Sam removed all the old appliances and installed the new ones. It took a little more than two hours to get it all finished and the food transferred into the new refrigerator, but everything gleamed; she couldn't wait to use it. Besides the double-door fridge, there was a brand-new, top-of-the-line stove, a microwave, a kitchen sink with a touch handle to turn it on, and a dishwasher. All of it was made of stainless steel, and she knew her mother would have hated it, which made Laura even happier.

She spent the remainder of her free time—which only meant free from her father, not free from work—answering fan mail and checking in with her assistant and publicist. She even managed to get a chapter written, not that she really liked it, but there were words on the paper, and that was what counted.

She had just closed down her laptop when her father came down to the kitchen around four thirty. He noticed the new appliances and stopped next to the table, staring at them. "Where did all this come from?"

"Mom wanted to update the kitchen." Laura shrugged as she lied through her teeth.

Her father's brow furrowed, and he slowly nodded. "I remember her saying something about that. Is she home yet?"

"Um, no... she was, but she went shopping. Something about new kitchen curtains."

"I'm going to my study. I don't want to be disturbed; I have work to do." He turned to shuffle out of the kitchen.

"Um, Dad?"

"What?" He turned back toward Laura, frowning.

"I made some iced tea... don't you want to read the paper on the deck?"

He paused and looked confused again, as if he wasn't sure what he was supposed to do.

"Look how nice it is. Let me pour your iced tea while you take the paper out and get comfortable."

He nodded, but still seemed uncertain.

Laura handed him the paper and opened the door to the deck. "I'll just be a minute with your tea."

Awkwardly moving through the door, he made it over to his chair and sank down, flipped open the paper and began to read.

Laura brought him a glass of tea a few minutes later and left him to enjoy the afternoon breeze and his paper. She noticed Sam's helper, a boy who looked to be around seventeen or eighteen using the weed-whacker along the edges of the path that led toward Sam's house. She watched him for a moment to make sure he wouldn't disturb her dad.

Seeing that he was moving away from the main house, she returned to the kitchen and put her laptop away. She pulled out the hamburger and began to prep everything for dinner. Tomorrow she would start looking for help.

7

Being Sunday, Laura decided she'd start her quest for help by researching exactly what kind of help she needed. First, though, she had to get her dad's breakfast made and him settled watching his business report so he wouldn't interrupt her.

Laura searched the house, trying to figure out where her father had gone off to. He wasn't in his study, as he normally was if he wasn't already in the kitchen. She went upstairs to see if he'd gone back to bed, but his room was empty. She made a mental note to change the bedding and clean up in there, before heading back downstairs. She searched the entire bottom floor and looked outside but didn't see him anywhere.

Exasperated, Laura pulled out her phone and called Sam. She impatiently waited as the phone rang several times before he answered.

"Hey, darlin', let me guess, your father is missing?"

Laura's brow furrowed. "How did you know that?"

Sam laughed. "He's in the garage. I was doing an oil change on the Rolls, and when I looked up, he was seated behind the wheel. We've been chatting for about fifteen minutes."

"Okay, thanks. I'll come get him." Laura hung up the phone and headed out to the garage.

Her father sat in the driver's seat of the Rolls Royce as though he was patiently waiting for the oil change to be finished so he could be off to wherever it was he imagined himself going. Laura closed her eyes for half a moment and asked for strength.

She put a smile on her face and headed for the car. "Oh, Dad, I'm so glad you're home. I've just made a ton of waffles; want to help me eat them?"

Her dad stared at her through the open window for a moment as if trying to figure out who she was and then nodded. "I could eat."

"Great, let's go inside and let Sam finish up working on the car."

He opened the driver's door and stepped out. Laura could see that he'd attempted to dress for work. He'd put on his suit pants and jacket over his pajama shirt but was also wearing his slippers. She bit her lip to keep from laughing. He'd be upset if he knew she found his attire amusing.

They headed back into the house and toward the kitchen.

"Why don't you take off your jacket. I don't want to accidentally get syrup on such a nice suit jacket, Dad."

Without saying anything, he slipped the jacket off and laid it over the back of a chair. When he sat down, Laura set his plate in front of him with the syrup and then removed the jacket and took it into the laundry room to hang up.

"Would you like milk or coffee?" she asked.

"Coffee." He picked up his fork and held it firmly as though it might jump out of his hand, staring at the waffles, which she'd taken the time to cut up for him, to make it easier. He stabbed a piece, dipped it in some syrup and slowly lifted it to his mouth, but at the last moment, the fork slipped from his hand, and the waffle splattered onto the plate.

Laura set his coffee mug down in front of him and then sat down next to him. "I'm feeling a bit silly. Let's eat like they did back in the Middle Ages..." With that, Laura picked up a chunk of her waffle, dipped it in the small bowl of syrup and then bit into it.

Looking around, her father said, "Well, maybe just this once, since your mother is at work and won't witness us eating like heathens." He smiled and then did the same with his own waffle.

"It will be our little secret." Laura inwardly cheered that he went along with her suggestion. It was moments like this that she actually enjoyed spending time with him. She regretted not doing so more often after her mom passed away.

Like Billy, she'd blamed her dad for not standing up to her mother, not stopping all the abuse she'd dished out to them all. Over the years since her mom had passed, though, her stance against him had softened some, which led to her being here now. He was still her dad. She could remember when she was little, maybe around three or four, that he'd pick her up and tote her around on his shoulders. He'd called her his little button. She'd spent time playing in his office while her mom was at school, or he'd take her to the park and they'd go out to get ice cream.

Of course, when her mom was home, he'd barely look at her, and that had always hurt her heart. She hadn't understood how jealous her mom was. She'd been about five when her mom had come home to see her dad playing with her out in the yard. They had been playing tag, chasing each other around, and Laura had been having the best time.

Her mother had stepped onto the back lawn and

demanded to know what was going on. Dad had stopped cold and told her to go in the house. Laura had scurried past her mother, afraid that she'd lash out at her, but it had been her dad whom she'd gone for. Laura had watched from the deck as her mom had begun to hit her dad.

After that, the outings with him stopped. Her mom had hired a nanny for her until it was time for her to go to school. She'd always wondered what it was that she'd done wrong for her dad to stop doing things with her. However, thinking about it now, she knew it wasn't because he hadn't wanted to do things with her; it was because her mother was a jealous, abusive woman who angered easily and had a mean right hook.

She hadn't thought about any of that in so long. Suddenly, she wished things could have been different. If they had, maybe now he would be more accepting of her being here, of her helping him through this illness.

Laura sighed. Maybe she'd need to bring all of this up with her therapist. She clearly still had issues about her parents and her relationships with both of them. She couldn't see it ever really improving, though, with her dad having dementia.

After breakfast and his medication, Laura suggested they use the new kitchen sink to wash up their sticky fingers, since it would be easier to clean, and then walked with him to his study and turned his Sunday business report show on for him. "There you go, Dad. I'll leave you alone so you can watch your report."

He looked at her with a confused expression. "Laura?"

"Yes?"

"What day is it?" He started to rise from his chair. "I should be at work—"

"It's Sunday, Dad. And you have another week of vacation. You can relax."

"I..." He shook his head as if trying to remember. He was stuck in that half-sitting, half-standing mode as he thought about it. "Sunday? Are you sure?"

"Absolutely." Laura nodded.

He nodded and sank back down in his chair. "All right, then."

She was just glad he didn't question where her mom was again. It wasn't as though she could tell him that she went to church, because her mother had never once set foot in a church. Not even when they had married. Instead, they'd gotten married at the courthouse with only her dad's older brother in attendance. Her mom had refused to tell her family that she was getting married; Laura had never even met them. It was as though her mother had no one prior to marrying Michael Radcliffe. However, Laura knew that wasn't quite true. She'd heard her mom once let slip that Michael was just like her own father, weak and malleable, which was why she chose him.

It had been during one of their epic fights after Billy was born. He'd probably been about two at the time. Dad had been overjoyed to have a son. It had been him talking about doing something for Billy's third birthday that had started it. Her mom had lashed out, threatening him and hitting him with something... Laura couldn't recall what it was, as her mother had always grabbed whatever was at hand to use.

When that started, Laura had taken Billy and gone outside to the backyard. It was still early in the afternoon. She'd taken him to the very back of the property, behind Sam's cottage—though it hadn't been his at the time—and she kept her brother away from the house for longer than she should have, because her mother had come to find them and dragged her back into the house. Laura recalled her mom screaming, and that she'd smacked Laura around and had hit her wrist so hard with the rolling pin that she'd broken it. She had cried for hours before her father had sneaked her out of the house and to the hospital to have it looked at while her mother slept.

Laura remembered that the whole time, she had been very worried about Billy on his own with their mom, since Mrs. Shepard went home after dinner on most days. Her dad had told her not to worry, though, that Mrs. Shepard had stayed and was looking out for him. Sure enough, when they returned home with Laura's wrist in a cast, Billy had been fine.

Laura tried to dismiss thoughts of her mom and all the things she'd done to them as she headed back to the kitchen and cleaned up their mess from breakfast. Once everything was in the dishwasher, which quietly hummed, she set up her laptop on the table and began looking up what kind of caregiver or nurse she needed to help care for her dad. Still, thoughts of her mom plagued her as she tried to work.

She'd made a list of everything that her father required, which included cooking, because if that was an option, she wanted to take advantage of it. She wanted someone who was strong and capable of helping him up and down the stairs, and someone who would eventually be able to help him bathe and take care of his bathroom needs when he started needing more help in that regard. Not only that, but she wanted to make sure that whoever she hired was caring and loving, and not someone like her mother. She wanted someone kind and gentle. Someone she could, maybe, end up being friends with.

Laura thought more about what type of person she was going to need and what she could afford to offer. There was plenty of room at the estate for her to offer room and board as well, so she knew that she could add that in as part of their salary. From Mr. Pippen, she had the figures of what her father could afford without draining the estate and knew that there was a limit to how much she could offer. She had to look for the people she needed in the price range that the accountant had given her.

She spent as much of the day as she could, in between making meals and taking care of her dad, looking into the available nurses and caregivers who either lived in the state or were willing to move. She made a list of all the ones she was interested in and made plans to start calling and interviewing throughout the week.

ON MONDAY, she invited one of her choices out to the estate for an interview. The woman had been a nurse for thirty years, and on paper she looked good. However, when she arrived, Laura found her voice harsh and her manner gruff. She knew that the woman would not be a good fit for her father. She reminded Laura too much of her mother, so Laura thanked her for her time, informed her that she had several other candidates to interview and she would be in touch to let her know one way or another. Of course, she already knew the woman wouldn't suit, but she didn't want her to know that.

On Tuesday, Laura went to her appointment at Dr. Fischer's office, leaving Sam in charge of her dad. That afternoon she had another two interviews, one in person and one over the phone. The latter was with a male nurse who lived in the Midwest. He sounded perfect over the phone, and she offered him the job; however, he wasn't willing to accept the salary she offered along with the move. So that put Laura back at square one. She was running out of candidates.

Wednesday, Laura didn't have time to make any calls or book any interviews. Her father had another tantrum, and it took her an hour and a half to get him up to his room for his afternoon nap. She was nearly falling over herself and decided that she, too, could use a nap, so she headed to her old bedroom and curled up on the bed. She was asleep within seconds. When she woke three hours later, it was time to cook dinner.

Thursday, after her appointment with her therapist, Laura worked with the maids to rearrange the living room. Anything breakable was carefully wrapped and put away, and the furniture was now set against the walls, leaving a wide open space through the center of the room. Once that was finished, she finally made some more calls and scheduled another couple of interviews. As she was looking at her search again, a new pair of names popped up on the list of available caregivers: a brother and sister team who specialized in dementia patients.

Laura couldn't believe her luck. She looked over their credentials and was amazed to find that their salaries fell right in with what she had available to offer. Having a good feeling about them, she decided to set up an interview for the following day if they were available.

Laura dialed the number provided and was pleasantly surprised when someone answered on the second ring.

"Hello? You've reached Bella Ormond; may I ask who is calling?"

Laura was flustered hearing the other woman's sultry voice. "Uh, hi, good afternoon. I'm... I mean, my name is Laura Radcliffe, and I'm calling to see if you'd be interested in interviewing for a possible in-home nurse caregiver position?"

"Well, I am available for a new position, but I'm afraid I'm a package deal with my brother, Andrei. You see, we like to work together to provide care to seniors in need. It just warms our hearts to be able to provide them with companionship and care."

"Oh, yes, I meant for both of you, of course. It's care for my father, Michael Radcliffe," Laura explained.

"Well, in that case, we would love to come for an interview. We've just recently lost our previous patient, such a sweet man, really. Died in his sleep, God bless him. So we are indeed looking for a new patient to care for. Did you have a day in mind?"

"Um, are you available tomorrow?"

"Of course. Would tomorrow afternoon work well for you?"

Thinking about the other interviews she booked for in the morning, she knew the afternoon would be better. "How about three o'clock?" Laura offered.

"If you'll give me the address, we'll be there."

Laura provided her with an address and hung up with a good feeling.

8

"Thank you so much for coming, Mrs. Keller. Your credentials are perfect... but—" Laura hesitated. She really was perfect except for the matter of two things. One, Mrs. Keller wouldn't agree to live on-site, and two, she could only work part-time.

"It's alright, I understand." Mrs. Keller smiled ruefully. "You're looking for a full-time, live-in caregiver."

"Yes. I'm sorry."

She laughed. "Don't be sorry for explaining what it is you need, especially when it comes to the care of a loved one."

"Thank you." Laura smiled at her. "Would you like another cup of tea before you go?"

"Oh, no, dear, thank you, though. If I have another cup, I'll be all jittery in an hour. I'd best be on my way. I do wish you luck in finding the right caregiver for your father. I'm sure they are out there."

"I certainly hope so." Laura shook her hand and walked with her to the door.

Once she was gone, Laura returned to the kitchen and cleaned their cups and saucers and then started making lunch for her and her father. She really hoped that the next interview would be the one. It was with Bella and Andrei Ormond, and she had high hopes that they would be the ones she was looking for.

At two fifteen, after having taken her father upstairs for his nap, Laura took a shower and washed her hair. She reapplied her makeup in the bathroom mirror and then got dressed. She still had dark circles under her eyes from the lack of sleep and the late hours of trying to work at night. She had a rapidly approaching deadline, and she was behind on her word count. She really needed this interview to go well and wanted to look her best.

When the doorbell rang, Laura rushed down the stairs to answer it. As she reached the door, she took a calming breath, ran her hands over her hair and then opened it with a smile. She was stunned by the two standing on the front porch.

Bella Ormond was gorgeous. She had lustrous auburn hair and blue eyes that sparkled and curves for days. Her brother, Andrei, was also extremely handsome, only his hair was dark brown. He did, however, have the same sparkling blue eyes. He looked as if he should be doing movies starring as the lead action hero. Laura could imagine him smirking for the camera as he was smirking at her, and a million women falling in love with him.

"H-hello... you must be Bella and Andrei Ormond?" Laura said, sounding breathless.

"We are. You must be Laura Radcliffe?"

"Yes, um..." Laura flushed. "Please come in." She opened the door wider, and they sauntered into the front hall as if they owned the space. "Let's head into the kitchen," Laura suggested. It was where she had all her notes and the place that she felt the most comfortable.

"You have a lovely home," Bella said sweetly as she gazed about the rooms.

"Thank you, though it's my parents', well, my father's home, not really mine, though I guess it is for the time being. I mean, I've moved back to help my dad..." Laura rambled as they all sat down around the table.

"What an amazing thing for you to do," Andrei said, speaking for the first time.

Laura about melted right there at the timbre of his voice. And the look he was giving her told her that he was very interested in her as well. Her heart raced, and her face heated at his attention. She took a deep steadying breath and waved away his compliment. "He's my dad."

"I so understand how you feel," Bella replied, laying a gentle hand over Laura's. "We lost our own father to dementia. It's what made us want to do this professionally. Take care of people together. Andrei and I make a great team." She looked at him fondly.

Laura nodded. "Well, before we get started, would either of you care for a cup of tea, or coffee maybe?"

"Oh, I'll have a bottled water if you have one?" Bella suggested.

"I'll have the same," Andrei added.

"Sure, let me just grab those." Laura hopped up and got them each a cold bottle of water and then returned to the table. "Can you tell me a little bit about your last patient?"

"Of course." Bella nodded. "Our last patient was my dear, sweet Jeremy Heath. He was such a lovely man." She sniffled. "He asked me to marry him after I'd cared for him for a short while, and I had just fallen head over heels for the man, he was such a gentle soul."

Laura blinked. She'd married her patient? "Um, how... how old was Mr. Heath?"

"Eighty-five." Bella sighed. "But he didn't look it, you know? He didn't look older than mid-fifties, and as I said, he was a real sweetheart. So of course I said yes, I mean, I didn't want to break his heart, and I did love him, God rest his soul. He had a bad heart along with the dementia, but we were managing it well. I still don't understand how he could just die like that in his sleep." She wiped away a tear.

Laura felt bad for her. She really seemed to have cared for the man despite the huge age difference. "I'm sorry for your loss."

Bella smiled gently. "Thank you. You're so kind."

"Um, so how many other patients have you cared for?" she asked.

"Well, you understand that we live with and care for patients long-term. Some we are with for more than a year or two," Andrei replied.

"If you hire us on, your father will be our fourth official patient, not counting our father, of course."

"I see." Laura nodded. "Can you tell me what kind of things you do with your patients?"

Bella said, "I like to provide nutritious meals for my patients. A healthy, balanced diet will help maintain the patient's mood—"

Andrei jumped in: "Along with a good exercise program, based on the patient's mobility, of course."

"We like to provide companionship as well as care. We'll take care of errands and appointments the patient needs, pick up medications, and provide twenty-four-hour care where we'll be there for him to gently guide him through these last few years of his life."

"We want to ease his burden, and yours," Andrei added.

Laura felt really good about their answers. "I know that as this disease gets worse, he'll need physical help with dressing and bathing. Will that be a problem?"

Andrei grinned. "I am very capable of helping gentlemen retain their egos in that area. We've learned that male patients don't like to appear weak in front of their daughters and wives, or even their female nurses." He winked at her.

Bella giggled. "The same could be said for our female patient. Lottie would have died of embarrassment if I hadn't helped her look her very best for Andrei."

"Lottie?" Laura questioned.

"Oh, she was another of our previous patients. She adored Andrei."

Laura looked at him, and he smirked back at her. She said, "Well, do you have any questions for me?"

"We haven't discussed rates," Bella began. "Since we do this because we enjoy it and want to give back to seniors, we only ask for minimum wage along with room and board. We aren't looking to bankrupt your father's estate."

"Oh, yes, I forgot to mention, there are rooms available near my father's room for you. One next to his and one across the hall. So if I hire you, that won't be a problem."

"That will be perfect. We do like to be close to our patients; it makes it easier for us to do things with them," Bella added. "I've prepared a list of references for you; do you need them?"

"Oh, yes, thank you, that's so helpful."

"And when would you be looking for us to start? Will there be a trial period?"

Laura nodded. "Well, as soon as possible, if your references check out, which I'm sure they will." She smiled. "And yes, perhaps a weeklong trial period? And if you both and my father seem to be getting on, then we'll have you move in. Does that sound all right?"

"That sounds perfect. It will give us some time to get our living situation handled before moving here."

"Oh, will you need more time?" Laura asked. "I mean, do you have a lease you need to get out of?"

"Oh, no, nothing like that. We have a pay-weekly apartment because we never know when we'll take a job. This just lets us know when to tell the staff we'll be leaving."

"Well, if that's everything, I'll give your references a call, and then if everything is good, I'll call you this evening. Does that work for you?"

"It does. I am so looking forward to helping you, Laura," Andrei said, taking her hand in his and gently shaking it.

"And I'm looking forward to meeting your father. I'm sure he's as lovely as you are," Bella added as they walked back toward the front door.

"Perhaps if this all goes right, you can both come by tomorrow and meet him?"

"That would be wonderful," Bella agreed. "I look forward to hearing from you this evening."

"Bye," Laura said, waving to them as they walked out to their Mercedes. She guessed that since they didn't have too many living expenses, they could afford that kind of car.

Once they were gone, Laura pulled out her phone and started calling. There were six references on the sheet that Bella had given her, so she started at the top. It had an out-of-state area code, and she worried that it might be too late to reach them, but they answered after the first ring.

"Heath and Mason... how may I direct your call?"

"May I speak to James Heath?"

"One moment."

"This is Heath," a man answered.

"Hi, my name is Laura Radcliffe. I'm calling to check the references for Bella and Andrei Ormond?"

"Ah, yes, Bella mentioned you might be calling. Such a beautiful lady; my father just loved her." He chuckled. "Well, he married her because he loved her so much. Though we all do, really. She was so good for him."

"I'm so glad to hear that, Mr. Heath."

"James, please call me James."

"And what of Andrei? Was he well-liked by your father, too?"

"Andrei was excellent with my dad. Got him to do things that I couldn't get him to do. Had him on a great exercise program and eating healthy foods. Seeing him those last few months with them, well, I'm just glad he died a happy man."

"I'm so glad to hear that, James. Thank you so much for your time."

"My pleasure, Ms. Radcliffe, my pleasure."

Laura hung up the phone feeling excited. It was seriously looking like she'd found the perfect pair to help her with her father. They were almost too good to be true. She had to set the references aside and start dinner, but as soon as they'd eaten, she'd get right back to it. She was anxious to get some of her life back, starting with getting a full night's sleep.

After the final reference check, where the brother-and-sister team were given a glowing reference, Laura was ready to call them and offer them the job. She was just about to call when she noticed Sam out in the garden again. She had noticed that he liked to do the watering as the sun was setting.

"Hi, Sam! Guess what!" Laura called as she went out on the deck and hurried toward him.

"Hey, darlin', what?" He turned the hose off and glanced at her with a smile.

"I think I've found the perfect pair to hire to help with Dad."

"That's great! Was it that redhead in the Mercedes with the dark-haired, movie-star-looking guy?"

"He does look like a movie star, doesn't he?" Laura laughed. "Yes. Bella and Andrei Ormond. Their references were amazing. The families loved them when they worked for them. They always work as a team and specialize in helping seniors with dementia."

"That's good to hear. So you're going to hire them?"

"Yes. I'm gonna ask them over to meet Dad tomorrow and have them start on a trial period for a week. Then if everything goes well, they'll move in and be here full-time."

"Sounds like you've got a plan."

Laura noticed a hint of something in his eyes as he spoke that looked a little like concern, but it was quickly gone, so she dismissed it. "You'll help me, right? Make sure they're getting on with Dad?"

"You can count on me, darlin'." He reached for her hand and squeezed her fingers gently. "You can always count on me."

Laura felt the heat from his fingers, and it warmed her heart. "Thank you, Sam. You don't know how much it means to me that you've been so helpful with all of this. I don't know what I would do if you weren't here."

"We'll never have to find out, will we?" He grinned.

"I hope not." Laura laughed. "Would you want to join us for lunch tomorrow and meet them? I don't know what I'm serving yet, but I'd be happy to have you join us."

"Sure, I can do that. What time?"

"Around noon."

"Sounds good." He nodded, then gestured over his shoulder. "I should finish this up and head home. You give me a holler if you need anything, and I'll see you in the morning."

He started rolling up the hose; Laura took that as her cue to head back inside. "Night, Sam." She closed the kitchen door and peeked in at her father, who had insisted he stay up to watch a movie. He seemed to be fine, so she headed back to the kitchen to make the call.

"Hello?" Bella answered.

"Bella, hi, this is Laura. Laura Radcliffe." She didn't know why, but Bella slightly intimidated her. Maybe it was her confidence or the way she carried herself, but either way, it made Laura stumble through her words, which wasn't great, since she was an author and words were kind of her thing.

"Laura, I was hoping you'd call. Did our references check out?"

"They did. Yes. They gave such lovely replies, I mean references, about you and your brother. They really seemed to have loved you. I'm... I am really excited to have you come and work with my dad. Can you come tomorrow afternoon and meet him?"

"Of course. What time would you like for us to be there?"

"How about around noon. You can stay for lunch with us."

"Perfect, we'll see you then," Bella replied before hanging up the phone.

Laura couldn't wait for tomorrow.

9

As her father sat down for breakfast, Laura made herself a cup of instant coffee and added a splash of French vanilla creamer. She drank it quietly as she waited for her father to finish eating so she could share her news. She was actually worried about how he would react to having a pair of caregivers in the house, but she wasn't going to back down. This needed to happen so that she could get back to some semblance of a normal life. Meaning, able to wake up late, spend the day writing and doing other author-related activities.

She'd posted a blog last night about how hard life had gotten recently, and how behind she'd become and asked for her fans to be patient while she sorted things out in her home life. The comments and emails had all been very supportive, thankfully.

Glancing at her father's plate, she noticed he only had a few bites left, so she got his morning pills ready for him. "Here you go." She held them out to him.

He grumbled but took the handful of pills and swallowed

them with a gulp of his decaffeinated coffee. "Hate taking these things," he muttered.

"I know." Laura sighed as she sank down into the chair next to him. "Dad, I have some news."

"What's that? Jim finally coming to get you?"

"What?" Laura was surprised that he actually recalled that she was married and whom she was married to. "No. Jim is definitely not coming to get me. Jim and I are no longer together."

"So that's why you're here; threw you out, did he?" he said suspiciously.

Laura nearly growled at him. "No. He stole all my money and left with some skanky nineteen-year-old."

"Could have told you he was no good, but you wouldn't listen," he muttered.

Laura took a breath and counted to ten. "Anyway, that wasn't my news."

"Oh?" He picked up the newspaper and opened it.

"Dad, can you put that down for a moment? This is important."

He sighed and rattled the paper, lowering it. "What is it, Laura? Can't a man enjoy his coffee and the paper in peace?"

"You have all morning to enjoy that paper, but I need to speak to you right now. So please, please set the paper down and listen to me."

Huffing, he folded the paper and set it aside. He crossed his arms and stared at her. "Well?"

"Thank you." She took another calming breath. "I wanted to tell you that I've hired some help—"

"What for? We're doing fine, we've got Mrs. Shepard and Sam and the cleaning staff that comes in twice a week. What do you need more help for?"

"Dad, Mrs. Shepard is no longer here. Sam is busy taking care of the estate itself. The help I've hired is to help you.

Bella and Andrei Ormond. They are both specialty nurses who have made a career of helping patients with dementia."

"What would I need them for? I don't have that... whatever you called it. I'm fine."

"Dad, you do need help, and you do have dementia. That's why you take those pills."

He frowned, his graying brow furrowing as he fell into a confused state. A moment later, he returned to being stubborn. "Don't need any blasted help. I'm doing fine."

"You'll like Bella and Andrei, I promise. They are coming to meet you at lunch today."

Shoving himself away from the table, he stood up. "I'm missing my business report. Call Williams and tell him I want an update on how things are going at the office." With that, he marched out of the kitchen and into the dining room. When he reached the living room, he called out, "And put this room back the way it belongs before your mother gets home!"

Laura sighed. He'd seemed so lucid just a little bit ago, but now he was back to thinking her mother was still alive. Gritting her teeth, she yelled back, "Mom is the one who changed it!" Everything she'd done was to make both of their lives easier, and she had to give her mother all the credit. It wasn't fair, but since when was life ever fair?

As she cleaned up the mess from breakfast, Laura contemplated what to make for lunch. She didn't want to serve sandwiches, which was what she normally made for her and her father. She finished up the breakfast dishes and started the dishwasher, then looked in the fridge and freezer to see what she had available to make. Grabbing a package of chicken breasts, she decided to fix grilled chicken alfredo and a salad. Hopefully that would be easy enough, and they would all enjoy it. She set the chicken in the cool water of the filled sink to defrost.

She still had a few hours before she would need to cook, so she pulled out her laptop and started going through her emails. She managed to get ten emails answered and a new blog post written, and she'd checked in with her personal assistant and publicist. She promised her editor, Erin, that she'd have something for her by Wednesday, since Bella and Andrei would be starting work on Monday. She'd just have to lock herself up in a room and spend the entire couple of days writing to catch up on where she was supposed to be. She was actually looking forward to it.

At eleven, she checked the chicken and saw that it had defrosted nicely in the cool water of the sink. After firing up the propane grill on the deck, she set about getting the water for the pasta ready. By the time Bella and Andrei arrived, she had everything ready to be served.

"Come in," Laura said, opening the door with a smile. "We're going to be eating in the dining room, if you want to go on through. I'll just be a moment. I need to get my father from his study."

"Just through here?" Bella gestured toward the living room.

"Yes, go through here, and it's on the left. Sam is already in there; he'll get you each some drinks."

"Sam?" Bella murmured.

"He takes care of the estate," Laura answered. "I'll be right back." She hurried toward the study and poked her head in. "Dad, Bella and Andrei Ormond are here, and lunch is ready."

"Still don't see why you had to go and hire strangers," he grumbled as he stood up. "Fine on my own."

"I know, you've told me a million times. I think you'll like them, though." She walked with him to the dining room.

Her father stopped in the doorway. "Is this gorgeous woman going to be my nurse?" he asked, clearly stunned.

Bella laughed. "Oh, Mr. Radcliffe, we are going to get on so well, especially if you keep those comments coming."

"You sure are a beauty. My wife is going to have a fit."

"Oh, I was under the impression that your wife had passed," Andrei said, looking at Laura.

Her dad's brow furrowed in confusion, and then his expression cleared. "That's right, she did. Guess you won't be causing her any fits." He chuckled as he moved toward Bella. "Come sit next to me and tell me all about yourself, Ms. Ormond."

"I'd be delighted." Bella smiled as she took the seat next to Laura's dad.

Andrei took the seat across from Bella and next to Laura's, while Sam took the seat on Laura's other side. Sam had yet to say anything, but he looked as though he was paying attention to the two newcomers.

"Let me go and get the meal. I won't be a moment." Laura started toward the kitchen.

"I'll help," Sam called after her.

When they reached the kitchen, Laura began fixing plates. "Sam, will you take the salads out? This one is Dad's; I've cut his up into smaller bites."

"Sure thing, darlin'." Sam gathered the bowls and headed toward the dining room. He returned a few moments later. "What else can I help with?"

"This is Dad's plate... and the French rolls, will you take these? I've got plates for Bella and Andrei; then we can come back and get ours."

"Sounds good." Sam nodded, taking the platter of rolls and her father's plate.

"Here we are," Laura said, setting a plate in front of Bella and one in front of Andrei.

"It looks delicious. You must be a fantastic cook. Your

father is a lucky man, having a beautiful daughter who can cook, Laura." Andrei gave her a sultry look.

Laura felt her cheeks heat. "Well, I hope it tastes as good as it looks." She headed back to the kitchen to grab her own plate.

Sam was close on her heels. "He's quite the flirt." He did not sound impressed. In fact, Sam made it sound like Andrei was a degenerate.

"I'm sure he didn't mean anything by it, Sam."

"I'm sure you're right, darlin'." Sam picked up his plate and followed her back to the dining room. "So, Andrei, what made you want to go into the field of nursing?" he asked as they sat down.

Andrei glanced at his sister and then Laura. "As we mentioned to Laura during our interview, our own father had dementia, and Bella and I cared for him. It made us want to continue to work together and help other seniors with the same disease."

Sam nodded. "It's good when families can work together like that." He took a bite of his pasta. "This is delicious, Laura."

"Thanks, Sam."

"Michael, are you enjoying your meal?" Bella asked.

"Not my usual meal, but it'll do," Laura's dad replied.

"Oh, you've got a little sauce... here, I'll get it." Bella popped up from her seat, took her napkin and dabbed the corner of his mouth. "There, that's better."

"Thank you," he murmured. "Messy meal, this." He pushed his plate away and then took a roll from the platter.

"I'll be sure to fix you meals that aren't messy," Bella said, with a giggle.

"You'll be doing the cooking?"

"Mm-hmm. I *am* a pretty good cook, if I do say so myself." Bella tittered.

"Bella can cook up a storm," Andrei complimented.

Laura's dad looked over at him, as if for the first time. "So what will you be doing around here?" he asked suspiciously.

"I'll be running errands, like picking up groceries and your medication. I'll help you in the mornings and evenings, getting dressed and grooming, those types of things, as needed of course. And during the day, we can exercise and converse about business, whatever you'd like."

Michael gave him a grumpy look but nodded.

Bella reached over and patted his hand. "And I'll be here to make sure you are well fed, have your meds and to entertain you."

"Now *that* I'm looking forward to," he replied, his eyes softening as he gazed at her.

Laura should have known that all it would take for her dad to behave was a beautiful nurse to take care of him. Bella was the complete opposite of her mother. She had always wondered what it was that had attracted her father to her mother in the first place. Of course, she had seen pictures of her mom when she was young, and she had been a beauty. It was just that all that beauty had left her within a few years of marriage. All that anger she had carried around didn't help.

The conversations continued for a little while after lunch was finished, and then Bella and Andrei left, promising they would arrive bright and early Monday morning, in time to fix breakfast and get her father up. Laura was ecstatic that she was finally going to have help.

Sam cleared the table for her while she gave her dad his pills and took him up to his room for a nap. When she returned to the kitchen, she asked Sam, "So what do you think?"

He leaned a hip against the counter as she began to rinse the dishes. "I think you've made a good choice; they seem to really enjoy conversing with your dad. And it seems like they want to help."

"They do, don't they?" Laura smiled as she handed him a plate to load into the dishwasher. "We still have the trial week to go through, but I think this is going to work."

"So where are you going to put them if they move in?" he asked as he filled the machine with the tableware she'd rinsed off.

"I think I'll give the room I'm staying in right now to Bella and put Andrei in the one next to Dad's." Laura had thought about it a lot. She really hated being in that room, but it was close enough to her dad's room if he needed her. However, with Bella and Andrei available to help him if he needed it, she could move to one of the guest rooms in the other wing of the house.

"Where will you go?" he asked as she put a dishwasher pod in the machine and closed it.

"I'm going to move my things to the blue suite in the other wing. It's all the way at the back, and it'll be quiet, so I can get some work done."

"I can help you start moving things if you'd like," Sam offered.

"Thanks, Sam. You really are too good to me."

"My pleasure, darlin'."

"I'll probably wait until Friday, make sure that everything is going well before I move anything."

"I'll make sure I'm free to help."

"Thank you. And thank you for helping clean up. You didn't have to do that."

"It gave me an excuse to stay and chat with you, darlin'; can't complain about that." He chuckled. "But I'd better head off now. Got some things to attend to."

"Okay, I'll see you later, Sam."

"Bye, darlin'." He waved and headed out the back door.

.   .   .

THE FOLLOWING week went by fairly quickly and smoothly. Bella and Andrei arrived every morning by six a.m., got breakfast made for her father, gave him his pills on schedule, spent the mornings with him in his study, took care of lunch and exercise and every other little thing that needed doing throughout the day. Laura couldn't have been any happier with how things were going.

The only major thing, if there was a major thing, was that Andrei flirted with her any time he saw her. Laura couldn't help but feel flattered by his attention. He was a very handsome man, after all. She was sure it was just his way, but when he looked at her with that sultry gaze of his, she felt drawn to him, and she ended up flirting back. She figured it was mostly harmless, but there were times when his gaze was a little too intense—it almost made her uncomfortable—but then he would smile, and it was as if she'd imagined it.

On Friday, she went searching for Sam to see what his thoughts were. She liked having him there as a sounding board, and he always gave her good advice. "Hi, Sam."

"Hey, darlin', how's the writing coming?" he asked as he turned off the mower.

"It's going really well. I'm caught up to where I need to be, and my editor is really happy with what I have so far."

"That's great."

"So, I wanted to talk to you about Bella and Andrei, get your thoughts..."

Sam shrugged and looked up at the house. "Can't find anything to fault them for, really. I could do without that Andrei flirting so heavily with you, but if you don't mind it, then I guess I shouldn't." He shrugged again.

Laura laughed. "Yeah, he is pretty flirty, but other than

that, Dad really seems to like both of them, and he seems to be happier. Guess I didn't realize he was so lonely."

"He's always been one to prefer being left to his own devices, so you couldn't have guessed. I think he just likes the attention of a pretty girl who isn't his daughter." Sam grinned.

"I think you're right about that," Laura replied. "I think I'm going to tell them they can move in on Monday."

"Still wanting my help to move your things?"

"Yes, that would be great, thanks, Sam."

"No problem. Let me finish up with the mowing, get a quick shower, and I'll be over to help."

"Sounds good. I'll see you in about an hour, then?"

Sam nodded. "Yeah, just got this little bit left to mow." He gestured toward a patch of yard that was taller than the rest.

Laura headed back to the house while he finished up. She found Bella and Andrei in the study with her dad, asking questions about his former business and what he recommended them to invest in. "Hey, guys. Thought I'd find you all here." She smiled at them from the doorway.

"Oh, hi, Laura. Something we can do for you?" Bella asked, glancing up at her.

"Well, I just wanted to tell you, since the trial week is just about over, I think this is going to work out well. Dad's really taken a liking to the two of you, and you've both been so great. So if you want to move in on Monday, I'll have the rooms ready for you."

"That's really wonderful. Monday is perfect."

"Absolutely looking forward to being here twenty-four seven." Andrei's eyes met Laura's, and he gave her a sexy smirk. "It will make things so much... better... being here full-time."

Laura's breath caught in her throat, and all she could do was smile. She swallowed hard and backed up a step. "Well,

um... I've got some work to take care of, so I'll see you later."
She turned and headed toward the stairs.

She hadn't actually unpacked anything since being at the estate, so moving things would be fairly easy. The only things she'd unpacked were the few outfits she'd worn and her work things. Everything else, she'd left in the boxes.

When Sam arrived, he helped her move everything except what she would need for the couple of nights she'd still spend in the room close to her dad. She planned to get up early Monday, pull the sheets and put on a fresh set before Bella and Andrei arrived.

10

Her alarm rang at five fifteen, and Laura groaned as she rolled over and hit the button to make it shut up. She'd only gotten to bed two hours before because she'd been up writing late into the night. She couldn't stop the roll she'd been on, not until she'd gotten the scene written out as she'd seen it in her head. Of course, now she was paying the price for doing that.

It was Monday, and Bella and Andrei were due to arrive within forty-five minutes. She needed to get the room cleaned up and the bed remade with clean sheets before they got there. She quickly got dressed, pulled the dirty sheets from the bed and then grabbed clean ones from the linen closet in the hallway.

She finished everything just in time. At five till six, she heard the front door open, and she hurried down the stairs to greet Bella and Andrei. "Hi, I'm so glad you're here. Let me show you to your rooms."

"Thanks, we're glad to be here too." Bella lifted a small suitcase and followed Laura up the stairs.

Andrei followed her, carrying two larger suitcases.

"As you know, this is Dad's room." Laura pointed at his door. "There is a room next to his that you might want to take, Andrei, and Bella, I think you should take this room."

"Isn't this your room?" Bella asked.

"Oh, well, I figured you should have a room close to Dad, so I've moved all my things to the other wing of the house. I'll still be close by if you need me, but out of the way. That way I can still get some work done without interrupting you guys."

"That's so generous of you," Bella murmured. "It's a lovely room."

"And, of course, the bathroom is across the hall."

"I'll just set my things down and go get breakfast started. Andrei, will you go wake Michael and get him ready for breakfast?"

"I'll leave you to it, then. Let me know if you need anything." Laura turned and headed back toward the stairs.

Andrei stopped her as she passed his room. "Where in the other wing will you be?" he asked softly, his voice husky as he invaded her space.

"Just, um... down that way and around the corner." Laura pointed.

"Good to know," he replied with a sexy smirk. "I'd better go get your dad up, but I'm sure I'll see you later."

Laura nodded and then fled down the stairs to the kitchen. His flirting first thing in the morning, before she'd even had her coffee, was almost too much. As she was fixing her mug, it dawned on her that the new side character she'd introduced into the story she was writing was a lot like Andrei. He was quickly becoming her muse in that regard; it made her giggle.

She set about making herself some breakfast, just some eggs and toast. Bella arrived just as she was cracking her eggs. "I'll be quick, I promise. Just making a couple of eggs."

"Oh, no worries, I was going to hard-boil a couple for your father and make him some egg sandwiches. It's much easier for him to eat that way. His hands are a little unsteady with utensils, I've noticed."

"Yes, I noticed that too. I think he'll like some egg sandwiches. He likes waffles, too."

"I know, but the syrup isn't good for him. Too much sugar."

"Oh, I hadn't thought of that." Laura frowned.

"Well, that's why you've hired me. To think of these things, isn't it?"

"Right." Laura nodded. She flipped her eggs and waited another thirty seconds, then slid them onto a plate with her toast. She turned off the stove, set the pan in the sink and then sat down to eat.

Bella hummed as she worked, slicing the bread and buttering it as the eggs boiled. Andrei and her dad arrived a few minutes later, just as Laura finished her breakfast. She made quick work of cleaning off her plate and the cooled pan she'd used to cook her eggs.

"Morning, Dad, have fun with Bella and Andrei today." She kissed his cheek and started toward the door.

"Where are you going?" he asked, confused.

"I'll be here, just upstairs working."

He nodded and picked up the paper, clearly dismissing her.

Feeling relieved, Laura headed upstairs to the suite she'd claimed for herself. It had been used for important guests when her father had entertained friends and work guests. The suite consisted of a bedroom, sitting room, and full bathroom with a shower and garden tub. There was also a large walk-in closet. Her father's bedroom consisted of the same.

Laura spent two hours hanging her clothes in the closet or folding them into the dresser. She also went about unboxing the rest of her things. The boxes she decided to keep, just in case she ever decided to move from the rooms, and put them folded up in the back of the closet, out of the way. Once she was finished, the suite actually felt like it was hers. She had her favorite blanket folded over the loveseat in the sitting room, her laptop set up on the desk in front of the window where she could look out over the back of the estate, her jewelry box and knickknacks on the dresser and scattered about the room, and all her favorite toiletries in her private bathroom. It was almost like an apartment. All she needed was her own kitchen.

Maybe she could buy a microwave to keep up here? Then shook her head. There was no reason to do that; she had full access to the house kitchen. She imagined if she did have her own microwave and mini-fridge, she'd almost never leave the suite. No, it was better if she didn't have those; that way she would have to make herself leave and go check on her dad. Not that she wouldn't, but she did tend to get distracted in her writing, and if she had those things up there, she would be more likely to extend her writing time and just snack instead of eating real food.

Since everything was finished, Laura finally sat down and did some writing. She managed to get a couple more chapters written, several fan emails answered and set up some promotional stuff with her assistant and publicist. She stood up and stretched, her eyes straying to the window. She could see Sam out by the pool, vacuuming it, and she decided a swim sounded good. It would be the first time she'd gotten to actually use the pool since being there. She had never been able to use the pool before, since her parents didn't put it in until after she'd left the estate, and generally when she had visited, it wasn't for very long.

She put on her swimsuit and her cover-up, grabbed a book, a towel and her sunglasses, then went downstairs and out through the kitchen door. "Hi, Sam. Is the pool safe to swim in?"

Sam looked over his shoulder at her. "The pool's in good shape, darlin'. I just like to vacuum it once or twice a week, keep it clean."

"Great." She set her things down on one of the lounges and walked over to him. "Now that I'm caught up on my chapters, I thought this would be a perfect way to get some exercise and relax a little bit."

"Have to admit, it doesn't get much use these days, but your father has always insisted it be kept up."

"Funny, I didn't think he liked swimming. We didn't have it when I was a kid. They put it in after I moved out."

"I think your father did it for Billy and for those guests of his. Your mother wasn't too thrilled at seeing the wives parade around in their bikinis, though." Sam chuckled.

"I'm sure she never let him hear the end of it once they were gone."

"No, she didn't. I think your father started inviting them more often just to get back at her."

Laura sighed. "I don't think I'll ever understand why he didn't divorce her. She really was an awful woman."

Sam shrugged. "Love is funny like that. I've never seen a more forgiving man when it came to her."

"I guess." Laura shook her head. "I just wish he would acknowledge how terrible and abusive she was."

Sam laid his hand on her arm and looked at her gently. "I know, but he can't help but be the way he is, and with his mind going, well, the more he's going to cling to that love he had for her."

"Yeah."

Chuckling, Sam added, "Doesn't mean he doesn't appreciate that beautiful nurse of his, though."

Laura snickered. "True."

"Well, I'll let you enjoy your swim."

Laura watched him go, half wishing he would join her in the pool. Once he was gone, she pulled off her cover-up, kicked off her sandals and dove into the deep end of the pool. She swam multiple laps, enjoying the feeling of the water flowing over her, and then just floated for a little while.

When she was tired of the water, she hopped out, dried off and lay down on the lounge. She put her sunglasses on and picked up her book. She was just through the first chapter when the kitchen door opened onto the deck, causing her to turn to see who it was coming out. Bella stood there staring at her.

"Hey, do you need me?" Laura called out to her.

"No." Bella's voice sounded a little abrupt, but then she smiled. "I was just catching my breath before I fix lunch for your father, me and Andrei. The pool looks inviting." She nodded toward it.

"It is lovely. You and Andrei are, of course, welcome to use it when my dad doesn't need you."

"I may take you up on that." A smirk touched her lips. "Well, back to work." She spun on her heel and re-entered the kitchen, shutting the door behind her.

Laura stared after her for a moment, but then shrugged and went back to reading but couldn't really focus on the story. She finally had her life back on track. She was feeling great for the first time in she didn't know how long. It dawned on her that she should call Kelly and let her know what's been going on. She hadn't talked to her since the move. They'd texted a few times, of course, but it wasn't the same as seeing her every week. She looked at the table for her phone and realized she hadn't brought it out with her. Sighing, she closed the book, picked up her things and returned to the house.

She needed to grab some lunch anyway, and she planned to spend the afternoon doing marketing for her upcoming novel, the one she was still in the process of writing. Then this evening, she would tackle edits on what she'd written this morning. She always liked to go back over and tweak the things she'd written while it was all still fresh in her head.

She tossed her cover-up over her shoulders, but didn't bother to button it up, and then strode to the kitchen door. When she opened it, she felt Andrei's eyes on her, and she glanced at the table, a rush of heat burned her face at the lecherous gaze he was giving her. Bella seemed oblivious, though, as Laura pulled her cover-up closed.

"That looks delicious, Bella; is there any left?" Laura eyed the baked chicken, tossed salad, carrots and pasta.

Bella glanced at her, a pleasant smile on her lips. "Oh, I didn't realize you were going to want to eat. I didn't make enough."

"Oh, no, it's fine. I didn't expect you to cook for me. It just looks so good, I had to ask." Laura smiled back. "I'll take care of my own lunch. Since you've made chicken for lunch, I'll make a meat loaf for dinner—"

"No!" Bella said sharply and then stuttered, "I-I mean, no, I have already planned dinner. You don't need to worry about fixing it. Just let me handle it. It is what you're paying me for, remember?" She grinned.

"Oh, um... okay. Well, do you need me to order anything from the store?"

"Not at the moment. I need to take a look through the cabinets and freezer, and I'll make you a list."

Laura nodded. "Okay, just let me know."

"I will. Or you know, Andrei can just go to the store."

"No need, we have a great delivery service." Laura hesitated, her eyes straying to Andrei and then back to Bella. She felt a little uncomfortable standing there in her bathing suit and wanted to escape to her shower. "Well, I'll let you all finish eating." As she passed by her dad, she paused and laid a hand on his shoulder. "Everything okay, Dad?"

He nodded, then looked at Bella. "She's lovely, isn't she?" he said, then glanced at Laura and smiled.

"Yes, Bella is very pretty," she answered, smiling back at him.

"Aw, you are so sweet, Michael," Bella simpered as she reached out to stroke his cheek.

"I'll be in the guest wing if you need me, Dad."

His brow furrowed. "What are you doing in the guest wing? You're not a guest. Those rooms are for clients. I have the Watsons coming to visit on Saturday—"

"Oh, Michael, you're so admirable. I just love hearing you speak about your job." Bella batted her eyelashes. "Oh, but we should finish our lunch first; then you can tell me all about it."

Laura watched in amazement as he quickly turned his diverted attention back to Bella.

"Right you are, Bella, my dear."

Mouthing the words, *Thank you,* to Bella, Laura gave her a finger wave and quickly left the room. She returned upstairs, tossed her wet towel in the hamper along with her cover-up and bathing suit, then took a shower.

Her stomach was grumbling when she emerged from her room an hour later. As she entered the kitchen, she noticed Bella going through the cabinets and writing things on a list. "Oh, you're doing it now?" she asked in surprise.

"Mmmm, yes. Well, Michael is sleeping, so I had time," Bella murmured, her head stuck in the pantry. She pulled out a box, looked at it, shook her head and replaced it. "There isn't much in here that he should be eating."

"Well, not all of it is for my dad."

Bella looked at her over a bag of Muddy Buddies, her eyebrow arched. "I should think not." She replaced it, her lips pursed in disapproval.

Laura felt her cheeks heat. "Sometimes I just need a little something sweet," she explained.

"I'm not judging," Bella replied, but it was clear from her tone that she'd like to. Still, she didn't say anything derogatory. "I'm just going to put this on this low shelf in the back. It's best not to put these kinds of things at eye level, where your father will see them and decide he wants them."

"Okay." Laura couldn't help but think that with them down there, even she would forget they were there. She promised herself she would move them up to her room later, along with whatever else Bella decided to hide away from her dad. Maybe she'd invest in that microwave after all.

By the following Monday, Laura was used to having Bella and Andrei around nearly twenty-four seven. She spent a great deal of time on her own now, and she was able to get a ton more written and only had to check in a couple of times of day. She was so much more relaxed, and she thought things couldn't be going better.

Of course, Andrei continued to flirt heavily with her, which was, if Laura was honest, extremely flattering. It had been a good while since she'd felt even remotely beautiful to anyone. Jim hadn't called her beautiful in who knew how long. Had he ever really called her beautiful? she wondered. Thinking back over their relationship, she recalled the handful of times where he'd said anything even remotely positive about her looks.

The first had been on their very first date, he'd said she looked very pretty. After that, it had mostly been compliments about her clothing, not necessarily her. The second time had been the day they were engaged, where he'd said she was lovely, and the final time had been on their honeymoon, when he'd precisely said, *"Beautiful, let's hit the tables,"* but now, as she thought about it, she wasn't sure he was actually calling her beautiful, or just anxious to get to the gambling tables in their Las Vegas hotel. He might have actually been looking around the casino when he'd said that.

She shook her head and pushed thoughts of Jim away. The asshole didn't deserve any of her thoughts. Instead, she turned her attention to Sam. She wanted to know what his thoughts were on the previous week. With him in mind, she went out the back door and strolled down the path that led to his cottage. The lights were on in the living room, so she knew he was still awake. She only hesitated a moment before knocking on the door.

When Sam opened the front door, he smiled at her with surprise. "Darlin', what brings you by?"

"Hey, Sam, can I come in?"

"Sure thing," he replied, opening the door wider.

She stepped over the threshold and paused in the entryway.

"Excuse the mess. I didn't expect to be having company," he commented as he quickly picked up a shirt he'd tossed over the back of the chair and shoved a pair of shoes out of the way. "Come on in." He gestured toward the sofa in the living room.

"I'm sorry, I should have texted you," Laura apologized as she moved into the room.

"Don't worry about it." Sam smiled. "Sit, please. Can I get you anything?"

"Oh, no, I just came by to get your thoughts on how this week went. I mean, if you noticed anything off, or... or anything." Laura shrugged.

Sam sank down in the chair opposite the sofa where

Laura had sat down. He shook his head. "No, can't say that I did. Notice anything off, I mean. Your father seemed happy; I didn't much notice any tantrums or anything like that. Bella seems to have him wrapped around her little finger."

Laura giggled. "She does. What about her brother?"

A look passed over Sam's face that Laura couldn't quite decipher. It almost looked like disgust to her, but it was gone so quickly, she figured she must have been mistaken.

"Well, I've seen him out walking the estate with your father. They seem to get along fine. I'm glad to see he's getting some exercise."

Nodding, Laura couldn't help but agree. "True. I think they've been a good hire. I just don't want to make a mistake, you know?" She shook her head. "I'm just so bad at judging people." Her words were quiet, almost a whisper. She glanced from her hands in her lap back up to Sam. "That's why I'm asking your opinion. I just... I don't want to be wrong."

Sam smiled across the coffee table at her. "You can ask my opinion anytime, darlin'. And so far, I think they're doing pretty well with him."

"Thanks, Sam. I trust your judgment." Sighing, Laura stood. "Well, I shouldn't keep you. I'm sure you've got better things to do than to entertain me and my insecurities."

Sam stood, too, and moved toward her. He reached out and touched her arm, drawing her eyes up to his face. "Don't." He stared into her eyes. "I've told you before, I'm always here for you, darlin'. You can come visit me anytime you want." He traced a finger from her brow down to her chin.

Laura bit her lip and gave him a slight nod. "Thanks, Sam." Her voice was breathy and soft. "I should still go, though," she whispered.

He hesitated for a moment and then dropped his hand,

stepping back. He walked her to the door and opened it. "Good night, darlin'."

"Night, Sam." Laura gave him a little wave as she stepped out to his front porch. She hurried back down the path and back up to the large estate house with a flutter in her heart.

11

"So, tell me why you haven't sought a divorce yet," Dr. Fischer asked.

Laura shrugged. She'd been in Dr. Fischer's office for nearly forty-five minutes, talking about her marriage and the train wreck that it had become. "I have signed the papers, but... well, Jim wasn't taking my calls, and I don't know where he's staying. And I've been so busy these last few weeks that I guess I just haven't tried again."

"But you do know where he is, don't you? Where he works?" She arched a brow, her pen poised over her notepad.

"I tried the community college where he was working, but they told me he was no longer working there." Laura sighed. "He was only there as an adjunct professor; I mean, he wasn't on a path for tenure or anything."

"I see." She made a note on her paper and then tapped her pen against it for a moment, apparently lost in thought. A moment later, she reached over to her desk and grabbed a card file. She flipped through it, pulled out a business card, and handed it toward Laura. "This is the number of a private investigator. I normally don't give out recommendations of this kind, especially to clients, but I do think it is important that you track Jim down and separate yourself fully from him. And I really think Angela can help you."

Laura took the card and looked at it. "Is she another client of yours?"

Dr. Fischer shook her head. "No, actually, *I* was a client of *hers.*" She smiled ruefully. "I shouldn't be telling you this, but I had an incident with a former partner threatening my life. The police wouldn't do anything, so I hired Angela to keep tabs on him. She saved my life."

"Oh, wow. I had no idea—"

"No, you wouldn't have. Nobody did, thankfully. I didn't want it affecting my practice. Let me just say that I completely understand what you've gone through with your mother and your husband, because I've been in a similar—but not exactly the same by any means—situation. Which is why I really would like to see you go through with that divorce. Remove him from your life completely so he no longer has a hold over you."

Laura nodded. "I don't think Jim would ever threaten my life, though..."

"I agree. I don't think he would hurt you physically; that's not his thing. He's an emotional abuser. He's manipulative and charming and very good at gaslighting you."

"Yes."

"And he will drain you of energy and money and anything else, but he won't kill you."

Nodding, Laura couldn't help but agree. "I know."

"So you'll call her?"

"Yes. Definitely. I wouldn't have known how to find him if you hadn't given me this." Laura held up the card. "It hadn't occurred to me to hire an investigator to find him."

"Why not?"

"Well, to be honest, I'm going to say probably because

before, I couldn't afford it, and since moving... well, there just hasn't been time."

"Angela isn't too expensive. She charges by the hour, but she is worth it. I have no doubt she'll be able to track him down quickly."

"Okay, I'll call her when I get back to the estate." Laura still had trouble calling it *home* and probably always would. It would probably never be her home in her mind.

"I'm glad to hear it. And we'll call that your assignment for today, then." Dr. Fischer set her notepad aside and stood up.

Laura took that as her cue to it being time to end her appointment. "Thank you, Dr. Fischer."

"We'll talk about what she finds out for you on Thursday." Dr. Fischer walked her to the door.

"I'll see you then," Laura answered, then shuffled through the doorway. She gave Amanda a wave and then left the office. As she got into her car, she looked at the card in her hand again.

Angela Downey, Private Detective.

It included an address and office number. As she drove home, Laura planned out what to say. She held an imaginary conversation in her head that seemed to be playing out like some 1940s detective noir. She was the dame looking for the deadbeat husband who'd left her high and dry, and Angela was the private dick who was going to find him for her. She pictured herself walking into Angela's dingy little office, wearing a tight red dress cut low and strappy heels. Her hair was, of course, perfectly curled and flowing down her back, and she had on just the right amount of makeup with bright red lipstick. Angela would be behind her desk, shadowed, wearing a long beige trench coat and a fedora.

"I need your help," Laura could hear herself saying in a breathy voice, playing the damsel in distress.

"Whatever you need, doll, I'm on the case," Angela would reply.

The entire scenario sent her into a gale of giggles as she punched in the code for the gate. Maybe she'd have to try her hand at writing a 1940s romantic detective noir. She didn't know what her fans would think of that, though. She'd have to ask them if they would be up to reading something of the sort. The idea made her grin. It was kind of exciting to think about.

She parked her car in the garage and noticed Sam tinkering with one of the mowers. As she opened the door, he slammed tools back into his toolbox.

"Hey, Sam. Everything okay?"

He glanced up as though just realizing she was there and sighed. "No, not really."

She strode over to him, her brow furrowed. She'd never seen him looking so frustrated before. "What's wrong?"

Huffing, he shook his head. "It's nothin', darlin'. Don't worry about it."

"Sam, come on, tell me what's bugging you, please?" Laura frowned. Sam was always one to have a smile on his face. He was nearly always happy, so to see him like this was very worrisome.

"It's that Andrei. I was on the mower, and the next thing I know, your father is in my path. I nearly hit him, and he started shouting. Said I tried to mow him down. But he wasn't even there two seconds beforehand. He and Andrei had been on the path. You know I always pay attention when I'm out on the equipment, Laura. I would never put anyone at risk."

"What?" Laura shook her head, horrified at what could have happened, but she knew Sam was always careful, so she trusted that he was telling her the truth.

"I'm sorry, Laura. I didn't mean to upset you." He looked even more upset than he had a moment before.

"It's okay, Sam, I know you would never endanger anyone. I'm just shocked is all. I mean, how did Dad get onto the lawn and into your path?"

Sam shook his head, a befuddled expression upon his face. "I don't know, honestly. Andrei said he just suddenly wandered away from him, claiming he had to talk to me about making sure to water the roses."

Laura frowned. That sounded completely strange; her father knew it was part of Sam's routine to water all of the garden around sunset. "What did Dad say to that? Did he actually say anything at all about the roses?"

"No, he was too busy yelling at me for nearly hitting him. He was very worked up and agitated. I haven't seen him in such a state in a while. So I decided it'd be better to just stop mowing while he was out there. I'll finish up later, I guess, when he's back inside and I know he's safe."

"I'm so sorry, Sam." Laura placed her hand on his forearm. "I know how much this bothers you."

"Not your fault, darlin'. Nobody's fault but the dementia, I guess." He shrugged, but looked a little better, more relieved that she wasn't angry with him.

Laura smiled, catching his gaze. "I'll ask Andrei to keep a better eye on him when they're outside. That could have been a really bad accident."

Sam nodded. "Yes, it could have been. Thanks, darlin'."

"You're welcome, Sam."

"How was your appointment?"

Laura thought about it, and a brighter smile lit her face. "Pretty good. Dr. Fischer gave me the name of a private investigator so I can track down Jim and get him to sign the divorce papers. Then I'll really be a free woman."

"You don't know where he is?"

Shaking her head, Laura explained, "He doesn't work at the community college anymore, and I don't know where he went when he left. Not to mention, he has been avoiding my calls. I gave up trying before I even made the move here, but now that I have more time, I think I should get this done, don't you?"

"Definitely." Sam nodded.

"Well, I'll let you go back to tinkering. I've got a call to make and a caregiver to speak to."

Sam winked. "Good luck."

Laura waved and headed into the house. She found Bella, Andrei, and her dad seated at the table. "Hey, um, I just ran into Sam—"

Before she could tell them what he'd said, Andrei jumped in. "Did he tell you he nearly ran your father over? The man needs to be fired. He obviously is careless about what he's doing out there!"

Laura was taken aback. His tone shocked the heck out of her, but she was determined not to let him cast Sam in a bad light. "He did tell me that Dad somehow managed to leave the path and wander onto the lawn, but that he managed to stop in time. I wanted to ask if you would make sure Dad stays on the path when you're out with him. I don't want him having any accidents because the dementia makes him do unsafe things."

Andrei gave her a slightly sullen look, but then nodded. "I'm sorry, I was just so panicked about him wandering off like that. It was so unexpected. I'll make sure he stays with me from now on. But you need to have a talk with that gardener. He was very reckless, mowing so close to us. He really should be fired."

Laura gave him a tight smile. "I've spoken to Sam. He's going to make sure to mow the lawn closest to the house when Dad is inside. That way, there won't be any more chances for him to get hurt."

"That's all I can ask, I suppose. We don't want to lose Michael to an accident like that."

"No, we don't. Michael is too precious to lose," Bella simpered as she looked at Laura's father, who remained quiet as he ate.

"Which is why it would be best if you make sure he stays with you. I mean, he could wander off and fall in the pool or the pond, or just get hurt going down the steps. Those pills of his make him very unsteady at times. I just don't want him to hurt himself."

Andrei nodded. "That's fair. We don't either, do we, Bella?" He glanced at his sister, and they seemed to share a look, then they both nodded.

"I made some extra sandwiches, if you want one," Bella said, hopping up from her seat.

"Oh, well, I was going to make my own from the leftovers last night—"

"Those are gone. Andrei ate them for a snack."

"Oh. Well, then, okay. What did you make?" Laura glanced toward the kitchen counter.

"Crab salad."

Sighing, Laura gritted her teeth. She'd been planning to use the crab to make a special dinner for her and her dad during Bella and Andrei's evening off on Friday. "Um, I think I'll pass. I have some work to do right now, so I'll just grab something later."

"If you're sure?" Bella blinked at her.

Nodding, Laura made her way out of the kitchen and upstairs to her suite. She sank down on the bed and dug her phone out of her purse. She was still holding the investigator's card in her hand, and she looked at it before dialing the number.

"Angela Downey, PI. What can I do for you today?"

"Hi, my name is Laura Radcliffe, and Dr. Vera Fischer gave me your contact information."

Laura could hear the smile in the woman's voice as she said, "Dr. Fischer is a very nice woman. I'm glad I was able to help her out. So what is it I can do for you, Ms. Radcliffe?"

Laura took a breath and then explained: "I need you to find my husband so I can have him served with divorce papers."

"I have an hourly rate plus expenses, and I'll need a bit more information before I can get started."

"Yes, Dr. Fischer mentioned that; what is your hourly rate?"

Angela quoted her a rate that made Laura's eyes widen, but it was still manageable. "Okay. I can do that. Hopefully, it won't take you too long to find him."

"I promise I won't waste your time, Ms. Radcliffe. Now, can you tell me his name and his last known whereabouts?"

"Jim Larson. He was an adjunct professor at the community college, but he doesn't work there anymore. I don't know where he's gone to. As for where he's living, I don't have a clue. I kicked him out for cheating on me and didn't really care where he went, as long as he wasn't in my space."

"I totally get that. Do you have a working number for him?"

"I don't know. I mean, I have a number, but he's not taking my calls. I don't know if he's screening me or if he's ditched it."

"Well, give me that, and I'll see what I can do with it."

Laura recited the digits to her. "Is there anything else you need?"

"Just your information and how to contact you when I find him." Once again, Laura could hear the smile in her voice.

"Sure," Laura replied. She proceeded to give Angela her current address and her cell phone number as well.

"Okay, I'll be in touch."

Afterward, Laura was surprised by how easy it was to hire her. With that out of the way, she went into the sitting room and sat down at her desk to get some work done.

AT SIX THE NEXT EVENING, her phone rang, and Laura recognized it as the detective's number. "Hello?"

"Ms. Radcliffe? It's Angela, the private investigator you hired to find your husband?"

"Yes, hi. Did you find him already?"

"I did! So, let me tell you. I was able to track his movements after you kicked him out. Turns out he was let go by the college for an inappropriate relationship with a student. Sorry about that."

"He was? I mean, I knew about his cheating with a girl from the school, but she was one of his students?"

"Yes. They gave him the option to end the relationship, but he wouldn't. When he was let go, the girl broke things off with him and kicked him out of her apartment."

"Oh?"

"Yes. It gets even more interesting from there. Turns out she wasn't the only one he was seeing. He just managed to move to another girl's apartment across town. A Lindsay Travers. I spoke to her; she's pretty young and naïve. He claimed he was divorced and that you got him fired."

"He what!" Laura fumed.

"Do you need me to repeat?" Angela asked, clearly unsure how to read Laura's reaction.

"No, I'm just pissed off."

"I can imagine. Anyway, he's been sending out new applications for work to various universities around the area.

I'm texting you the address he's staying at, so you can get your lawyer to send the divorce papers to him as soon as possible."

"Okay, great. Thank you so much, Angela. What do I owe you?"

"It only took me a total of two hours to actually track him down. The computer did most of the work." She chuckled.

"No expenses?"

"Not at this time."

"Okay, great. I'll transfer you the money if that works for you?"

"It does indeed." Angela gave her the banking address to send it to and waited as Laura made the transfer. "I've got it. Let me know if you need me again. I appreciate the business."

"Thanks, Angela. I will definitely let you know." Laura hung up. She felt overwhelmed by disgust for her husband's actions. She couldn't believe the nerve of the man. He'd been cheating on her with not only one nineteen-year-old, but two!

She was so pissed off, she couldn't even think about going back to writing, so she saved her work and headed downstairs to find something to calm her nerves.

12

Laura wandered downstairs and into the kitchen. She'd declined eating earlier with Bella, Andrei, and her dad, but now she was hungry. With her emotions boiling over because of the news she'd just heard, Laura decided she needed ice cream and maybe something stronger. She grabbed a carton of fudge ripple from the freezer and then went to the drawer and pulled out a spoon.

Just as she was reaching for a glass to pour some of her father's Tennessee bourbon into, Bella came into the room.

"Oh, I didn't know you were down here." Bella stopped short.

Laura set the glass on the counter next to the ice cream, then headed for the liquor cabinet. She pulled out a bottle of Heaven's Door and returned, pouring a good amount into the glass.

"Bad day?" Bella asked, eyeing her.

Laura nodded, held the bottle up and said, "Want some?"

"Sure." Bella nodded. "Want to talk about it?" she asked as Laura pulled another glass down.

"Not especially." She handed over the second glass, then

picked up her own, taking a gulp. "Just my fucking husband is a sleazebag," she muttered.

Bella took the glass and sipped it. "Oh! I didn't even know you were married."

"Separated." She opened the carton of ice cream and stuck the spoon in, scooping out a bite. "Bastard was cheating on me with not one, but two teenagers! Can you believe it?"

"Oh my God! What an asshole! Teenagers?"

"Nineteen-year-old students from the college he taught at." Laura snickered. "He got fired, though, and one of the girls dumped his ass."

"How did you find out?" Bella leaned a hip against the counter, watching her over the rim of the etched, double old-fashioned glass.

"Had to hire an investigator to track him down. I didn't know where he went after I kicked him out," she said, through a mouthful of ice cream. "Now that I know where he is, I can have my lawyer drop off the divorce papers." She set the carton down and picked up her bourbon, taking a gulp, then refilled the glass. The bourbon was smooth and had a vanilla and oak taste with a tiny bit of spice. It went really well with the fudge ripple.

"Gosh, I'm so sorry you're going through that with him. Was he staying here, too?"

"Oh God, no." Laura shook her head. "I kicked him out of our apartment before I moved back here. He left me in basically financial ruin, the asshole. Ran up a bunch of credit card debt and took out loans in my name... just... I don't know what I saw in him, you know?" She held the spoon halfway to her mouth, her thoughts drifting to when she first met him. She shoved the spoon between her lips and let the ice cream melt on her tongue.

"Let me guess, he was a charmer?"

"Oh yeah." Laura nodded. "And good looking. I thought I

was the luckiest girl to have found him." Laura sneered and rolled her eyes. "I was so stupid!"

Bella set her glass down and moved closer. "Aw, don't say that; you're not stupid. Some people are manipulative, and you just can't see it happening. I've dated my share of men who take advantage of vulnerable women. Luckily, I figured it out before I married them, but... well, that doesn't mean it couldn't have happened to me too. Besides, I have Andrei to look out for me, as well."

Laura sighed and sipped some more of the bourbon. It was mixing with the saltiness of the tears that she hadn't even realized were streaming down her cheeks in anger. She dashed her palm across her wet cheeks, brushing them away. "God, I'm a mess." She sniffled.

"You look fine, just upset." Bella smiled. "Oh! I just thought of something..."

Laura was moving beyond tipsy to being full-on drunk, so Bella's exclamation had her frowning, wondering what it was that Bella could have thought of that had to do with her being a mess. "What? Do I look worse than I thought?"

"What?" Bella glanced at her, then shook her head. "Oh, no, not that... about your husband. I mean, if you're going to divorce him, you should make sure you change your will and life insurance papers. I mean, if I were you, I wouldn't want him collecting anything if something happened to me."

Laura blinked slowly, processing what Bella was saying. She was right. "That's smart. I hadn't even thought of those." She slowly nodded. "I'll call my lawyer before my therapy appointment tomorrow."

"You go to therapy? I've always wondered about therapists. I mean, who wants to sit around and listen to people complain all day about their problems." Bella shuddered.

Frowning, Laura stared at her.

"I don't mean to say that *you* do that, of course..." Bella blinked wide, looking at her as though she hadn't meant to give offense.

"It's okay. And, well, I just have a lot of things to work through, and Dr. Fischer helps me sort through it all. She's very kind."

"I'm sure she is, sweetie." Bella nodded. "I mean, she'd have to be, right? For you to keep seeing her."

"Yeah, I guess?" Laura was confused. She couldn't remember why she'd even brought up Dr. Fischer in the first place. Her mind was fuzzy and clouded. She looked down at the carton of ice cream in her hand, which was now slippery with condensation. The ice cream that was left in the container was getting soupy, too. "Ugh, I shouldn't have eaten all this." She felt sick to her stomach.

"Looked like you needed it, though."

Laura shook her head and put the spoon in the sink and the lid on the carton, then tossed it in the trash. She finished off the bourbon in her glass, not because she wanted it, but because she didn't want to waste it and couldn't put it back in the bottle. Once she had drank it all, she rinsed the glass and spoon and shoved them in the dishwasher. "I think I'm going to head up to bed."

"Oh, already?" Bella pouted. "We were just getting to know each other."

Were we? Laura thought. "Sorry, I'm just feeling really light-headed and queasy. I think I am going to take a bath and just go to sleep."

"Aw, okay. I wouldn't want you feeling bad. Just don't forget to call and get those changed tomorrow. That jerk doesn't deserve to be able to take anything else from you. I mean, he seems like a really shady character."

Laura nodded. "You're right, he doesn't deserve any more from me, and he *is* a shady character. Thanks, Bella. And thanks for letting me vent to you. I know listening to my problems isn't really part of your job description."

Bella giggled. "No, but I had hoped we could be friends, and friends talk to each other."

"They do," Laura agreed. "Well, thanks. I do appreciate it." She laid a hand on Bella's arm gently. "I really do."

"I'm glad I could be here for you." Bella smiled. "Now go on and get up to bed. Don't spend too long in the bath."

Laura gave a small laugh. "I won't. Night, Bella."

"Goodnight."

Laura made her way up the stairs slowly. Her head was spinning. She couldn't remember if she'd returned the bottle of Heaven's Door to the liquor cabinet or not, and she nearly turned around to make sure, but she felt horrible, and just the thought of having to go back downstairs made her stomach roll. She decided she'd just set her alarm for five thirty so she could go down and clean up before breakfast, and before her father caught sight of the more-than-half-empty bottle.

13

"Ugh, God, stop..." Laura groaned at the beeping that was making her head pound with the worst headache she'd had in some time. She shoved her pillow over her head, trying to block out the sound, but it just continued its monotonous and insidious noise. It took her nearly ten minutes to realize it was coming from her alarm clock. It was time to get up.

Blinking her eyes as she came fully awake, she sat up and glanced at the clock. It was five forty-one. She quickly turned it off and then grabbed a bottle of ibuprofen from the bathroom cabinet and dumped two pills in her hand. She swallowed them down with a glass of water. Her mouth tasted like sawdust, and all she really wanted to do was crawl back into bed, but then she remembered why she had set her alarm to wake her so early.

She needed to get downstairs and make sure the liquor was put away before her father came down. He didn't need a reminder that he was no longer allowed to drink. The liquor cabinet was generally out of the way, but if he saw the bottle out on the counter, especially his favorite bottle of bourbon, he'd demand to know why. Laura didn't want to explain that she'd just found out her cheating bastard of a husband was living it up at some girl-child's apartment. That would be too much. So she quickly dressed and hurried down the stairs to the kitchen.

She found the bottle on the counter where she'd left it. Picking it up, she hurried over to the liquor cabinet and slipped it inside behind a couple of drink mixer bottles. She debated going back upstairs to bed, but her stomach chose that moment to rumble, and she realized how hungry she really was. All she'd eaten last night was the ice cream, so now she was truly ravenous.

She figured protein would be the best to get rid of the remainder of her headache and hangover, so she pulled out some eggs and sausage and started cooking.

"Something smells divine." Andrei strolled into the kitchen. "Breakfast smells pretty good, too. Is any of that for me, gorgeous?"

Laura blushed at his words. "Oh, do you want some? I can make you some, too. I just didn't know anyone was up yet."

"Well, I missed out on drinks and ice cream last night," he pouted, but his eyes twinkled. "So I would love to have breakfast with you, just the two of us... it will be special."

Laura felt her belly tighten. It had been a long time since a man other than Jim had spoken to her in such a way. It made her a little giddy. "I'll just add a few more of each, then." Her cheeks pinkened as she reached for two more eggs and cracked them into the pan, then added more sausage to the pot of boiling water.

"You're gorgeous, you know that, right?" He quirked a brow at her. "Especially when you blush like that." He touched her cheeks gently and stroked his finger down it as he leaned forward to whisper in her ear, "I really like it."

Her breath caught as he pulled back and gazed into her

eyes. She bit her lip, and her blush deepened. She had no idea what to say. A million replies raced through her mind, but all of them sounded corny or cheesy, and then the moment passed, because she had to take care of the eggs or they wouldn't be eating anything, because it would be ruined.

"Should I make the coffee?" he asked.

Laura still hadn't found her voice, so she nodded.

Andrei snickered as he strolled to the pantry and pulled out the coffee. He hummed as he made it, putting a small pitcher of water in the microwave to get it hot enough for their instant coffee. It was then that she noticed that he was only wearing a pair of basketball shorts and no shirt.

He caught her staring at him and smirked at her, but she quickly turned back to the stove. Her face felt like it was on fire. In her head, she scolded herself for being so taken by him.

"I like when you look at me like that," he murmured, from directly behind her.

Laura shivered as she felt his breath on her neck and the heat from his body at her back. She cleared her throat. "Um, breakfast is ready... just have to put it on plates." She glanced up and over her shoulder at him.

He smiled and took a step backward, watching her for a moment. Then he went back to finish making the coffee. "Coffee is just about ready, too."

As Laura filled the plates and brought them over to the table, he carried over the coffee, setting hers down in front of her. "Oh, I forgot the forks," she said, hopping up and right into his arms. "Uh—" She dragged her gaze up his rock-hard abs to his pecs and then to his face, knowing her own had to be scarlet.

He smirked again and took a step back, barely enough to allow her to pass between him and her chair. He watched her with a sexy gaze as she scurried to the drawer, grabbed two forks and returned to the table.

"Um, here?" She held the fork out to him.

"Thanks," he murmured, still watching her.

Laura scooted by him again and slipped into her seat. "Um, sit down and eat before it goes cold."

He chuckled. "Do I make you nervous, Laura?"

"No!" Laura squeaked out, completely embarrassed. "No. No, I'm fine. Just fine..."

"You're more than *just fine*, pretty little Laura." He winked at her as he took a seat.

Not knowing what to say, Laura picked up her coffee and took a drink, almost immediately burning her mouth. "Argh!" she gasped, choking as she tried to fan her mouth.

"Oh, damn, was it too hot? I'm sorry! Let me get you some water."

Tears burned her eyes as she took the cup from him and guzzled the water. The roof of her mouth and tongue felt raw. "Ugh. I hate when I do that. I'm going to feel off all day," she groaned, staring at her plate.

"I should have warned you it was still hot." He gave her a puppy-dog look, and she couldn't help but forgive him.

She shook her head. "Not your fault. I knew you heated the water in the microwave." She gave him a weak smile. "You should eat; it's gonna be cold if you don't eat it now."

"Can you eat?"

Shrugging, she picked up her fork. "I can try." She managed to eat most of her food, but she could hardly taste it because of the scalding her mouth had taken.

"I'm glad I didn't ruin your breakfast; it was really good. You're a fantastic cook," Andrei said when he finished.

"Thanks." Laura stood and picked up their empty—well, mostly empty, in her case—plates and walked to the sink.

"I've got this if you want to head upstairs to wake my dad?" She glanced over at him.

"Sure. He's probably already up by now."

Laura looked at the clock. "Probably, but I know you've been helping him, and he might need you." She slid one of the plates into the dishwasher and glanced up through her lashes, catching what might have been a flash of annoyance crossing his face, but it was quickly gone.

"You're right; I'll head on up there. Bella will be down anytime to start her and Michael's breakfast anyway. I'll let her know I've already eaten." He moved toward her and took her hand, bringing it to his lips. "Thank you for cooking for me. It was delicious."

"You're welcome," Laura answered, a new blush forming on her cheeks.

She watched him saunter out of the room, then finished cleaning up. Afterwards, she returned to her own room and pulled out her phone. Andrei mentioning Bella had reminded her she needed to call her lawyers and not only give them Jim's address so they could serve him the divorce papers, but also so she could ask about changing her will and life insurance beneficiary.

Only she'd gotten up so early that it was still too early to call. They wouldn't be in their offices for another hour at least. So she moved to the sitting room, setting her phone next to the computer, and decided to work on edits for the novel. It was nearly finished—well, the first-round draft was nearly finished, at any rate. She only had two more chapters to write before she could send it off to Erin.

Once she finished the daily edits, she began writing up a blog about her idea of doing a 1940s romantic noir mystery and set up a poll for her fans to see if they would be interested. She was rather excited about it and went into detail about it for them. Explaining it would be from the female detective's point of view, as she would be the heroine of the story. She hadn't yet decided who the hero counterpart and love interest would be, or exactly what the mystery was yet, but she was already imagining interviewing Angela and basing the heroine on her, and maybe some of her experiences... of course, she still had to get Angela's okay, but that would come after her fans gave her the yea or nay on the idea.

She was really hoping for a yea.

With that finished, she picked up her phone and dialed her lawyers' offices.

"Hartman and Keene, may I help you?"

"Hi, Maggie, this is Laura Radcliffe. May I speak to Mr. Hartman?"

"Let me see if he's available this morning, Ms. Radcliffe."

Laura waited for a few minutes as Maggie put her on hold. The music was light instrumental Muzak, songs she knew but couldn't remember the words to.

"Ms. Radcliffe, this is Wayne Hartman; what can I do for you?"

"Good morning, Mr. Hartman. I wanted to let you know that I've located Jim if you want to send someone over with the papers for him to sign."

"Oh, great. I'll have someone get right on that. Was there anything else?"

"Yes, actually. A friend reminded me I need to change my will and life insurance so that Jim isn't on them. Do you have time to squeeze me in for that?"

"Today?"

"Sure, if you can fit me in?"

"Let me check my schedule, and I'll have Maggie give you a call back."

"That's fine." She proceeded to give him Jim's address and thank him for his time.

"I'll have Maggie call you soon. Take care now, Ms. Radcliffe."

When she hung up, she decided a shower was in order before she went to her appointment with Dr. Fischer. By the time she finished, she had a voicemail waiting for her. "Damn, I missed the call," she muttered as she called her mailbox. She listened as Maggie informed her that Mr. Hartman would see her at two p.m. if she was able. If not, she could call back, and they could reschedule.

Two was perfect for Laura. She would just stay in town after her appointment and have lunch, then make the drive to the lawyers' offices, which were back near her old apartment building. Thinking about it, she decided to text Kelly and see if they could have lunch together before the appointment, since she would be close by. They made plans to meet at noon at their favorite Mexican restaurant.

At her appointment, Laura shared the information she'd gotten from Angela about Jim and how she'd broken down over it. Dr. Fischer commiserated with her and said it was okay to break down occasionally, but not to make a habit of it, and that it was good she'd had someone there to talk with about it all. She also said that Bella must have a good head on her shoulders to have thought about the will and life insurance. Laura had agreed.

"I think we're making good progress, Laura. You've dealt with a lot over the last few weeks. How are you sleeping, overall?"

Laura thought about it. "Not too bad. Being in the different wing of the house is nice. It's an area that I was rarely in as a child, so it doesn't have any bad memories. And with the kitchen redone and the furniture rearranged in the living room, it almost feels like... well, like a ghost-free space, if you get what I mean?"

"I do. Not being reminded of the bad memories with your

mother can be very freeing. Still, I think I'd like you to start journaling about your dreams as soon as you wake. We might gain some more insight into your subconscious that way, make sure you aren't backsliding."

Laura nodded. "I can do that."

"Good. Well, our time is up for today, but I'll see you next week, right?"

"I'll be here." Laura stood.

"Have a good weekend." She held the door open for her.

"Thanks, I hope you do too."

From there, Laura got in her car and drove the forty-five minutes to meet Kelly at their favorite restaurant, Del Toros. It was a small family-owned restaurant that was hidden away, that mostly only locals knew about. Laura really liked the atmosphere, and the staff was so friendly.

"Ms. Laura, it's so good to see you," Jose said.

"Hi, Jose. I have missed this place! Do you have a table for me and Kelly?"

He sucked his teeth and rolled his eyes. "Of course I have a table for you and Ms. Kelly. Come sit." He grabbed a couple of menus and took her to the booth she normally shared with Kelly when they came to eat there. "I'll have Maria bring you chips and cheese, and a sweet tea, yes?"

"Perfect, thanks."

He left her, heading to find his wife, who was bustling about the room helping other patrons. Laura watched him speak to her and point to Laura's table. Maria followed his finger, and her face lit up when she saw Laura, and she waved. Then she held up a finger and pointed from herself to the kitchen.

Laura just nodded and smiled. It was like being home, sitting there. The Del Toro family was more real family to her than her own father had ever been.

A moment later, Maria arrived at the table with a big

basket of chips, a bowl of spicy white cheese and a large, iced tea. "Come, give me a hug!" Maria said after setting it all down.

Laura stood and hugged her. "Hi, Maria."

"We've missed you around here, Ms. Laura! How is your father doing? He well enough you come visit more often?"

"I've missed being here with you all, too. My dad's doing okay, I guess. I hired some help, so, maybe?" She smiled. "How's Theresa?"

Maria tutted and looked annoyed for a moment, but then smiled. "That girl. Oh. The trouble she gives me. Took up with that boy again, that Stavon. Troublemaker, that one." She shook her head. "She'll be sorry she missed you."

"You'll tell her I said hi?"

"Of course." Maria nodded. "You want me to put in your order, or you going to wait for Ms. Kelly?"

"I'll wait. She should be here in a minute. I got here a little bit early."

"Okay, I'll be back. You tell Ms. Kelly I'll bring her Diet Coke when she gets here."

"I will." Laura smiled.

Maria patted her shoulder and bustled off.

Laura ate a few chips, being careful of the roof of her mouth, which was still tender after its scalding that morning, and then Kelly turned up. Maria reappeared seconds later and set down a diet soda, then hugged Kelly and asked how she was doing. They spoke for a few minutes, and then Laura and Kelly placed their orders.

"I'll be back with those soon," Maria said.

Kelly's gaze stayed on her as she hurried away. "I love that woman."

Laura giggled. "Me too. I swear she, Theresa, and Jose are like family."

"I've always thought so." Kelly nodded. "So, speaking of,

how's your dad? How are the nurses working out? How's *Sam*?" She wiggled her eyebrows when she spoke his name, knowing Laura had always had a crush on him.

Laughing, Laura said, "Sam is fine, just his usual self, I guess. Still good-looking and sweet. Dad's doing okay. Bella has been so nice—God, she let me cry all over her after that phone call with the investigator. She says she wants to be friends. I guess it would be nice to have someone up there I can talk to."

"Hey, what am I? Chopped liver?"

"You know what I mean." Laura rolled her eyes. "She's not you; she's not going to ever take your place as my best friend, Kel. It's just... she's nice, and she seems lonely, and we're both there, you know?"

"I get it. I wish you weren't so far away. I mean, it's not like forever away, but with work and your dad... well, I just miss hanging out with you."

Laura nodded. "Me too."

"So what about the brother... what's his name?"

"Andrei." Laura felt her cheeks go hot, and she raised her hands to cover them.

Kelly quirked a brow and smirked at her. "Something you want to share?"

"Oh my God, Kel, he is so hot," she hissed, leaning across the table and keeping her voice low. "I mean, the man has been flirting with me, and his looks could melt butter on ice. Half the time I'm tongue-tied around him; it's so embarrassing! I mean, I'm supposed to be good with words, but damn!"

Kelly laughed. "So he's sexy and living on the estate with you... and Sam... look at you, stuck between two gorgeous men!"

Laura shook her head. "Hey now, Sam is just a fantasy; I mean, he doesn't notice me like that. But Andrei... well... something could happen there... maybe." She grinned.

"So... what are you saying? If Sam *were* interested, who would you choose?"

Laura bit her lip. She didn't know; she couldn't even imagine it. "I mean... Andrei would be great for, like, a fling... but I... I can't see Sam... I mean, I would love to see Sam, but you know not for a fling... you know? Sam is special."

"So? Have a fling with Andrei. You deserve to have a good time after what Jim did to you."

"I don't know. He's taking care of my dad; it's kind of weird. And I think he's a bit of a player."

"Which makes him perfect for a fling, right?"

"Maybe." Laura bit into another cheese-covered chip. "Mmmm, I have missed these so much."

"You should take some back with you. Tell Maria."

Laura nodded. "I think I will if it will keep while I talk to Hartman."

"Why? What's up?"

"Changing my will and life insurance. Taking Jim off them."

"Ohhh, good idea," she said as Maria brought their food.

"Yeah, so, Bella was the one who thought of that," Laura said once Maria had bustled off again.

"Good on her. I'm glad she's looking out for my girl." Kelly grinned as she began to eat.

"Well, more looking out for my dad... but yeah, she did suggest it."

"So have you found Jim yet?"

"Yes; and get this..." Laura told her everything Angela had found out.

"Oh my God, he's, like, down the street from my office!"

Laura nodded.

"I swear I haven't seen him. You know I'd have told you if I had."

"I know."

"I can't believe that asshole. Please tell me you are making him pay you back for the credit card and loan payments, right?"

"Well..." Laura hedged.

"Laura!"

"It's in the divorce decree that he doesn't get anything from me, and that I want him to cover the credit card payments."

"You should have put the loans in there, too. Or, at the very least, taken his car."

"I know, but... I kind of just want to be rid of him."

Kelly sighed. "I get that. Still can't believe you're letting him get away with it."

They spoke for a while longer as they finished their meal, and then Kelly had to get back to her office, and Laura needed to head to Mr. Hartman's office. She hugged Maria and Jose before she left, carrying half the restaurant with her because Maria said she needed it to go with her carton of cheese. She had promised to come back again soon and visit.

She spent the next two hours in Mr. Hartman's office going over her will and life insurance. There was still no word from Jim on the divorce papers, because he hadn't been at the apartment when their runner had stopped by with them. Mr. Hartman assured her not to worry.

"We'll make sure he gets them by Monday at the latest."

"Okay, thanks," Laura answered. "And thanks for fitting me in today to make those changes. I appreciate it."

"No problem. You have a safe drive back."

"I will." Laura waved her fingers as she left his office. She climbed into her car, which now smelled like she was a delivery driver for Del Toros. The scent made her mouth water, and halfway back to the estate, she cracked open the container of cheese and the bag of chips.

When she got home, she put everything in the fridge,

planning to eat it for a late dinner. And probably for lunch again the next day, Maria had sent that much back home with her.

"Mmm, that all smells good. Where did you go?" Bella asked as she prepared dinner for Laura's father.

"Del Toros. It's about an hour from here."

"Why did you go so far?"

"Oh, I took your advice and met my lawyer to change my will and life insurance."

"That's great; I'm so happy for you. Did you get that jerk to sign the divorce papers?" Bella asked, her back to Laura as she stirred a pot on the stove.

"Not yet. They missed him at the apartment, but said he'd have the papers by Monday at the latest."

"Good. I'm glad to hear it. It must be so stressful waiting to hear that he's signed them."

"You have no idea." Laura nodded, even though Bella couldn't see her.

"Oh, I'm sure I do," Bella murmured.

"Well, I'll let you finish up down here. I'm going to go up and see if I can get those last two chapters finished up tonight. My deadline is Saturday to have it to my editor. I want to be early."

"Okay, well, see you later, then." Bella glanced at her over her shoulder but didn't smile. She just turned back to the pot on the stove.

Shrugging, Laura headed upstairs to her sitting room and got to work.

On Friday, she edited everything she had written the night before, went over the entire book one last time and then sent it off to Erin, along with an email:

Hey look, I'm twelve hours early! LOL

SHE TOOK the weekend off to relax by the pool and, admittedly, flirt with Andrei. She spoke to Sam, too, usually in the evenings when he was out in the garden, but she didn't see a lot of him, as he was busy with estate stuff. On Monday, she got the call from Hartman and Keene that they'd managed to put the papers in Jim's hand, which she was grateful for, but he'd said he needed to read them over and have his lawyer look at them. Laura took that as a good sign.

Soon she would be a free woman. Free to have a fling with the flirtatious and delicious-looking Andrei if she so chose. She was still on the fence about that, though. He definitely made her feel attractive and desirable, and being with him would most definitely be a hot experience, but she wasn't sure she was ready for something like that yet. Maybe she'd be more ready once Jim signed those papers. She'd just have to wait and see.

14

"Jim's refusing to sign the divorce papers."

"What?" Laura screeched into the phone. "What do you mean?"

"He showed up at our office this morning, demanding that Maggie show him into my office," Mr. Hartman said. "He said he wasn't going to let you go."

Laura was hyperventilating. She sank down to the floor, her hands shaking with fury. "No. No, no, no! He can't do this!"

"I'm afraid, at the moment, he can."

"But I want a divorce! I want my life back!"

"Calm down, Ms. Radcliffe. You can still divorce him; it's just going to take longer. I suggest you try speaking to him first. In the meantime, I'll start getting the paperwork ready to file a petition to the court, just in case he continues to refuse. We have to wait thirty days from him initially being served, though, to file."

"Okay, okay. I'll talk to him." Laura nodded.

"He's got a new number, by the way. Maggie's got it; I'll have her text it to you."

"Thank you, Mr. Hartman."

"Don't give up, Ms. Radcliffe. We'll make it happen one way or another." He hung up.

Laura sat there on the floor for another minute and then realized she needed to see a friendly face. She left her room and headed down to the kitchen, her phone in her hand, as she waited for Maggie to text her.

"Hey, not used to see you down here around now. What's up?" Bella asked.

"Jim is refusing to sign the divorce papers."

"What? Why?" Bella looked as frustrated for her as she felt.

"I don't know. Told my lawyer he didn't want to let me go, like he has a choice. I mean, the nerve of the man!"

"What are you going to do?" Bella demanded.

"I'm going to call him, but I have to wait for Maggie—my lawyer's assistant—to text me his new number."

"Well, how long is that going to take?"

Laura shook her head. "I don't know." She shrugged. "I figured I'd have it by now."

Bella pressed her lips together in a thin line and folded her arms over her chest. "That is so unfair! I mean, what are you supposed to do? Just stay married to him?"

"Yeah, it is. And no, Mr. Hartman said we can petition the court, but we have to wait thirty days, and it would be easier if I could talk Jim into signing."

"Then you'd better do it!"

Laura blinked at how vehemently she'd answered. "You seem almost angrier than I am about it." She giggled.

Bella dropped her arms and started giggling, too. "Well, I'm just upset for you. I mean, you should have your life back. He's not being fair to you. I just hate it for you." She reached out and hugged her.

Laura smiled. It was nice to have a friend to hug when she

was upset. "Thanks," she said as her phone beeped. "Oh, that might be Maggie." She moved back from the embrace and pulled out her phone. "It is." She turned and grabbed a pencil and paper from the junk drawer and copied down the number. "Okay, I'm gonna call him."

"Want me to stay with you, give you some courage not to back down?"

Laura felt a wave of support coming from her and smiled. "That would be nice."

Bella nodded. "I got you."

Taking a breath, she picked up the rarely used phone in the kitchen and dialed his number, then waited.

"Hello? Jim Larson speaking."

"Jim, it's Laura. What is this about you not signing the divorce papers?"

He chuckled. "Laura, it's so good to hear your voice, babe. I've missed you so much."

"Cut the crap, Jim! This isn't a 'gee, how are you, I've missed you' call!"

"That's right, you tell him, Laura," Bella whispered next to her.

"Why haven't you signed the papers?"

"Well, I've been thinking about it, and I want to keep my options open..."

"Your options open? You don't have any options, Jim!"

"Don't be like that, Laura. We are so good together, don't you remember? Remember our Vegas honeymoon? How we snuggled on the balcony and watched the sunset?"

Laura growled. "I remember you saying the casino was gorgeous, and then spending half the night gambling away our money for the entire trip!"

"Oh come on, it wasn't like that. We had a great time."

"No. *You* had a great time!"

"Come on, Laura, don't be like th—"

"Shut up, Jim!" Laura screamed. "Just shut up! I never should have married you! You are a user, a manipulator, and I am never, *ever* going to get back together with you! Not ever! Do you hear me?"

"Laura, you're hurting my feelings. Don't you care about me at all? I mean, the least you could do is take me back after you got me fired from the college."

"I didn't get you fired! *You* got you fired! You and that nineteen-year-old beauty pageant queen!"

"She was pretty, wasn't she?" He sounded wistful.

"Oh my God! You are such an asshole! Why the hell would you think I would ever in a million years take you back?"

"Because, baby, that's all over, I swear. I ended it right after I was fired. I want you back."

Laura started laughing hysterically. "*Over?* Sure, that little affair is over, but what about the one with Lindsay Travers?"

"How do you know about her... I mean, who?"

"I know everything, Jim! All of it! Now get this through that extremely thick skull of yours, okay? I am never, not ever, not even if you were the last man on planet Earth or in the universe, I am not going to get back together with you! Do you understand? Sign the freaking papers!" Laura screamed into the phone and then slammed the receiver down.

Bella hugged her immediately. "You did so good. I'm proud of you."

Laura was fuming. She couldn't believe him. He'd tried to gaslight her all over again, but she'd stood up to him, told him off and demanded he sign the papers.

Bella pulled back and looked at her. "You okay?"

Laura nodded, but she was still angry, and her heart was racing. "Yeah. Just mad."

"But you were so awesome on the phone with him."

Laura felt a smile tug at her lips. "I was, wasn't I?"

Bella nodded.

"I never do that..." She started shaking. "I never yell like that... I just... I was so angry..."

"Well, he deserved that and so much more. Now, you should go relax, do something fun."

Laura nodded, but she didn't know what.

"I know, why don't you go for a swim?"

A swim actually did sound kind of nice. It was still sunny out, and the pool did look inviting. "You know, that sounds like a good idea. I think I will."

"Just be quiet when you get upstairs. Your father is still sleeping."

"I will. Thanks, Bella. You're a good friend."

"Anytime, babe." She smirked as she patted Laura on the shoulder.

15

L aura dove into the pool and enjoyed the feeling of the water sluicing over her. It was as if the water scraped away all of her troubles while she moved smoothly through it. She could be calm out there, be in the moment and just rejuvenate herself. And the sun on the water made it just the right temperature; it was so refreshing.

She swam for a while and then lazily basked in the sun on a float that she'd bought in town after one of her appointments with Dr. Fischer. When she got too hot, she'd just roll off the float and into the water, do a couple of laps and then climb back on it again. It was the most relaxing afternoon ever.

She was about to get out when her father and Andrei came outside. "Hi, Dad." She waved.

He squinted at her, and Andrei whispered something to him, his eyes on her. "Laura? What are you doing here?"

Laura closed her eyes behind her sunglasses and sighed softly. "Visiting, Dad."

"Where's your mother?"

"Shopping for dinner."

"Bella's cooking dinner!" he shouted.

"Yes, I... sorry, I meant shopping for the dinner at the school, it's, um... some kind of fundraiser."

Andrei arched a brow and smirked at her, his eyes roaming over her bikini-clad body.

"Right, right." Her father nodded.

She really hated lying to him, but she just wanted him to be happy. And apparently thinking her mom was alive did that for him. "So where are you two off to?" she asked, eyeing Andrei, who looked amazing in a pair of basketball shorts and tight blue shirt. She licked her lips as her eyes roamed his chest.

"We're getting some exercise, aren't we, Michael?"

"Thought I was showing you around the estate?" Her dad seemed confused.

"You are." Andrei chuckled.

"Well, have fun." Laura smiled.

Her dad batted his hand through the air as if he couldn't bother with anything like fun and started marching off toward the garden, telling Andrei about the roses as they walked.

Andrei kept his eyes on her for as long as he could, then finally moved out of her range of sight.

Laura debated getting out now or waiting until they returned. She really liked watching Andrei—who wouldn't? The man was *GQ* cover material, after all—but she also wanted to shower and get the chlorine out of her hair. Still... they wouldn't be gone that long, so she decided to wait.

Twenty minutes later, they returned, and Andrei grinned at her. "Still floating, I see."

"It's just so relaxing out here," Laura answered. She couldn't very well tell him that she'd been waiting to see him again.

"It really is. The whole property is just gorgeous," he

agreed as he and her father walked down the path by the pool. "Let me get Michael to Bella, and I'll be right back. I want to ask you something." He winked.

Laura felt a little flutter build in her stomach. He wanted to ask her something? What could it be? "Sure."

It took another three minutes to get her dad inside. In that time, Laura maneuvered herself and the float to the pool steps. She was setting it aside near the cabana when Andrei returned.

"So, what's up?"

He grinned at her and put a hand on her waist. "I was wondering if you'd like to take a stroll with me tonight? The moon is going to be full..."

The fluttering in her stomach intensified. "I'd... I'd like that." She nodded.

"Great." He dropped his hand from her waist. "I'll see you out here on the deck around eight?"

"Sounds good."

"I'd better get back in there. Bella doesn't like me to leave Michael alone with her when she's cooking." He grinned and jogged back to the kitchen door, blowing her a kiss on his way.

Laura blushed and bit her lip as she waved at him. She couldn't believe her luck. She'd stood up to her asshole of a husband and landed a date with the very hot and available Andrei Ormond. Giggling, she hurried over and grabbed her towel and cover-up, then let herself into the house, rushing upstairs to shower and change for her date.

She took extra care blow-drying her hair so that it hung in waves over her shoulders. Then she pulled out a nice summer sundress to wear that would show off the nice tan she was getting and a pair of sandals. She added some mascara to her lashes and some gloss to her lips but didn't bother with any other bit of makeup.

She was too nervous to eat dinner, so she decided to spend the time before her date checking her blog and the poll she'd set for her followers. So far it was seventy-eight percent in favor of her writing the noir. She decided to go for it, so she wrote out a blog to let them know that she would be starting the outline in the next couple of days. She was really excited about it.

At five till eight, she headed downstairs and out to the deck, where she'd agreed to meet Andrei. She didn't have to wait long.

"Wow, you look amazing," he greeted her.

"Thanks." Her eyes ran over him in his beige chinos and polo. "You look nice yourself."

He smirked and took her hand, threading it through his arm. "You know, your garden here is one of the nicest I've seen."

Laura smiled. "I think so, too." She didn't want to say that it was all thanks to Sam, but she thought it.

"Your dad says your mother chose the roses?"

"Yes." She didn't want to talk about her mother and the roses that she would pull up by their roots if she ever got the chance. Her mother had loved them more than she had ever loved her or Billy.

"He said she won prizes for them?"

Laura gritted her teeth. "She did, yes." She nodded tightly. "Um, would you mind very much if we don't talk about my mother? She's a bit of a sore point for me."

"Oh, sure. How about you tell me about you?"

Laura relaxed a little bit more, feeling more comfortable with this topic than that of her mother or the roses. "Not a lot to tell. I mean, you know I write romances for a living."

"Sure, but why do you do that? Do they sell well?"

"I love it. I love weaving a story that draws readers in and gives them that romantic happily-ever-after that you can only get in fictional stories." She looked away and then up to the moon and sighed.

Andrei paused on the walk and slid his arm around her waist, pulling her against his chest. "So you don't believe they are possible in real life?" he whispered softly as he gazed down at her.

Laura felt her breath catch as she held his gaze.

Andrei leaned in closer, his gaze moving to her lips.

"Laura!"

Laura blinked and turned her head. Sam was hurrying toward them, a strange look on his face in the moonlight. She took a step back from Andrei, who sighed at the intrusion.

"Sam? What's wrong?" she asked as he joined them.

Sam reached for her and pulled her from Andrei's side and behind him. He glared at Andrei. "You keep your hands and your lips to yourself, you Lothario!" he demanded.

Andrei laughed. "Look, you jealous little man, Laura wants to be with me, so I'll kiss her if I want!"

Laura blinked. *Sam is jealous?*

"You're just another player who wants to make her a notch on your belt! You don't want her because she's a good, sweet, caring person. All you see is a beautiful woman to seduce and throw away. Laura deserves better than that!"

"You don't know what you're talking about!" Andrei growled.

Sam thinks I am good and sweet and beautiful? Is it possible Sam likes me? That Sam is jealous of Andrei because he wants me for himself?

"I see right through you. You're just like the soon-to-be ex-husband of hers. She doesn't need another one of you deceitful leeches taking advantage of her sweetness. She deserves to be treated like a lady, and not by the likes of you!"

Andrei laughed harshly. "What, and someone like you

can give her that? What a joke you are! You're nothing but a gardener; paid help!"

His words made Laura step between them. "Hey! That's enough out of both of you! I am not some prize the two of you get to fight over. I am a person, and right now, I don't want to hear any more out of either of you!" With that, Laura turned and stormed off back to the house.

"See what you did?" Andrei said, from behind her. "We were having a perfectly nice—"

Laura ran until she couldn't hear them anymore. She entered the house, and though she wanted to slam the door, she didn't, knowing her dad was probably asleep. She didn't want to wake him. Instead she went up the back stairs, the ones that had allowed the staff to be out of sight when her father entertained, and wound her way to her suite.

She flung herself into a seat in the sitting room and clicked on the TV. As she scrolled through channels, she kicked off her sandals and thought over everything Sam had said. In a way, he was right. Andrei was a bit like Jim, but she wasn't looking at marrying him. He was just hot and would probably be fun to have a short fling with. But Sam. Sam was precious. Sam was everything she'd ever wanted, and that she had hoped Jim would be. Had *thought* he was, up until she'd actually married him. And tonight, she'd found out that Sam—her Sam—actually liked her.

Actually thought she was beautiful.

Actually thought of her as more than just his employer's daughter.

Thought of her as more than just a friend...

Her Sam wanted her back.

Laura bit her lip. She'd dreamt of him wanting her for so long she couldn't even believe that her dream was coming true. Was it possible that she had misinterpreted his words this evening?

Maybe.

She wasn't sure, but she thought he'd blushed when Andrei had called him out for being jealous. And his gaze had softened when he'd looked at her...

Still, she wasn't too pleased with how they'd turned into little boys fighting over their shiny new toy. Sam, she was willing to forgive though—just not tonight. Tonight, she'd let the two of them stew, because they'd ruined a perfectly good evening stroll to argue with each other rather than be with her.

She shook her head and turned her attention to the TV. She'd landed on an old Bogart and Bacall movie and settled in to watch.

16

A few days later, Laura was putting the finishing touches on her outline for the 1940s romantic mystery. She was really excited to get started on it, but she knew she needed to wait until she finished the edits on her last book. It was still currently being edited, though, and wouldn't be ready for her to tackle for another few days. It was always such a process. Normally, she went through about three rounds with her editor, going back and forth after the initial edit; then it was off to her beta readers, which were a group of avid fans who loved reading advance copies that were probably 90 percent ready to go to market. They would leave comments and find any little technical stuff they thought was wrong or needed fixing, and about 75 percent of the time she would agree. Then Erin would look it over again, and finally it would head to pre-sales.

That meant she wouldn't really be able to start the noir yet. She might get a free moment here or there and write a scene, but it would be at least a month before she could really tackle it, focus on it alone. And people wondered why she charged what she did per ebook edition and paperback. They had no idea how many hours actually went into creating a well-put-together novel.

Seven bucks for a coffee? Sure, no problem. Six for an ice-cream cone? Yeah, down for that. But oh my God, you want eight dollars for an ebook and sixteen for a paperback? How dare you! Like, I'll just wait until you put it on sale. Laura sighed. It was a no-win situation. You couldn't argue with people like that. She would just smile, shrug her shoulders and tell them that was their choice, all the while silently screaming.

Her fans, of course, always preordered as soon as they went up. And, thankfully, she had been lucky to gain a good following with the first book she'd ever written, and that following continued to grow because her fans shared her books with others. Not that marketing and ads and the like didn't help. Of course they did. They were a huge part of her success. Writing was either an expensive hobby or a somewhat lucrative career. Of course, there were writers who hit it out of the park and made millions, but Laura hadn't quite reached that level. She was somewhere above expensive hobby, but maybe only halfway into lucrative career.

So after finishing the outline, she messaged Erin to see how the edit was going, and then her publicist, Jacklyn, and her personal assistant, Tori, to work on marketing. She was finished by noon, which left her with the rest of the day free. She debated going into town to do some shopping, but she didn't really need anything, so she put on her swimsuit and decided she'd go out to the pool. But at that moment, her stomach grumbled, and she decided to grab some lunch while she worked out her afternoon plans.

She went down to the kitchen and pulled out the fixings for a peanut butter and jelly sandwich. As she returned the jelly to the fridge, Andrei showed up, smirking as usual in that dead sexy way of his. "Hey," she said as she closed the fridge. "What's up?"

He leaned his hip against the counter next to her and folded his arms. He looked over his shoulder toward the door and then turned back with a smile. "Your father's sleeping, not feeling too well today, so I'm just heading out for a jog. I wondered if you wanted to join me." Then he gave her that bad-boy, sexy grin of his, and his eyes raked over her, bringing heat to her cheeks.

"Oh, um... I don't really jog, you know? I'm more of a get a few laps in the pool and then float for a few hours kind of girl." She laughed.

He chuckled. "Okay, but how about we do something this evening, since we were interrupted so rudely the other night? Maybe a movie?"

Laura felt a thrill race up her spine. She loved the idea of a fling with Andrei, but knowing Sam liked her the way she liked him had her hesitating. Still, Sam hadn't asked her out, and it wasn't as if he hadn't had a chance to do so. She'd seen him since his and Andrei's childish argument over her, but he hadn't brought up going on a date or even apologized for breaking up her stroll.

"Okay, a movie sounds nice."

"Great, I'll see you in the entertainment room around seven thirty?"

Laura hadn't actually been in that room in years. It had originally been her and Billy's 'playroom,' but her mother hated to call it that and rarely allowed any toys in there. It mostly consisted of a large couch with a coffee table and side tables, a mounted TV that nearly resembled a projection screen, it was so large, and a pool table and other various tables and chairs, for playing cards or board games.

"Okay, I'll see you there. Um, enjoy your jog." She picked up the jar of peanut butter to return it to the pantry.

"Can't wait." He winked and headed out the back door, pulling his shirt off as he went.

Laura watched him through the window as he tossed the shirt onto a deck chair and headed out toward the path. She put the peanut butter away and ducked down to the bottom shelf to dig behind stuff and find a bag of chips. Finally she came up with one and took it and her plated sandwich to the table.

As she ate, she decided to go into town and see if she could find something to wear tonight. Even though the 'date' was in the house, she still wanted to look nice. So when she finished eating, she ran upstairs and grabbed her purse, then back down to the garage. She spent the entire afternoon in town, browsing through little boutiques, and finally came across a really cute chambray shirt and shorts set that were turquoise. They were perfect, and she even had a pair of slip-on sandals that would match.

She headed back to the estate after eating a quick burger and fries at the local diner, so she could get ready for her date with Andrei. She took a shower and washed her hair. Once it was dry, she pulled it up into a messy bun and added a cute pair of starfish clips. She put on a bit of mascara and some gloss, then slipped into the turquoise top. The neckline was scooped and had little cutouts of shells and starfish. The shorts fell to mid-thigh, with the hem having the same cutouts as the neckline.

She slipped on her matching sandals and headed downstairs and turned to the right, going in the opposite direction from the kitchen, and then stopped short, thinking maybe some popcorn and a glass of wine would be nice with their movie, so she turned around and headed to the kitchen. She quickly tossed a popcorn bag in the microwave, grabbed a large bowl and two wineglasses. When it was popped, she dumped it in the bowl. In the pantry, which was rather large, there one of those cooling wine racks that kept certain bottles chilled. She grabbed a bottle of *Schmitt Sohne Rheinhessen Ice Wine,* which was a delicious dessert wine, then returned to grab the goblets and popcorn before heading to the entertainment room.

She was setting everything down on the coffee table when Andrei arrived. "Um, hi?" Laura smiled bashfully. "I thought we could use some snacks."

"Sure," Andrei agreed as he walked over to her. "Don't you look adorable."

"Thanks." She blushed and looked down at her feet. "Do you want to choose a movie?"

He shrugged. "Sure, but you know, why don't we sit first?"

Laura nodded, taking a seat on the couch.

Andrei sat down next to her, sliding over so his thigh was less than an inch from hers. "That's better." He reached for the remote control and pulled up the On Demand movies and selected one. "This will do."

"*Mr. and Mrs. Smith*?" Laura said doubtfully. It was an older movie that she'd seen numerous times.

"Sure, why not? I've seen it before, but it's a decent enough movie, and we can talk while we watch." He winked. "You've seen it before, right?"

"Well, yeah." Laura nodded.

"Great, then it won't matter if we miss parts." He smirked. "Let me pour us some of this wine." He grabbed the bottle and looked around. "Corkscrew?"

"Oh, I forgot it." Laura hopped up. "Give me a minute, and I'll go grab it." She swiftly left the room for the kitchen, grabbed the bottle opener and then headed back to the entertainment room. Andrei didn't even look as though he had moved. "Got it." She held it up.

Andrei took it from her and poured them each a glass. "You know, your outfit reminds me of one worn by a girl I met in Mallorca." He sighed.

"Oh? Where is that?" She frowned. She didn't really like the idea that she was reminding him of some other girl.

"One of the islands off the coast of Spain in the Mediterranean Sea. So you've never been, I take it?"

Laura shook her head. "No, what's it like?"

"Gorgeous. Beautiful beaches, beautiful women. I stayed longer than I should have, but it was so lovely... and the girl, Camile, she was exquisite."

"Did you date her for long?" Laura asked, feeling just a little bit uncomfortable.

"No, just for a blissful week or so. We made love four times a day, she was so addicted to me." He smirked and then sipped his wine as he moved a little closer to Laura. "She had hair like yours, long and lovely, but she wore it down, not in a bun."

"Oh?" Laura murmured as his fingers trailed over her neck lightly.

"Mm-hmm. Bella did not join me on this trip, and she was quite irritated with me for not returning to US on time to join her for a job. But Camile, my sweet, lovely Camile, she begged me not to go. Of course, in the end, I had to. It is so sad, really; the poor girl was beside herself with grief over my departure."

"Have you not seen her again? Written to her?" Laura couldn't believe he'd not kept in touch.

"I couldn't. As I said, the poor girl was so upset, she walked out into the sea and drowned herself after my plane left."

"Andrei, that is so sad!" Laura gasped.

"Ah, it is, but I am still here and with a beautiful woman... life goes on, does it not?" He traced a finger down her cheek as he leaned toward her, his lips whisper close. A moment later, he sealed his lips to hers, his hand moving behind her head, holding her close. He swiped his tongue over her lips and pushed into her mouth.

Laura felt unsure about the kiss. At first, she'd thought it was sweet, but then he got a bit more forceful with it, demanding, and she just wasn't ready for that. Still, she didn't pull away right away. She allowed him to continue to kiss her, but she wasn't really kissing him back. When he finally came up for air, Laura licked her lips and pulled back a little, sliding just an inch away.

"You taste delicious," he murmured.

She gave him a smile, but didn't say anything, just reached for the bowl of popcorn and pulled it into her lap as her eyes strayed to the TV. She ate a few pieces and then gave him a side glance as she tried to think of something to say. Finally, she came up with, "So do you do a lot of traveling?"

He slid his arm across the back of the couch and picked up his wine again. "Some. I especially love the islands. Sandy beaches, sunny skies. Those are my favorites. What about you?"

"No, not really. I've been to a few places around the US for book tours, but that's about it."

His fingers tickled the back of her neck. "We'll have to go to a beach sometime. You'll love it."

Laura shifted uncomfortably but smiled. "Maybe..." Her eyes strayed back to the screen. "Oh, I love this part."

From that moment on, she paid more attention to the movie than to Andrei, but she couldn't help it. He was making her uncomfortable. She could feel this whole vibe coming off of him, like his ultimate goal was to get her into bed and that was it. It made her feel, well... kind of like Sam described it. Like a notch on his belt. Just one more girl to add to the list of ones he'd seduced.

She wasn't so sure she wanted to join that list.

17

L aura stood on the path outside Jim's office. *She was frozen there, staring into the window. She couldn't believe what she was seeing. She wanted to scream, but her throat was closed up. She wanted to run in there and drag him off the girl he was pounding into, her ass in the air and her hands planted on his desk, but she couldn't make her feet move. All she could do was stand there and stare at them.*

Her Jim, in the throes of passion, driving that blonde beauty queen wild. She'd never felt so devastated in her life. Her heart raced, pounding in her chest in the same rhythm as Jim thrust into the teenaged hussy. Other students walked by her as though she weren't even there. It was as though she were a ghost.

A ghost chained to that one spot, forced to revisit this one scene of her life over and over and over again.

Laura shut her eyes, willing the scene to change. Pleading with whoever would listen to make it end, make it go away. And when she opened her eyes, it had. But this wasn't any better.

Now, she was hiding with Billy in the upstairs linen closet. She had him wrapped in a blanket, rubbing his back and rocking him back and forth as her mother stormed through the house. She could hear things shattering against the wall downstairs. Her mother's temper was up. Laura couldn't hear whom she was angry with, which meant it had to be her father. He was always mild-mannered. Just taking her mother's ire.

"Shhh, Billy, we don't want Mama coming after us," she murmured to the six-month-old.

Laura had no idea what time it was, sometime after ten at least. There had been guests for the past couple of days, staying in the off-limits wing of the house, but they were gone now. She could hear her mother screaming something about Tom's wife, but she didn't understand what she meant or what lounge ray *was.*

Really, she just wanted it to stop, wanted to go back to bed and hide under her covers, telling herself a story that she could disappear into and forget the world she was living in. A moment later, the front door slammed. Laura held her breath, waiting to see what would happen next.

She heard gentle footsteps on the stairs. Her father's. Which meant it was her mother who'd gone. She relaxed for the first time in an hour. Holding onto Billy, Laura slowly opened the linen closet door and peeked out. She saw her father, his face bloodied and his eye bruised as he headed for his bedroom. Tears filled her eyes as she watched him touch his busted lip and go into the bedroom.

As quietly as she could, Laura left the closet and returned Billy to his crib. She placed a kiss on his forehead and crept across the hall to her own room.

LAURA WOKE up tangled in the sheets and shaking. She hadn't had a dream like that in some time, and it worried her. Was she backsliding? She wasn't sure, but she quickly picked up the dream journal that Dr. Fischer had told her to start, and wrote down everything she could remember from both troubling dreams. First the one with Jim, which was part dream, part memory of that day she'd seen him with his little nineteen-year-old mistress. Or one of them, at least. She sighed. Then she recorded the second dream, which she couldn't be sure was a memory or if it was just a combination of various events that had taken place in her childhood.

She'd have to talk to Dr. Fischer about it all. Maybe the doctor would have some insight into why she was dreaming about all this now. Feeling absolutely sluggish, she crawled out of bed, nearly tripping on the sheets tangled around her legs. She stumbled into the bathroom and decided to take a shower before going down for coffee.

After dressing, she decided to use the front stairs, going by her father's room. He hadn't been doing well the last few days. He seemed groggier, more tired and off balance a lot. He was slurring words and having tantrums. It was really troubling to her; she worried that maybe something else, beyond the dementia, was wrong.

She made her way down the hall and turned the corner. She could hear her father shouting from there, so she walked faster, toward his room.

"No!" he shouted. "You're trying to poison me! I won't take it! I won't!"

Laura opened the door to see her dad flailing his arms. "Dad!" She hurried toward him.

"Michael, it's just your regular morning pills." Bella tried to remain calm but was clearly frustrated.

"Dad?" Laura moved closer to the bed. "Come on, Dad, this isn't good for you. Why are you shouting at Bella? You like Bella."

He gave her a mutinous glare. "She's drugging me!"

"Dad, she's not. Look, it's just your normal meds. You take them every morning." Laura took the pills from Bella and held them in her palm for her dad to see. "Come on, take them now before you get all worked up again."

"I'm not getting worked up! She's trying to poison me, and you're in on it! You just want my money!"

Laura sighed. "No, Dad. I really don't. I have my own money." Not that it was anywhere near his millions, but she was comfortable for the most part and really didn't care about her father's money.

He grumbled some more, but eventually held his hand out for the pills and swallowed them. "Stop badgering me and leave me alone."

Bella just stood there the entire time, watching with a satisfied little smile on her lips. "Thanks," she whispered once he calmed down and drifted off to sleep. "He was really giving me fits this morning."

Laura frowned at the fact that her father had fallen asleep shortly after taking the pills. Normally, the morning pills weren't so strong that they knocked him out like that, but she supposed after the tantrum he'd thrown, he was just all tuckered out. Still, she wanted to call Dr. Temple and check in with him.

"He's starting to worry me, Bella. I mean, he was doing so well, he was on a routine, and now he's not even leaving his room, and he's sleeping more..." Laura looked worriedly down at her father.

Bella moved toward her and laid a hand on her arm. "It's like that for some dementia patients. They are fine for a while, and then it's like a light switch gets flicked and they spiral down. But don't worry; it could be temporary. We'll just have to wait and see, okay?"

Laura nodded. "Okay. I just hate seeing him like this."

"Me too." Bella nodded. "Go on and get some breakfast. I'll sit with him."

"You're sure?"

"Yes, I've already eaten."

Laura finally agreed and headed downstairs, but instead

of going to the kitchen, she headed for her father's study. When she reached it, she closed the door and locked it, then went and sat at her father's desk. She hadn't bothered to grab her phone before leaving the room, so she decided to call Dr. Temple on the landline. She found his number again in her dad's phone book and called.

"Dr. Temple's office, how may I help you?"

"Hi, this is Laura Radcliffe; is Dr. Temple available?"

The receptionist sighed. "Hold one moment and I will see if he can speak with you, Ms. Radcliffe."

"Thank—" Laura started but was cut off by the hold button. She didn't take the woman's manner personally; she was probably just overworked and underpaid.

A few minutes later, the receptionist came back on the line and said she'd transfer her over to his phone.

"Ms. Radcliffe, what can I do for you this morning? Is your father well?"

"Hi, Dr. Temple. He's... well, I'm not sure." She went on to tell him about what was going on and what his nurse, Bella, had said, and that she just wanted to be sure they weren't missing anything important.

"I see. In general, his nurse—Bella, did you say her name was?"

"Yes, sir."

"Okay, well, she's correct. These things can happen like that with dementia patients. Sometimes they'll come back out of it and resume a period of reasonable lucidity, and others, not so much. Just keep an eye on him, and if his condition worsens, let me know. Perhaps we can try a change in his medicine."

Sighing, Laura replied, "So you also think this is a natural progression of the disease?"

"I do."

"All right then, thank you, Dr. Temple. I didn't mean to take up your time."

"It's no trouble at all, Ms. Radcliffe. I understand your worry. Right now, there isn't much we can do."

"Okay," she said softly.

"Call me if you feel he's getting worse. Otherwise, I will see him at his next appointment."

"Yes, Doctor." Laura hung up and sat back in the chair.

The day had only just started, and she was already thoroughly exhausted. She wished she could crawl back into bed and start over, but there was too much to do. She had her appointment with Dr. Fischer to attend, and she'd gotten the first-round edits back from her editor and had to start going through them.

Her normal coffee wasn't going to cut it this morning. She needed something stronger. With that in mind, she headed back upstairs for her purse and laptop. After her appointment today, she would work from the little coffee shop in town, where she could have a double espresso. It was the only way she was going to make it through the day.

18

Tired, Laura headed home. Her appointment with Dr. Fischer had gone pretty well, even with the crazy nightmares about Jim and her mother that she'd had. Dr. Fischer explained that they had probably been brought on and made so intense because of stress, and that she wanted Laura to try some meditation.

On top of that, she hadn't gotten as far into the edits as she wanted; she'd been too distracted with worry over her dad. She knew that both Bella and Dr. Temple had said it was a natural progression, if a little early, but that sometimes it happened that way. Still, it bothered her.

She pulled up to the gate and punched in the code, then went up to the garage, where she maneuvered her car in and parked it. She could see Sam tinkering with the mower again. She smiled as she watched him for a moment. He really was handsome, in that rugged outdoors kind of way. He wasn't slick like Andrei, he was more... well, you could just tell that his muscles weren't built in a gym, but from hard work, and his tan didn't come from a tanning salon but from the sun... she supposed the word she was looking for was *real*. Andrei was like a fantasy, but Sam was real. And she liked that about him.

"Hi, Sam," she said as she climbed out of her car. "What's wrong with the mower?"

"Not sure," he said, "but I'll figure it out."

"I'm sure you will. Hey, can I talk to you for a minute? It's about my dad."

"Sure, darlin', you know I'm here for you." Sam set down his wrench and moved over to her.

"I know, I just... I think he's getting worse. I don't mean like just another tantrum, but really bad, Sam."

Sam took her hand and led her over to a pair of extra deck chairs that were being stored in the garage. He gestured for her to sit, and he took the other seat but didn't let go of her hand. "You know, my mom had dementia before she passed. That's how I recognized the pills." He shook his head. "It's not pretty. It's like a nightmare, so I understand why you're worried. My mom's didn't start getting really bad until the last six months of her life. She really went downhill after that."

"But Dad shouldn't be getting this bad already, should he? Not with the meds he's on, right?"

"I don't know. I mean, I have heard it can happen pretty fast for some people, but for most, yeah, the meds should help quite a lot. As long as he's taking them when he should be."

"I'm sure he is; Bella keeps track. What if he's on the wrong dosage?" Laura bit her lip and shared what she'd been worrying about. "Or the wrong pills for his system?"

"They were working fine before, though, right?"

"Well, yes..." She sighed, looking down at their entwined fingers. "But it's still a possibility, right?"

"It could be. Have you called his doctor?"

Laura nodded. "This morning. He told me basically the

same thing Bella said. That he could snap out of it, or it could be the beginning of him getting worse." She felt tears prick her eyes.

"You could always get another opinion. Call another doctor or ask a pharmacist."

Laura licked her lips and slowly nodded. "I could do that..."

Sam brushed a stray loose hair from her cheek. "You look like you haven't been sleeping. Is everything other than your father okay?"

Her mind flashed to the previous night's dreams, and she shuddered. "I haven't been sleeping well. I've been having nightmares again."

"Want to talk about them?"

She bit her lip and looked down at the cement floor as she scraped her toe over a rock and marked the floor up. "Not especially."

"Sometimes it helps."

"I know, but... one was a memory of finding Jim with... finding Jim cheating," she bit out. "The dream—well, more of a nightmare really—was worse than the actual event. I mean, when it happened for real, I turned around and left, but in the dream, I couldn't move. It was like I was stuck there."

"Come here." Sam reached for her and hugged her. "You know he can't hurt you anymore, right?"

She nodded. "Well, he can't hurt my heart anymore, at any rate."

"So what was the other dream?" he said, pulling back to look in her face.

"It was about Mom and Dad, mostly. Only I don't know if it really happened, or if I mixed up several fights of theirs and just put them all together into one nightmare, or what." Laura sighed. "But honestly, I don't really want to talk about it, if that's okay? I mean, I've talked to Dr. Fischer about it, but..." She didn't know why she was so hesitant to share that part of her nightmare with Sam. He'd known her mother and would understand what she'd been through. "You know how Mom was, so you can probably guess some of the things that happened in real life and in my dream."

Sam nodded. "Your mom was pretty abusive, especially to your dad those last few years. There were days he'd have a black eye or a bruised cheek, and he'd say he ran into a door. I knew she'd done it, though. I could hear them occasionally from the garden. Your dad would always try to get her to be quiet, but she'd just get louder."

"Yes, that's true; she would. In my dream, she was throwing things, and I was hiding in the closet with Billy. He was just a baby. She was screaming at my dad about some man's wife and—" Laura paused and finally realized what it was her mother had said. She blinked up at Sam. "She was talking about Tom's wife wearing lingerie!" she exclaimed. "In the dream, I couldn't figure it out. I thought she said *lounge ray*, but retelling it to you, it just hit me."

"Do you remember anything else?" Sam asked, sounding curious.

"I remember hearing the front door slam and seeing Dad come up the stairs. She'd beaten him up. Black eye, busted lip, and a swelling bruised cheek... and that was just what I could see." Laura shook her head, her eyes wide.

"Yeah, I saw him that way a few times too. He always tried to hide it under sunglasses when he could, but I could always tell."

Laura sighed. "I wish he would remember what she was like and admit that Mom was abusive."

"I know."

"It's not going to happen, is it?" Laura looked at him sadly. She hated the fact that her father didn't acknowledge the damage her mother had done to all of them.

"Probably not. Not if he's diminishing like he is," Sam commiserated.

Laura huffed a breath. She felt better for having talked to Sam, but the topic of her father and her mother was depressing. "I should go in. I've still got a ton of edits to fix from my editor."

"Is that where you went after your appointment? I wondered why you were gone for so long."

"Yeah, went to a coffee shop afterwards to work today. The view wasn't as great, but the double espresso was just what I needed." She smiled as she stood up.

Sam touched her chin. "Well, don't stay up all night working. You need to sleep, too."

"I won't. Thanks, Sam."

"Anytime, darlin'."

Laura grabbed her laptop and purse from the car. She felt his eyes on her as she headed into the house. She sluggishly made her way up the back stairs, avoiding the kitchen and living areas, where she might have run into Bella or Andrei. She really didn't feel like chatting with either of them. She just wanted to sit down at her desk and get back to work.

As she had promised Sam, she shut everything down by ten, took a relaxing bubble-filled bath in the garden tub, and then was in bed and asleep by eleven. She was either too tired to dream, or the dreams were too vague to remember after... but at least she was able to get some decent sleep.

19

"Laura, this is Maggie from Mr. Hartman's office."

"Hi, Maggie, what's up?" Laura answered, with a slight bit of worry piling up in her stomach.

"He was hoping he could either schedule a time for you to come in or, at the very minimum, a phone call."

"Um, sure—though, if it's at all possible, the phone call would work better for me. We could do a Zoom call if that works?" Laura had often used Zoom with her editor, publicist, and personal assistant, since none of them even lived remotely close to each other.

"Oh, I am sure that will work fine. He said if you chose a phone call, he'd prefer it to be after two. Would two fifteen work for you?"

"Sure. Just text me if he wants to make it a video call."

"Will do. Have a good day!" Maggie hung up.

Laura wondered what that could all be about. Had Jim gone in and signed the papers like she asked? If so, why not just have Maggie tell her? She started to fret as she pulled up her manuscript to work on. She still had six more chapters to go through and adjust before sending it back to her editor.

However, now she couldn't focus on it at all. Now, all she could do was sit and stare at the screen, wondering what Jim was doing to fuck up her life yet more. She couldn't believe it would be good news.

That just wasn't how her life went. At least not her family or personal life, at any rate. It was as though only one part of her life could be going fairly well at one time. And right now, that part was her work life. At least, mostly well, except for the part where she was so distracted that she couldn't do her edits.

"Argh!" she muttered and closed the laptop. There was no point in doing edits while she was distracted; she'd just mess something up. Instead, she moved over to the sofa, grabbed the remote and turned on the TV. Maybe she could find something to distract her until her phone call with Hartman.

She flipped channels and finally landed on a cooking show. She wasn't the best cook, but she did like to watch other people do it. Especially those wanting to be one of those outrageous chefs, the ones who made such phenomenal dishes and were celebrated by other famous chefs. Sometimes, she daydreamed there was a show like that for writers.

Like, she would have to create particular scenes given certain elements by the master writers. Of course in her head, those master writers were people like Jane Austen, Agatha Christie, Shakespeare and Mary Shelley, none of whom were alive, but it was her fantasy; she could have them be whoever she wanted.

Somehow, she drifted off to sleep and dreamt that she'd won the competition with her final action scene. The master writers were all gathered around her, applauding so loud it caused a buzzing to vibrate through her.

Suddenly she came awake, realizing that the vibrating

buzz was her phone in her pocket. She hurriedly picked it up and answered.

"Hello?"

"Laura? It's Hartman."

"Oh, um, hi, Mr. Hartman. I'm sorry, I must have fallen asleep." She wiped her eyes and clicked off the TV. "So what did you want to talk to me about?"

"It's not great news, I'm afraid. Jim had his lawyer send over an amended divorce settlement."

"Wait, what? Can he do that?"

"Well, he can, but you don't have to accept."

Laura was afraid to ask, but felt she needed to know. "What did he amend?"

"I read it over several times and then called his lawyers to see how he came to the settlement he's asking for... you're not going to like it, and I recommend not agreeing to any of it."

"Just tell me, what is he asking for?"

"It seems that Mr. Larson has claimed that because you are a famous author and come from a wealthy family, that he deserves to be kept in a fashion that is equal to when you were married, with you paying for his apartment, utilities and give him an allowance of five hundred dollars a week."

"Is he insane?" Laura shrieked into the phone.

"As I said, it's completely out of line, especially given the fact that you are more than ten thousand dollars in debt because of him."

Laura was seething. She couldn't even see for all of the blinding red taking over her vision. "No, absolutely not! I'm not giving him anything! Not one blasted cent! If anything, he should be paying *me*!"

"I knew that was how you would feel, but I had to tell you what he's countered with, anyway. Shall I draw up a new document and make changes, or do we go to arbitration?"

Laura didn't know what to do. "I... I don't know. What do you suggest?"

"I personally don't advise backing down on what you've asked for. He needs to be responsible for some of the debt incurred during the marriage. And I especially don't advise giving in to his demands for alimony. Which means I think we should go to court."

Laura groaned. She didn't want to have to go to court, but it looked like Jim was going to fight her every step of the way. "Okay... let's do that."

"I will see what kind of dates we're looking at and have Maggie give you a call once we have it all set up."

"Thank you, Mr. Hartman."

"Goodbye, Ms. Radcliffe. We'll be in touch."

Laura clicked her phone off. She wanted to dial Jim and strangle him through the phone lines, but that would be impossible, and even if it weren't, she'd go to jail for murder, and she didn't want to do that, either.

Instead, she went downstairs for the fudge ripple. Ice cream was always her solace whenever she became so upset and worked up. Add to that some bourbon, and she could blot out Jim being his usual asshole self for at least five minutes. She hesitated, though, remembering the last time she'd had some bourbon and ice cream. She'd woken with the worst hangover and hadn't gotten much accomplished at all the next day. Still... the edits could and would wait. Her editor was pretty lenient, knowing what was going on in Laura's life. She would completely understand her need to get drunk and drown her sorrows.

Because of that, Laura headed for the liquor cabinet first. She grabbed a bottle of Jim Beam instead of the Heaven's Door this time. Then she went to the kitchen for the ice cream and a spoon, as well as a glass. She took all of it to the table and poured herself a healthy glass of the Jim

Beam. It wasn't quite as expensive as the Heaven's Door, so she could actually drink the bottle and still afford to replace it.

She was a little more than halfway through the bottle of bourbon and the carton of fudge ripple when Bella strolled into the kitchen. "Uh-oh, what's happened?" she asked, sitting down next to her. "Spill it, sister."

Laura wiped her cheek, feeling the stickiness of the ice cream there. "My bastard of a husband is what happened!" she slurred as she took another gulp, finishing off what was in the glass so she could pour some more. So far, the alcohol wasn't doing much to make her forget about what her husband was doing. She needed more.

"Wanna tell me about it?" Bella asked.

Laura ignored her for a moment as she took another swig of the alcohol. She didn't offer Bella any, and Bella didn't ask, thankfully. Laura figured she was going to need it all to make herself forget, at least temporarily.

"Can you believe that asshole wants me to pay him alimony!" she said, only it probably came out sounding like the adults in the *Peanuts* cartoons. All wonk-wonk-wonka-wonk or something, but she didn't care.

"He doesn't! What a jerk! I am so glad you already changed your will and life insurance. I mean, what a dick move after everything he's done. Can you imagine what he'd do if you left him on them?"

Laura didn't bother to answer that. She just continued with her complaints. "And he knows I don't have any money from the estate. Billy and I both have had to do everything for ourselves. Dad always thought it was better for us to earn our own way, which I am sure he got from Mom. God knows who he's leaving this place to since Mom's gone. I mean, it's probably all going to some charity or to Mom's school or some other weird place." She gulped another glass of Jim Beam and poured a new one, though most of the bottle was gone now.

"Billy? Who's that?"

"My baby brother," Laura muttered as she dug into the ice-cream container to scoop out some more of the fudge. "He worked his ass off to get into college on a full scholarship. He did it, too, no thanks to Dad. Gonna be a vet."

"Is that so?" Bella replied, but she sounded weird to Laura's intoxicated mind.

"Mm-hmm."

"So how come we haven't met him yet?"

"Oh, he won't come here. Hates Dad." Laura was distracted by the fudge on the spoon and trying to get it all off with her tongue. "Not 'cause of the money. Because of the abuse, you know," she leaned toward Bella to whisper loudly. She nearly fell out of her chair, but Bella grabbed her shoulders and pushed her back upright in her chair.

"Abuse?"

Laura nodded. "Mom used to beat the shit out of us," she slurred, her gaze glassy as memories of her mom smacking the crap out of her and breaking her wrist and doing a dozen other terrible things to her passed through her mind. Tears slid down her cheeks as she recounted numerous times that her mother had lost her temper on her or Billy or her dad.

"One time, Mom beat Billy with one of her shoes so hard, she broke four of his ribs and gave him a busted nose and two black eyes. Told the doctors he *gotted* into a fight with a neighborhood boy she *dinn't* know. She always lied, and they always believed her." Laura grimaced. She knew some of the words that were coming out of her mouth weren't quite right, but she didn't care at this point; she was too far gone. "We knew *bedder* than to contradict her. She'd have *beatened* us worse. An' Dad *dinn't*, did-n't do a thing. Not a thing. Nothing. Zero. Zip. *Naddda. Juss* told us to behave *bedder*." Laura rolled her eyes, but then had to shut them because the room started to spin.

"That's terrible," Bella murmured.

Laura picked up the bottle of Jim Beam, and instead of pouring the last of it into her glass, she just drank it straight from the bottle. "Billy *hard-lee* ever calls me anymore. He's *anger* I'm here." She sniffled and wiped her nose with the back of her hand.

"That's too bad. He should be glad that you are here taking care of Michael so he doesn't have to be," Bella murmured. "So where is he? Which college, I mean."

Laura shrugged. "University of California, Davis-Davis."

"Pretty nice school."

Laura nodded. She turned the bottle of Jim upside down. "It's empty."

Bella snorted. "You drank it all."

Sighing, she tilted the ice-cream carton toward her face and said, "An' the ice cream is gone too."

"Looks that way."

She blinked over at Bella and gave her a watery smile. "Thanks for listening, I'm sorry I'm such a mess." Her words were even more slurred, and her *s* letters were coming out with a distinct 'sh' sound. "I think I need my bed."

"Want me to help you upstairs?"

Laura shook her head violently. "No. I got it." She waved as she started toward the door, but she was a bit wobbly. "G'night."

Bella giggled. "Night."

She stumbled on the steps and hit her knee, but she finally made it to her room. She didn't bother to get undressed. It seemed like too much of a hassle. Instead, she fell on the bed face-first and fell asleep where she landed.

20

Laura woke with a pounding headache to the sun glaring through her open curtains. "Ugh," she muttered, rolling over and pulling the pillow over her face. She attempted to go back to sleep, but the pounding in her head was relentless.

Finally, she tossed the pillow and pushed herself up on her elbows, blinking rapidly at the clock. It was nearly ten a.m. She was going to be late to her appointment. Feeling like crap, she reached for her phone and dialed Dr. Fischer.

"Dr. Fischer's office, how may I help you?"

"Amanda, this is Laura Radcliffe," she whispered into the phone because even her voice was too loud for her own ears. "I'm going to have to cancel today's appointment."

"Oh, I'm sorry to hear that. Has something happened? Are you safe?"

Laura nodded, then grabbed her head, because even that action hurt beyond reason. "I'm okay, and yes, something has happened, but I'm safe. There is no emergency. I had a bit too much to drink last night and just woke up a few minutes ago, so I can't make it in."

"Let me get Dr. Fischer. She's not with a patient at the moment, since you are due to come in."

Sighing, Laura agreed, "Okay." She only had to wait a moment before Dr. Fischer came on the line.

"Laura, is everything all right? Amanda said you are unable to come in?"

"Yes, I'm okay. I just got some really bad news from my lawyer yesterday afternoon, and I made the mistake of drowning my sorrows in bourbon and ice cream."

"I see. I'm glad you see that as a mistake, honestly, but it is sometimes a natural reaction, as long as you recognize that it's an unhealthy one."

"I do," Laura said softly.

"Do you want to talk about it? What drove you to do that?"

"Jim wants me to pay him alimony consisting of his rent, utilities and a five-hundred-dollar-a-week allowance. I guess I just lost it. I was—I still *am* so upset and angry. All I want is to be free of him, and him to pay his share of the debt."

"That is a completely reasonable desire for you to have. He, on the other hand, is continuing in his emotional abuse toward you and trying to control you. My guess is, he is asking for something outrageous in the hopes of pushing you into speaking to him. Did you?"

"No. My lawyer, Mr. Hartman said we could just take him to court, and recommended that I not give in to his ridiculous demands."

"Good. I'm glad to hear you have someone competent working in your favor. So what was it that pushed you over the edge last evening?"

"Stupidity?" Laura said, with a grimace. "I just wanted to blot out the whole thing for, like, five minutes, but the more I drank, the worse my thoughts got..."

"Okay, so you realize that wasn't the best way to go about things, correct?"

"Yes. I just... I feel... unempowered. Miserable. Unlovable," she softly replied.

"I can understand the feelings. However, you realize that you are neither unempowered nor unlovable, don't you? As for miserable, that one is understandable. You are going through several difficult things at the moment. Dealing with your dad's declining health, being in a home that caused you so much pain, the breakdown of your marriage... those are all the things causing you misery. But once you recognize those things, you can look at the things that are good in your life and attempt to focus on those. Tell me five things that are good in your life."

Laura sat there for a moment, thinking about what was possibly good in her life. "Um, I have a fairly successful career that I love?"

"You do indeed. That's one. Four more."

Laura bit her lip. "I have good friends?"

"Who and why are they good friends?"

"Well, Sam... he always listens and gives me good advice, and he's sweet and caring. Kelly, she's been my best friend since college, we love doing things together, and we have a lot in common. Bella, she's kind of a new friend, but she's been a great help with my dad, and she listens when I need to vent and is very supportive..."

"And would you say any of these friends would call you unlovable?"

"No..."

"So that's two, name three more..." Dr. Fischer urged.

"I'm physically healthy?"

"That is always a blessing. Two more."

"I have a place to live while I get back on my feet financially?"

"A very positive way to look at your living situation. One more."

"Despite all the stress of the last two months, I was able to meet my deadline and finish my novel?"

"Another very good positive going on. You see? You are more empowered than you think, Laura. You have people on your side who are willing to support you, and you have a good lawyer who is going to help you free yourself from an abusive relationship. You have a roof over your head, food on your table and a job you love, with fans who love you."

Dr. Fischer's words made Laura smile in spite of the headache that was still rapping on her skull. "You're right. I have a lot to be thankful for."

"Now, when you start feeling so overwhelmed that you want to blot out part of your emotions, or the world, I want you to make another list of the positive things going on in your world and understand the misery of the moment is just that, of the moment. It won't last, but the positive things in your life, they will. All of the things you listed as positives are things that will continue to bring you joy."

Laura's smile widened. "Yes, that's true. Thank you, Dr. Fischer."

"You're welcome. Now, seeing as I am sure you are not feeling well after last evening, I want you to drink plenty of water, as I am sure you're dehydrated, and get some rest. Keep writing in your journal, and I'll see you in my office soon, okay?"

"Yes, you will. Thank you."

"Take care, Laura."

Laura hung up the phone and sighed. She actually did feel better for having talked to Dr. Fischer. Of course, she still had a headache, but she could fix that with a shower, ibupro-fen, food and, as Dr. Fischer had mentioned, plenty of water. With that in mind, Laura headed to the bathroom. She swallowed a couple of pills from the medicine cabinet, took a long, warm shower and then went downstairs for food.

By the time she'd eaten, her headache was pretty much gone, and she was feeling much better. Even good enough to tackle the last of the edits she needed to do. She returned upstairs to her suite without seeing or hearing from anyone else in the house.

Several hours later, she sent the file back to her editor and called it good. It was past seven, and she knew Bella, Andrei and her father had already eaten dinner, so she went and scrounged up her own and brought it up to her room to eat. It was just a microwavable burger and some chips, so it wasn't too much of a mess.

She sat in front of her TV and ate while she caught up on one of her favorite shows, then brushed her teeth and got ready for bed, even though it was barely ten o'clock. Just as she was about to drift off to sleep, there was a light rap upon her door.

Laura shoved her hair out of her face and got out of bed to answer it. "Andrei?" she murmured, peering up at him. "What's going on? Is my dad all right?"

"Sure, he's fine. Don't you look delicious," he said, smirking as he took in her slinky nightgown.

Laura blushed. "Um, so what are you doing here?"

"I came to see you, beautiful. I missed you today, stuck up here in this room, all by yourself." He moved forward toward her, his hands going to her hips. He kicked the door closed behind him as he leaned down to capture Laura's lips in a hot and hungry kiss.

Laura slid her arms up around his neck. The man was extremely attractive and made her skin sizzle. He was very hard to resist, even though she knew she should. Knew that he just wanted to add her to his collection of women. Still, was that really a bad thing if she knew it going in? She wasn't looking for forever, not with him. She was just looking for a hot little fling, which he was perfect for. So she kissed him back with as much passion as she could.

Andrei maneuvered her backwards until her legs hit the side of the bed, and then they both tumbled backwards. Laura giggled as they landed. She pushed against his chest a moment and then whipped the nightgown over her head.

Andrei leaned in and brushed kisses against her neck, which drove her wild. He moved down her body, taking her nipple into his mouth, sucking it as he fumbled with the button on his jeans. He began shoving them down to his knees, then reached for her panties. Laura eyed his large erection and drew in a sharp breath at the sight. He was bigger than she'd thought, definitely bigger than Jim. She shoved that thought away. She didn't want to be thinking of him during a time like this, but it was enough to make her hesitate and come back to reality for a moment.

She didn't want to stop, not at all. But she didn't want to deal with any consequences of this fling, either. She knew he'd been with multiple women, and they'd never talked about health status, and she really didn't want to get pregnant either. So she glanced up at him and murmured, "Condom?"

Andrei shook his head and dove back down to her neck.

Laura struggled against him, pushing at his shoulder. "Andrei, no. Not without a condom!"

"But I want you now," he whined. "I don't want to wait."

"And I want you too, but I'm not having sex with you without a condom." She reached for her panties and pulled them back up as she wiggled her way out from under him.

"You're on the pill, right? What's the big deal?" he pouted.

"I'm not. Can't take it; I break out in hives."

He sank down on the bed. "Well, this sucks. I want to feel you, babe, not some stupid condom."

"Well, that's not going to happen. I think you should go."

Laura reached for her nightgown and pulled it back over her head.

"Don't be like that, babe. Come on, it'll be fun," he urged, reaching for her.

"Andrei, I said no."

"Least you could do is suck me. I mean, look how hard I am." He gripped his cock and stroked it a few times, as if that would entice her.

Laura did her best not to roll her eyes. "I need to go to bed. You need to leave. Now."

He gave her a mutinous look and pulled his pants up. "Didn't know you were going to go all frigid on me. You're a cock tease." He pulled up his pants as he sneered at her.

"I am not! I was totally willing to have sex with you if you just put on a condom!"

"Whatever." He shook his head at her and strode to the door. He looked over his shoulder and said, "Last chance..."

"Goodnight, Andrei."

He yanked the door open and strode through, not bothering to close it behind him. As if he expected her to watch him walk away and regret her decision to tell him no.

Laura silently closed and locked her door. She thought about the entire scene, and all she could think was that she was actually glad that things had turned out the way they did. She wasn't really cut out for a fling, especially when her heart was already engaged elsewhere. Even if that man didn't want to acknowledge the fact that he felt the same for her.

With not one ounce of regret, she slipped back into bed and drifted off to sleep. The next morning, she awoke feeling completely refreshed. She hadn't had a nightmare and had slept very peacefully, though she did recall dreaming about a certain estate manager who had always made her heart flutter.

Dressing, she headed downstairs to make herself breakfast. The kitchen had a stack of dishes in the sink, which was a little annoying, but she went ahead and rinsed them off, then put them in the dishwasher before pulling out a new frying pan to make herself some scrambled eggs.

As she sat down to eat, Andrei slunk into the kitchen, pointedly ignoring her, while still pouting like a teenage little brat who didn't get his way. He slammed a cabinet as he pulled a mug out, then proceeded to make as much noise as possible to draw her attention.

Laura did not give him what he was after. Instead, she continued to eat in silence, ignoring his behavior. She was finding him less and less desirable the more he acted this way. She kept her eyes averted as he left the room, but she could feel his glare on her.

Later that afternoon, when she went out to the pool, he tried a different tactic. He suddenly acted as though the night before, and earlier this morning, never happened.

"Hey, beautiful. Can I join you in the pool?"

"Aren't you working?" She arched a brow at him.

His brow furrowed for a moment, like he didn't understand her question. "Um, well, I guess, but I don't have to be. Bella can—"

"I'm sure Bella would love for you to help her with my dad. I know he's been pretty cranky at her."

"Yeah, but—"

"It's okay, I'm fine on my own. You don't have to entertain me."

"Uh, okay?" The look on his face was one of disbelief. As if no woman had ever told him no before. "I'll just go see if Bella could use a hand. See you later?"

"Sure," Laura said, but didn't really mean it. She planned to do her laps and relax up until right before dinner, and then she'd head back up to her suite and ignore him for the rest of the evening. She really didn't know what she'd seen in the man to begin with.

Of course he was hot, but looks could only take a person so far. The more she talked with and learned about him, the less attractive she found him. She just couldn't even see herself being drawn to him anymore. It was as though someone had taken the rose-colored glasses from her eyes and given her a reality check.

It had happened that way in her novel too, as it happened. She wondered if maybe her subconscious mind had picked up on all those signs that she'd written about. In the story, the character she'd created in his image had turned out to be a player out to 'nail'—as he put it—as many women as he could. He had no real love for anyone but himself. Her heroine, of course, figured him out much quicker than Laura had, and had chosen her real love, the hero of the story, to fall in love with. Not that Laura hadn't wanted that to happen; she did. But giving her a challenge in the character based on Andrei had been an interesting twist. It had allowed the heroine and hero to fall even deeper in love than she'd pictured by the end of the story.

That was one of the major takeaways from her editor that she hoped her advance readers would pick up on. The thought made her smile. Maybe someday soon, she'd be just as happy as her heroine and hero.

If only Sam would make a move.

That thought had her diving into the pool to start her laps. She shouldn't even be thinking about men at the moment. She had a husband to divorce, and too many other things to do, without getting involved in a new relationship. Still, the thought of Sam asking her out made her smile, and she knew she'd say yes if only he were to ask.

.

21

L aura had been doing her best to avoid Andrei. It was difficult with them living in the same house, but Laura managed for the most part. She stayed in her suite for most of the morning and ate at odd hours. In the afternoon, she headed out to the yard and set up a lounge near the pond where she couldn't be seen from the downstairs windows.

She was set up under a shady tree, reading a book. She could hear Sam out and about working on the yard, getting it ready to mow. She waved to him as he headed to the garage for the riding lawn mower. A few minutes later, he was on the other side of the path, making passes over the yard. She loved watching him work. Not that she ever told him that.

As she watched, she heard a change in the mower's engine, and then suddenly something clanged. The hood of the mower flew up, and Sam was hit by something that knocked him from the seat. It all happened so fast that Laura could hardly take it in. Screaming, "Sam!" she tossed her book and frantically ran toward him. "Sam! Sam, are you alright?"

She reached his side as he lay groaning on the ground. His head was bleeding pretty badly from a cut to his temple. Laura yanked her shirt off over her head and pressed it to the wound.

"Stay with me, Sam," she murmured as she dialed 9-1-1.

"9-1-1, what is your emergency?"

"Hi, yes, I need an ambulance right away! My friend has been injured by a riding lawn mower accident!"

"Yes, ma'am, if I can get your address, we'll dispatch an ambulance immediately."

Laura gave the information. "Please hurry!"

Sam was trying to sit up and dissuade her from having an ambulance sent, but Laura was having none of it. She pressed one hand to his wound, holding him down to the ground, while she spoke on the phone with the other. The operator had stayed on the line, telling her to keep 'the patient' calm.

"Sam, hush. You're bleeding really bad; you're going to the hospital and that's it."

Finally the ambulance arrived, and she hit a button on her phone, opening the gate for them. She had explained to the operator that they'd need to follow the path around to the back, past the house, through the garden toward the pond. A few minutes after the ambulance got there, the paramedics arrived pushing a gurney. Two of them rushed over to them.

Laura was too worried about Sam to care about not having a shirt on. "He's got a really bad cut on his head. I'm worried," she explained.

"Let us take a look, ma'am."

Laura allowed the medic to take over as she thanked the operator for their help. She stood back, her arms hanging by her sides.

Sam caught sight of her and frowned. "Darlin', you need a shirt."

The EMT glanced from Sam to Laura; she caught the

quick smile on his face that swiftly disappeared before he turned back to Sam. "I believe she used it on your head, if I'm not mistaken."

The other medic held it up. "'Fraid it's ruined."

"I don't care about the blasted shirt! Is Sam okay?"

"He will be. We're going to take him in to the hospital. He'll need a few stitches, and the doctors might want to check him for a concussion."

"I'm coming too," Laura said as they helped Sam onto the gurney.

"No, you're not—" Sam started to argue.

"Ma'am, perhaps you'd like to drive behind us? That way, he has a ride back?"

Laura took a moment to process what he was saying, but then nodded. "Yes, okay. I'll just run in and grab my keys—"

"And a shirt!" Sam called out as they started to wheel him away.

Laura didn't bother to answer. Trust Sam to be more worried about her reputation rather than his injury. She raced back up to the house, grabbed her keys off the rack, made a pass through the laundry room and grabbed a shirt from the dryer, then headed out to the car as she pulled it on. She had the car out of the garage by the time they had Sam loaded into the back of the ambulance.

She followed the ambulance from the estate into town and straight to the hospital. She was a nervous wreck, terrified that Sam had more than just a superficial injury requiring stitches. She was afraid the mower had done more damage than he believed.

As the ambulance pulled up to the emergency entrance, Laura pulled into a nearby parking place, slammed the gearshift into park, and tore her keys from the ignition. As soon as the car was locked, she sprinted for the door.

Sam was no longer in sight, so she rushed to the front

desk. "My friend, Samuel Willoughby, was just brought in by ambulance. Where did they take him?"

"And what is your name, ma'am?"

"Laura Radcliffe," she answered. "Please, where is Sam?"

"He's being seen by the nurse, but since you aren't family —" the receptionist started.

"Look, ma'am, I know I am not family, but Sam doesn't have any family. I'm all he has; now please, let me see him!"

At that moment the paramedics returned, saw Laura was arguing with the receptionist, and joined them. "Mr. Willoughby is asking for her, says she's the closest he has to family."

The receptionist frowned, but then nodded. "Very well. Just go through those doors; he's in station number four."

Laura looked at the men who'd brought Sam in. "Thank you," she murmured as she headed straight for the doors.

She pushed through and speed-walked to the curtained area with a number four above it on the wall and tentatively said, "Sam? Are you in there?"

"You can come in. The nurse is just taking my information," Sam said from behind the curtain.

Laura popped her head into the little cubby. She breathed a sigh of relief, seeing he was okay. "Oh, Sam." She sighed as she sank into one of the guest seats next to the bed.

"I'm fine. Probably would have been fine without all this fanfare."

The nurse snorted. "You need stitches. Ten, if I had to guess. But I'm pretty sure the doctor is going to want to send you for a CT scan and an MRI. Can't ever be too careful with a head injury like that. Dr. Becker will want to make sure you don't have any skull fractures or internal bleeding."

"It doesn't even hurt," Sam argued.

"That's because the EMT gave you some numbing

medication." She rolled her eyes. "Now, sit still, and Dr. Becker will be in shortly."

Laura reached for his hand. "I'm glad you at least feel okay, Sam. You scared the crap out of me."

"Scared myself, honestly. I don't understand what went wrong with the mower. It was running perfectly last night when I checked it over. I cleaned the engine and tuned it all up." Sam frowned.

"Could you have left a part out?"

Sam looked at her like she'd just asked if the moon was made of cheese. "No. I've taken that mower apart and put it back together so many times I could do it in my sleep, darlin'." He looked troubled for a moment. "This isn't the first piece of equipment this week to malfunction after I've cleaned it, though," he said quietly.

"What do you mean?"

Sam sighed. "What I mean is... I honestly think someone is tampering with my equipment."

"What? How?"

"I don't know how. Not yet. But I will."

"Well, either way, I'm buying you a new mower. Something safer than that old one you've been using for eight years."

"It was working just fine until today. I'm telling you, someone messed with it."

"Knock, knock." A man in a lab coat poked his head in. "I'm Dr. Becker, the attending ER doctor. I understand you've got a bit of a head injury? How about I take a look?"

"Sure, Doc," Sam agreed.

Dr. Becker examined Sam and then, just as the nurse predicted, said he was sending Sam for CT and MRI scans, just to rule out further injury. When Sam returned, the doctor looked over his scans and cleared him from any fractures or internal damage, sewed up his head and told him he'd have a nice scar, but that the stitches would dissolve on their own.

"Thanks, Doc." Sam shook his hand.

"Take care now. No more mowing injuries, all right?"

"Do my best," Sam answered as he followed Laura out of the cubicle.

Laura waited patiently as he checked out, then walked him to her car. They were quiet until they were on the road. "Sam, what do you mean you think someone tampered with your equipment? Who could be doing it?"

"I have my suspicions, but I don't want to voice them until I have proof, if you don't mind?"

"Okay. I can understand that. But how are you going to get proof?"

"I was hoping you'd allow me to install a camera. I'll even pay for it—"

"No, you won't. The estate will pay for it. And we'll get some for anywhere you think they're needed."

Sam smiled. "Thank you, darlin'."

"Don't thank me. I was terrified that you were hurt. If this was sabotage, I want to know about it."

Sam reached for her hand. "I really do appreciate your concern for me." He raised their linked fingers and kissed the back of her hand.

Laura nearly melted. The gesture was so sweet, and it made her even more upset that someone had hurt her Sam. He could have been killed! A tear slid from her eye, and she sniffled a little.

"Hey now, what are you getting all teary for?"

"You could have been killed, Sam." Laura didn't bother to wipe away the few tears that had slipped down her cheeks.

"I'm fine, darlin'. Sore, but fine. We'll figure this out."

Laura nodded. She settled her nerves, and as they pulled

back into the estate, she said, "Let me park, and then I'll walk with you over to your cottage."

"You don't have to, darlin'."

"I want to. I need to know that you are okay, all right?" She looked at him across the car seat, willing him to see how much she cared about him.

Sam touched her cheek. "Okay."

As they walked, Laura said, "I think, until we know what's going on, you need to tell your helper that he's on vacation."

"But—"

"Sam, hear me out. I can't have you or anyone else getting hurt. I need to know what's going on."

"Okay. I'll let him know."

"I'll even make sure it's a paid vacation."

"He'll appreciate that."

"And I want you to take it easy for a few days. Take some time to get those cameras ordered and installed. And pick out whatever mower you want for the estate. I'll clear the expense with Dad's accountant."

"I don't need a few days—"

"Please. Humor me, Sam."

"All right, I'll take it easy," he said as they reached his door.

"You sure you'll be okay?" Laura was worried about leaving him alone.

"I'll be fine. I'm gonna have some dinner, put the game on and go to bed early. I promise."

"Okay. I'll come check on you in the morning." Laura nodded. "Night, Sam."

"Night, darlin'."

Laura headed back to the house. She couldn't figure out who would have a reason to hurt Sam. He was one of the nicest men she knew. It troubled her that someone could be targeting him for some reason. It seemed unlikely that anyone on the estate was behind it. What would their motive be? Sure, he and Andrei had butted heads, but she doubted that Andrei would try to harm him over it. That was just ridiculous. And Bella, she was too nice to do something like that. No, it had to be someone sneaking onto the estate. She just hoped they could stop whoever it was before they hurt him worse.

22

L aura woke up gasping for air and tangled in the sheets, her heart racing as though she'd been running a marathon. It was just barely light out, the sun having just broken over the horizon. She'd forgotten to close her curtains again and could see it getting lighter out through the light, gauzy sheers. She took a few deep breaths, her hand going to her chest, willing her heart to calm down.

She hadn't dreamt of her mother this time, or even about Jim. This nightmare had been about Sam being injured, only it was far worse than just a few stitches to his temple. The dream had started out nice enough. With her working at her desk, peering through the window, watching Sam as he went about cleaning the pool. The next thing she knew, someone whacked him over the head with a shovel and pushed him into the pool and then held him down under the water with the pool skimmer. She couldn't see who it was; they had been dressed all in black, their face obscured. She had screamed at them and then attempted to race down the stairs to get to Sam, to rescue him, but the stairs were never ending. They just went on and on, and she could see the pool through a set of glass doors just past the bottom of the stairs, but she couldn't reach them.

It was quite strange, thinking about it now, because that was not how the house was set up. Neither set of stairs enabled a person to see out to the pool. The main set were in the front hall, which led to the front door, and the back stairs, which would be considered the servants' stairs, were to the side of the kitchen, just before you went into the laundry room. The only thing you could see was a wall and a corner of the kitchen, or partially into the laundry room if you were in the right spot.

"It was just a nightmare. Sam's fine," she told herself. "He hasn't drowned; nobody hit him or held him underwater. It was simply a nightmare," she continued to murmur. It helped to calm her down some, but she was still fretting and knew she would be until she went to check on him.

With that in mind, she got dressed and went down to the kitchen to make some coffee. She fixed enough for a couple of cups and poured it into a thermos to carry over to Sam's cottage. Then she opened the fridge, took out half a dozen eggs, a package of bacon and grabbed a loaf of bread from the pantry. She also grabbed a handled basket and put everything inside it. She was going to go over to Sam's and cook him breakfast.

As she headed to the door, Andrei entered the kitchen. She gritted her teeth, knowing he was going to keep her from leaving the house and make her talk to him. She gave him a tight smile as she headed for the door, praying he would just say good morning and nothing more.

"Where are you off to so early in the morning, beautiful?"

Laura had her hand on the door. She glanced over her shoulder. "Sam is supposed to take it easy for a few days, so I'm headed over to see how he is and make him breakfast."

Andrei moved toward her and put a hand on her hip,

turning her toward him. "He's a big boy. I'm sure he can handle it himself." He smirked as his gaze raked over her in a leer. "You look extremely edible this morning. Why don't we head back up to your room?"

"Um, thanks, but no. I have a bunch of things to take care of today, and I really do need to make sure Sam is all right. I promised the doctor that I wouldn't let him be too active, but knowing Sam, he'll be trying to go overhaul the mower and figure out what happened."

"The man is incompetent. You really should just fire him and wash your hands of him, baby. I mean, he was probably drinking on the job or something, and that's how he got hurt. You can't coddle people who work for you. They'll just take advantage."

Laura could feel herself getting angry. "I appreciate your advice, but in this particular case, you're wrong. I've got to go. I'll see you later." With that, Laura pulled away and yanked open the door. She was across the deck and down the steps before he could accost her further. She really didn't appreciate him speaking badly about Sam. He didn't know him at all. Sam was like family; he'd been with them for years. If anyone was taking advantage of her goodwill, it was Andrei himself, not Sam!

She hurried down the path that led to Sam's cottage and knocked on the door, looking over her shoulder as she did so to make sure Andrei hadn't followed her. She was still grumbling internally about him when Sam opened his front door.

"Darlin', what are you doing here so early? You should still be sleeping," he said with a smile.

Laura smiled back but felt a wave of concern as she looked him over. His eyes were droopy, and he looked as though he hadn't slept at all. "Nonsense. I'm fine; it's you I'm worried about." Her brow furrowed as she moved from foot to foot on his front porch. "Can I come in? I brought stuff to make for breakfast."

Sam's smile widened. "You're going to cook for me?" he asked as he stepped back. "Well, I won't say no to that, darlin'."

Laura shook her head and gave him another quick smile. "It's the very least I can do after you were injured on the property, Sam. You have no idea how worried I've been." She moved into the cottage and past him toward the kitchen. "I brought coffee, too."

"Let me get a couple of mugs, then. You are joining me, aren't you?"

Nodding, she tossed him a glance over her shoulder as she emptied her basket. "Yes. You don't mind, do you?"

"Not at all." He set the mugs he pulled from the cabinet down on the counter. "Can I help?"

"No, you need to rest. Go sit down."

"I'm not an invalid, darlin'. Just had a knock to the head. I'm fine."

"And the doctor said you needed to take it easy, so go sit down." Laura pointed to the kitchen table and chairs.

Sam sighed, but leaned forward, kissed her cheek and did as she asked. "Very well, but I'm not happy about this."

Laura glanced at him as she bustled about his small kitchen. "I know. Thank you for humoring me." She pulled out a frying pan and a pot, which she filled with water. She set both on the stove. "So did you sleep at all?"

"A bit, off and on. And for the record, I wasn't planning on doing much today. Just looking into ordering the cameras and the mower, like you asked."

"Good." She cracked a couple of eggs into the skillet and dropped the sausage into the pot of water. Once that was started, she poured the coffee into the mugs and brought his over to him. "Got milk?" she asked.

"In the fridge. Should be half a gallon."

Laura pulled the fridge door open, grabbed the milk and added some to her mug. "Want some?"

"I'm good." He sipped the coffee as he watched her. "You know you really didn't have to do this."

"I know. I wanted to, though." Laura was silent after that as she cooked the eggs and checked the sausage. She opened the bread loaf and added a couple of pieces to Sam's toaster and set it. It didn't take long for everything to cook, and she quickly plated it all and brought the plates to the table along with utensils. She returned for her mug of coffee and then joined him. "I was really worried about you, Sam."

Sam reached for her hand and squeezed it, causing her to look at him instead of her plate. "I know."

"I want to know who sabotaged the mower, and if they are planning anything else. Do you have any idea who it might be?"

Sam picked up his mug and took a sip, avoiding the question. "This is good coffee," he murmured instead.

"Sam." Laura looked at him. "You do have a suspicion. Tell me."

He shook his head. "No. That's all it is, a suspicion, and until I can prove it, I don't want to say anything. I could be wrong."

Laura frowned. "Okay, but you'll tell me, won't you? The minute you find out?"

"Of course, darlin'." He nodded and picked up his fork. "You'd better eat; your eggs are getting cold." He smiled at her.

Sighing, Laura grabbed her own fork and began to eat. "It's much nicer eating here with you than up at the house by myself."

"Why aren't you eating with your dad?"

"He's been worse lately, so Bella has been bringing his

food up to his room. I've hardly seen him except for the few times I pop in to check on him, but usually he's asleep when I do. I just don't understand it, Sam. He was doing fine. Had a routine, his tantrums had lessened, but it's like a switch went off and he just declined to the point where he rarely even gets out of bed now. It was so fast." A tear slipped from her eye. She dashed it away.

"That is worrying. Maybe that scare with the mower triggered it?" Sam fretted.

Laura reached out to him. "You know my dad; that wouldn't have triggered him. Don't even think for a second that incident is to blame. No, it had to have been something else." She finished eating and picked up her plate, carrying it to the sink. "I'm calling the accountant in a little bit to clear the purchases for you," she murmured as she cleaned the dish and pans that she'd used.

"What else is on your agenda for today?" he asked as he joined her at the sink.

"Some marketing stuff, and I might write a chapter or two on the new series I'm starting." Laura paused, then added, "But now that I think about it, I might have to do a bit of research first. I have an outline for it, but with it being a period piece, I want to make sure I have my setting and everything perfect. It's a bit different than what I normally write."

"I know; I saw your blog about it. I'm looking forward to reading it." He grinned and bumped her shoulder with his.

"I keep forgetting that you read my blog," she exclaimed, her cheeks heating. "Kelly doesn't even read my blog, and I think she's only read, like, one book—and she's my best friend."

Sam chuckled. "What can I say? I enjoy reading."

"I'm glad you enjoy them, Sam." Laura blushed even harder. She could feel the heat creeping down her neck and knew her skin was probably bright pink. She handed him the last dish to add to the dishwasher and said, "I should probably go."

"I know you have a bit to do today." Sam laid his hand on hers. "I really enjoyed having breakfast with you."

Laura's breath caught in her throat at the look he was giving her. "I did too, with you, I mean." She wished he would lean in and kiss her, but for some reason he was still holding back, and then the moment passed. She stepped back and cleared her throat. "I... I'll check in with you later... let you know what Mr. Pippen says."

"Sure."

She turned from him, put the thermos back in the basket and walked to the door. "Bye, Sam."

He followed her, and when she stepped out onto the porch, he followed her. "Be careful, darlin'," he murmured as she stumbled down the step.

Laura waved and began quickly walking back toward the estate house. She couldn't believe how awkward she was being. She felt like kicking herself for allowing the moment to pass. She was perfectly capable of initiating a kiss with him, but for some crazy reason, she wanted... no, she *needed* him to make that first move.

Distracted by her thoughts, she didn't notice Andrei standing in the kitchen as she entered. She had entered the door and gone straight over to the counter next to the kitchen to rinse out the thermos and then put it and the basket away.

"How was... *breakfast?*"

Startled, Laura dropped the thermos in the sink. She glanced over at the kitchen table, where Andrei was sitting. The way he'd said 'breakfast' had somehow made it sound sleazy and dirty. She frowned as she looked at him, then turned back to the sink to pick up the thermos. "It was fine. Sam's doing better, if you were meaning to ask."

"I wasn't. I don't care about him." Andrei pushed back

from the table and stalked over to her. "I care about you," he said softly from behind her.

His hands went to her hips and turned her around. He attempted to lean down to kiss her, but Laura turned her head before his lips could connect with hers. He backed up and stared at her for a moment.

"What's the matter?" he asked, looking hurt and sounding a little pouty.

Laura didn't want to hurt his feelings, but the more jealous and hurt and pouty he acted, the more turned off she was by him. She sighed. "I just... I have a lot on my mind right now, you know? Between work and Jim and my dad and now Sam being injured... I just... I can't do this right now. I need some time," she replied.

Andrei dropped his hands from her hips and backed up a step. "Fine then. Whatever." He turned on his heel and strode from the room.

Laura didn't even bother to call after him, knowing that was what he wanted. He probably wasn't used to women turning him away for any reason, but she just couldn't make herself follow through with him now, not after everything. She was extremely grateful that he hadn't had a condom that night he'd visited her room. She couldn't even imagine how he would be acting if she had actually had sex with him already.

She quickly finished cleaning up the thermos and then put it and the basket away in the pantry before heading up to her suite. She had a call to make and then work to do. She wasn't going to waste any more time thinking about Andrei.

23

A few days passed, and everything seemed to be back to normal—well, as normal as it had been prior to Sam's injury. The new mower and the cameras had arrived, and Sam had installed them late in the evening when everyone had gone to bed. They were hooked up to his computer system so he could monitor them or review them daily.

As far as Laura could tell, nobody else in the household was aware of the new cameras, and she was grateful she didn't have to explain that they suspected someone was getting onto the estate and tampering with things. She didn't want to worry Bella or Andrei; after all, they were living there too and expected to be relatively safe.

She hadn't gone over to Sam's again after the morning after his injury, not because she didn't want to, but because he insisted that he was fine and she didn't need to. She had wondered if he just didn't want her around, but he had also insisted that wasn't the case. He said he knew she was getting stressed out over everything, and he just didn't want her worrying about him. What he didn't understand was that Laura worried about him anyway. Still, she did as he asked.

After she dressed that morning, she headed downstairs to see about making breakfast for herself, only to find Bella in the kitchen early. "Oh, I didn't know you were awake yet."

"Good morning!" Bella smiled brightly. "I couldn't sleep, so I thought I'd come down and make a big breakfast that we all can enjoy."

"Oh, well, um, thanks?" Laura replied. "Anything I can help with?"

"No, I've got it. It'll be ready in just a minute." Bella grinned. "So? Have you heard from your lawyer yet? What's going on with your divorce?"

"Oh, well, we're going to court, but the courts are backed up right now, so it's gonna be, like, another month or so before we can get in. Mr. Hartman said he's trying to work through Jim's lawyer to get him to see there is nothing for me to give him. But so far, we're at a standstill because Jim is an asshole and won't listen to reason." Laura sank down into a chair at the table and put her head in her hands.

"That's too bad. You don't think he's trying to get some of your inheritance from your father, though, right?" Bella asked. "He can't do something like that, can he?"

"No, but even if he were trying to do that, he'd get nothing. Besides, I haven't inherited anything, and I hopefully won't for a long time. I fully expect my dad to live well past the finalization of my divorce." Laura smiled as Bella plated the food and brought it over to the table for her. "This looks great, Bella. Smells good too."

"Thanks. I watched a video on how to make it and just couldn't help but try it. Let me know how it tastes."

Laura picked up a spoon and scooped up some of the egg fried rice, peppers, onions, mushrooms, and sausage and took a bite. "Mmmm," she murmured as she chewed. "It's great."

"I'm so glad you like it. Oh." Bella hurried back toward the counter. "I forgot your coffee. Just a splash of milk, right?"

"You didn't have to make that too, I could have—"

"It's my pleasure. You just enjoy. I'm going to take your dad up some. It's got everything he needs in it nutrient-wise, it's colorful and not too bland, so he should eat it. Be back in a jiffy." She picked up another plate and headed out of the kitchen.

Laura ate in silence, enjoying the flavor of the rice mixed with egg and what she thought might be soy sauce. She was about halfway through when her eyes started to droop. Suddenly she was extremely tired. It was as though everything from the past couple of months had just dropped on her shoulders and was weighing her down.

"How are you doing? Is it not good?" Bella asked as she came into the kitchen and stood next to her. "You've only eaten half of it." She frowned.

"It is good. I just... I'm so... so... sleepy." Laura shook her head, trying to stay awake. She picked up her coffee and gulped it, hoping it would wake her up some, but after a moment she was more dizzy and could barely hold her head up.

"Sweetie, maybe you should go back to bed? I mean, you've just got so much going on; maybe it's all just taking its toll on you."

Laura nodded, but her head felt wobbly. She tried to stand, but it was as though her limbs were weak and didn't want to work properly. She stumbled against the table.

Bella reached out and steadied her. "Oh, golly. You must be super exhausted. Why don't I help you up to your room?"

"Thanks," Laura murmured, or at least she thought she

did as Bella wrapped an arm around her waist and helped her walk.

It took a bit, but they finally made it up the stairs and down the hallway to her room. "Here we are. Let's get you tucked into bed."

Laura felt herself flop onto the mattress. She felt Bella lift one of her feet and pull her shoe off; then she did the same to the other. A moment later, she was tucked under the covers, and her eyes closed and would not open. It was as though a blackness descended over her and was holding her hostage. She couldn't think, let alone move, and after a moment she didn't care. She just drifted in the darkness.

Laura had no idea how much time had passed when a noise woke her. She shifted in her bed, her mind a complete fog as she came awake. The sound happened again, and she recognized it. A creak of the floorboards in the middle of her room. But that couldn't be right, because they only creaked when she stepped on the board, and since she was in her bed, she couldn't have made the board creak.

She blinked her eyes in the dusky light of the afternoon, feeling another presence. "Hello?" she murmured. "Who's here?"

Nobody said anything. It was if they wanted her to believe she had imagined it.

Laura knew that wasn't the case, though, so she rolled over, which was slightly difficult, as her limbs felt extremely stiff. She forced herself to sit up and looked around the room. "Bella?" she asked, her gaze landing on her.

"Oh, darn. I'm sorry. I was trying not to wake you."

"What are you doing in my room?" Laura shoved her hair from her face groggily. "Crap, how long was I asleep?"

"I was just checking on you. I got worried because it's almost dinnertime and you've slept all day."

"All day?" Laura shook her head. Some of the stiffness

was leaving her body, finally. She shifted again and did her best to focus on Bella. "I don't understand."

"You came down early for breakfast and just got so tired. I think you've been overworking yourself. That must be why you slept all day. How are you feeling?"

There was a weird taste in Laura's mouth. It was like it was filled with cotton. "Strange. Everything is muffled, and I can't focus well."

"Maybe you're coming down with something?"

Laura wasn't sure what was going on, but she didn't feel sick. Not like any kind of sick that she'd experienced before at least. This was different. "Maybe," she answered anyway.

"Well, I should get back down and check on dinner. Do you want some?"

"No, thanks, though." She watched Bella head for the door.

"No problem. There'll be plenty if you decide you want some later." She smiled and walked out.

Laura's eyes drifted around her room and to the door to the sitting room. She moved to stand up and swayed a bit but righted herself. Walking toward the sitting room, Laura paused. Her dresser drawer was slightly ajar. She knew she hadn't left it like that.

Had Bella been looking through her things?

Frowning, Laura opened the drawer. She could see that things inside had been shifted around. It wasn't a mess—it was almost exactly how she'd left it—but there were just a few things not quite as she'd set them in there. Feeling suspicious, she opened the other drawers and noticed that they were also slightly off.

She was moving more now, gaining the feeling back in her stiff limbs as her foggy mind began to clear some. She headed for the sitting room and went right to her computer. She tapped the mouse and looked at the screen. Thankfully, it didn't come on. Of course, Bella could have attempted to turn it on and discovered it was password protected. She had set it to lock up for ten minutes after three incorrect log-in attempts... so she switched it on and checked it. Sure enough, it said it was locked for another two minutes.

"Son of a bitch," she whispered, not wanting anyone to overhear her. She couldn't believe that Bella would go through her things and attempt to log onto her computer. Just what was she looking for? Laura wondered. And then another thought hit her.

Did Bella drug me?

24

L aura spent the rest of the day in her room, thinking about the breakfast she'd eaten and the deep sleep she'd fallen into. She didn't feel well rested, either. The more she thought about it, the more convinced she was that Bella had drugged her. But why?

She started wondering if Bella and Andrei were as trustworthy as she'd thought when she'd first hired them. Was it possible that they were planning some kind of theft? Maybe they thought they could get into her father's accounts and take his money? But everything went through the accountant... maybe they weren't aware of that, though, she thought.

She was still feeling very lethargic, so she didn't leave her room at all until the next morning. Having contemplated what the two were actually doing, Laura decided she needed to keep a better eye on them. With that in mind, she dressed and headed to her father's room the next morning. She wanted to be there to watch the two of them interact with her dad.

When she entered, her dad was still asleep, looking frailer than she remembered. She headed for the dresser where

Bella had his medicine bottles lined up and began looking them over, reading the prescriptions. She noticed a change to them. They were the same pills she had been giving him, but the dose was stronger.

When had that been changed? she wondered. Did Dr. Temple increase his meds without her being aware? How? She realized she needed to make a phone call and find out what was going on. She left her dad's room and quickly returned to her own for her phone. It was too early to call though, so she just grabbed it and headed back to her dad's room.

She decided to let it go for the moment. She would call Dr. Temple and discuss it with him once Bella and Andrei did their morning routine. She could hear them moving around in the hallway, and a moment later the door opened.

"Gorgeous, what are you doing in here?" Andrei asked as he sauntered in.

"Thought I'd sit with my dad today. I haven't spent much time with him, and since I am finished with my edits for now, I thought I would take today to spend with him."

"Huh. Well, he's not going to be much fun. I mean, all he does now is sleep, really."

Laura narrowed her eyes. "And why is he always sleeping?"

"Oh, beautiful, I'm sorry; it's just how this disease goes. Once the patient starts to spiral, it's just best to let them wear themselves out so they'll sleep."

That didn't sound right to Laura, but she didn't say anything. "So if he just sleeps all the time, why are you here?"

"Oh, well, I was going to give him a quick bath and change his clothes."

"I see. Will he wake up for that?"

"Oh, yeah, of course he will. He's not in a coma, silly girl. He's just sleeping."

Laura felt herself getting irritated with him. "Then I'll stay."

"O-kay." Andrei nodded. He headed into the bathroom and started running the bathwater in the tub. A few minutes later, he came back and shook her dad's shoulder until he groggily came awake.

"Go 'way..." he muttered, trying to drift back to sleep.

"Michael, it's Andrei. I'm here to give you a bath."

"No. Don't want one," her dad grumbled, but his voice sounded weak and faint.

"Come on, Michael, up you get. I've already got the bath at a nice warm temperature for you." Andrei forced him to sit up and then slid his legs to the side of the bed. He ran his arm behind her dad's back and made him stand.

"Leave me alone!" her dad cried out. "Leave me alone!"

It broke Laura's heart to see him like this. "Dad, it's okay, Andrei is just going to give you a quick bath, and then we'll have some breakfast together," she said as she rushed over to him.

He stared at her as if he didn't recognize her. Before he could say anything, Andrei ushered him into the bathroom.

Laura returned to the chair, crossing her arms over her chest as she worried about her dad. She didn't want to go in there and see him without his clothes, but she worried about how Andrei was treating him. She got up a couple of times and started across the room, only to turn around and return to the seat.

Finally, the two emerged. Her dad was dressed in a different pair of pajamas as he shuffled across the room to his bed.

Andrei helped him back onto the mattress, then pulled the blankets over him. "There you go, Michael, fresh as a flower."

Her dad just glared at him.

"Well, I'll go see if I can help Bella, since you're here, lovely Laura." Andrei smiled at her and then headed for the door.

When he was gone, her dad looked at her, leaned closer and whispered, "They're trying to poison me, Laura! Make them leave."

Laura sighed. "Dad, I don't think they are poisoning you, but I'm going to call Dr. Temple later and find out what's going on with your pills." Despite her words, she had to wonder if Bella could be sedating him, since she suspected that Bella had drugged her.

"He's in on it!" He sucked his teeth and sank deeper into the bed.

"Dad, you've been seeing Dr. Temple for years, haven't you?"

He grumbled but didn't say anything else.

A few minutes later, Bella entered with her dad's food. She'd made him oatmeal and toast. "Good morning, Michael, how are you feeling?"

Her dad's face lit up despite the fact that two minutes ago he'd claimed Bella was poisoning him. "Morning, Bella," he murmured, eyeing the tray of food.

Seeing him light up at Bella's appearance had Laura dismissing his claims of being poisoned, but she still didn't rule out Bella sedating him.

Bella set the tray in his lap. "Oh, Laura, I didn't see you there."

Laura arched a brow. *Really? You didn't notice me sitting right in front of you?* she wanted to say but didn't. "Good morning. Didn't Andrei tell you I am planning to spend the day with my dad today?"

"No, I haven't seen him since I went down to make breakfast."

Laura frowned. "But he said he was going down to help

you."

Bella rolled her eyes and snorted. "Andrei is a bit scatter-brained, if I'm honest. He probably found some other chore to do on his way to the kitchen."

Laura didn't say anything to that, but she did wonder what chore he could have found that needed doing right at that moment. It seemed unlikely that there was really anything for him to do. It wasn't like she asked them to clean the house; the maids took care of that. And they didn't have to do any yard work, because Sam and his helper took care of all of that. The only 'chores' they had were in regard to her dad, and she was in here with him, so she knew he wasn't doing whatever it was she was paying him to do.

Maybe Sam had picked him up on the cameras? she wondered.

As Laura sat, thinking about where Andrei might be, Bella had continued to speak to her father. She held the spoon out for him and fed him a few bites as she chatted about the morning. "Oh, don't spill. We don't want to have to change your pajamas again," she said, with a distinctive giggle in her voice. She finished feeding him and then went over to the dresser. "Laura, did you touch these?" She turned and looked over her shoulder at her and frowned.

Laura glanced up. "Yes, just checking them."

"Hm, well, I'd prefer if you didn't touch them. I have them in a particular order, and I don't want to screw up and accidentally give your dad the wrong ones at the wrong time." She began moving things around, but they ended up in the exact same order that Laura had set them back down in.

"Right."

Bella poured a couple of pills into a small paper cup from three bottles and then returned to Laura's dad. "Here you go, Michael; swallow them all down like a good boy."

He took the cup, poured the pills into his mouth and then

drank from the cup she held out to him. "Business... report..." he said slowly.

"Oh, not today, sweetie. You're much too tired for that, aren't you?" Bella said softly as she stroked the hair from his forehead.

"Ye—" He didn't even finish the word before his eyes drooped, and he began to softly snore.

Bella looked at Laura and smiled. "You know he's going to sleep for several hours; you might not want to hang around."

"Oh, I'll be fine. It's actually kind of relaxing, just sitting here." Laura leaned back in the chair, preparing to wait it out.

"Well, if you're sure...?" Bella seemed uncertain as she picked up the tray with the mostly finished breakfast.

"I'll be fine. If I get bored, I can grab one of the books over there to read." Laura nodded at the bookshelf that used to be her mother's.

Bella smiled again and then left the room.

"Finally," Laura muttered. She hopped up and went over to the door, putting her ear to it so she could listen to see if either Andrei or Bella were out there. She couldn't hear anything, so she cracked the door and peered out. Over the top of the stair railing she saw Bella heading toward the kitchen. She closed the door and locked it.

Returning to her chair, she dialed Dr. Temple's office and asked to speak with him.

"Ms. Radcliffe, what can I do for you? Your father isn't still giving his nurse trouble, is he?"

Laura paused. "What do you mean?" she asked cautiously.

"Well, she called a few weeks ago to speak about his condition, and given that we'd spoken not long before that, I agreed that perhaps an increase of his pills was in order."

"But he was doing fine until that increase; I don't understand. Now he won't even leave his bed. He can't; he doesn't stay awake long enough to do anything."

"I have my notes right here. Nurse Ormond explained that he was being extremely defiant, trying to bite and hit her, and throwing things. She was afraid that he might do himself an injury, especially given his wandering into the path of the riding lawn mower, and I had to agree with her. Keeping him calm when he starts to get agitated is best for him, so I wrote out a new script for her to give him when he starts to go into that state."

"Wait, she's only supposed to give him the extra dosage if he's getting agitated?"

"Yes, exactly."

"I see." Laura frowned. "Okay, well, thank you, Dr. Temple."

"Call anytime, Ms. Radcliffe."

Laura hung up. She was extremely pissed off. Bella had been dosing her father with the extra daily rather than waiting to see if he did get agitated. She decided to go and confront her. She found her in her father's study, watching a soap opera, but she didn't know which one since she never watched them herself.

"Bella, can we talk?"

"Right now?" Bella shot her a glance, then turned right back to the TV.

"Yes. Right now." Laura tapped her foot impatiently.

Bella sighed, clicked off the TV and stared at her. "Well? What is it?"

"I just got off the phone with Dr. Temple."

"So?"

"So, I asked him about my dad's meds. He said you are giving him too much. You're only supposed to give him the extra if he's getting agitated, which he's not!"

Bella rolled her eyes and stood up. "Look, I am a trained

professional, and I know what I'm doing. Your father has been on a downward slope for weeks now, and his irritation levels have grown. He gets agitated at the slightest thing—and maybe you didn't see it, but he was agitated by you being there this morning. It was a change in his routine, and he was acting irritable. I did what I thought was best. He is my patient. I am here to treat him, not your feelings." She huffed and put her hands on her hips.

"But he seemed fine. I mean, he wasn't upset or even getting upset—"

"Perhaps you don't know him as well as you think you do. You haven't been around him in a long time, and before you moved in, you only saw him, what, once a year? Maybe twice? I've been with him every day for most of the day since I got here. I can tell when he's getting upset better than you can."

Laura was taken aback at her vehemence. Was she wrong? Had she somehow missed her dad getting irritated with her? She frowned. She couldn't be sure if what she thought or what Bella was saying was true. Because of that, she backed down. "Okay, I guess you could be right..."

"Of course I'm right. Now, since I rarely get to watch this soap, can I go back to it?" she asked impatiently.

Nodding, Laura left her alone. She had some more thinking to do about this situation, and she knew she couldn't do it standing in the doorway with some silly soap opera playing in the background.

THE NEXT MORNING, Laura decided to give Bella the benefit of the doubt. She went down to get breakfast and once again found Bella at the stove. "Good morning."

Bella smiled at her. "Oh, good morning. Sleep well?" she asked.

Laura returned her smile. "I slept okay. You?"

"Like an angel. I'm making waffles; would you like one?"

Laura hesitated for just a moment, but then decided she was determined to believe Bella and not hold a grudge over what she thought had been going on. "Sure. Thanks."

"No problem. I love to cook," Bella claimed. A few minutes later, she set a plate down in front of Laura. "There you go. I'm just going to take these up to your dad. Andrei is going to help him, so I'll be back down in a few minutes."

"Great." Laura picked up her fork and cut into the waffle. She lifted the bite to her mouth without syrup and started to chew, but as she did, she felt something was off. The waffle had a strange taste to it. It was almost bitter. She spit the piece back out onto her plate, grabbed the whole thing and then hurried to the kitchen door. She dumped it into the garbage can on the deck, rushed back in and silently closed the door and poured a bit of syrup on her plate, scraping it around with her fork. She then waited to hear Bella on the stairs and stuck the fork in her mouth, licking it clean.

"Wow, you must have been hungry!" Bella exclaimed seeing the cleared plate.

Laura acted a bit droopy and nodded. "I was. Don't know what's going on with me, but... I'm so tired now."

"Oh no. I hope you aren't coming down with something," Bella replied.

"Me too, I'm going to go lie down." She stood up and unsteadily made her way upstairs. She was probably overacting, but she wanted Bella to think whatever she'd put in her waffle was working.

"Get some rest," Bella called.

That did it. Laura was now convinced more than ever that Bella was up to something. She had been ready to think she was wrong, but no, now her suspicions were up even more than before. When she reached her room, she pulled out her phone and dialed the one person she knew could help her.

25

"Angela Downey, private investigator. How may I help you today?"

"Hi, Angela, it's Laura Radcliffe."

"Laura, hello! Are you having trouble locating your husband again?"

"Oh, no, this isn't about that. I've got a different kind of problem." Laura kept her voice down. She didn't want Bella or Andrei to overhear her.

"All right. What can I do for you?"

"Well, you know how my dad is sick? I explained that, right? And that I'd hired a nurse and caregiver to help with him?"

"Yes, I recall you mentioning that in our conversations."

"Okay, good. Well, I did check their references, and they were perfect, absolutely glowing, but..." Laura trailed off, unsure of how to explain what her gut was telling her.

"But you think they aren't who they say they are, or that the references were faked somehow?"

"Maybe, but it's more than that. It's just a feeling I've got, a sense of dread that something isn't right. I think... I think

Bella may have drugged me? And I think she tried to do it again, but I managed not to eat what she gave me, and when she left the room, I tossed it outside in the garbage can on the deck."

"If you suspect she's drugging you, definitely stop eating anything she's fixing. That's number one."

"Right. Yes. But can you help me?"

"I can. I need everything you have on them, and anything else you think might be pertinent to the situation."

"Okay. There've been a few other strange things..." Laura hesitated. "I don't know that they're connected, but something is telling me they are. I just don't have any proof."

"Well, tell me, and when I look into things, I can determine if you should be even more cautious."

Laura explained about her dad's condition: How he was fine one moment, and then Bella claimed that he was getting worse and had his meds upped to the point where all he did was sleep. From there, she spoke about the two frightening incidents—the first one where her dad had ended up on the lawn in front of the lawn mower and the second, when Sam had been hurt by the sabotaged mower.

"Scary to think how dangerous that could have been. Is there any reason to think that the Ormonds are responsible for the sabotage?"

"Well, Andrei—that's Bella's brother—he's been very flirtatious, but he also acts jealous whenever Sam is around, or if I'm talking to Sam..."

"So you think he might be trying to take out a rival?"

"I know it sounds insane, but yeah. Not that I'm interested in Andrei, not really. I mean, I was when I first met him, he is very good-looking, but he is also childish and manipulative and sullen..."

"So he's exactly like your ex."

"He is!" Laura agreed. "He's just like that."

"I think I've got enough to get started. I'll see what I can dig up. In the meantime, keep an eye on them, don't eat anything you aren't one hundred percent sure is safe, and don't be alone with either of them."

"Okay, that's good advice. Thanks, Angela."

"I'll get back to you as soon as I can."

"Thanks." Laura hung up and tried to sit down at her desk to get some work done, but she kept wondering what Bella and Andrei were up to. Would it be too obvious for her to sneak around the house peering into rooms to observe them? Probably. She frowned and wondered how she was supposed to keep an eye on them, and then she remembered the cameras that Sam had installed. Maybe he had picked something up on them.

She needed to go see Sam. She closed down her computer and hurried out of her room and outside without running into either Bella or Andrei. She wound her way down the path to Sam's place, only to see Bella standing on his porch in a very short dress that was cut low. Her hair was done up, and she was wearing more makeup than usual. Frowning, Laura slowed her pace as she moved quietly closer.

Neither Sam, who was standing in the doorway, nor Bella, who was touching his chest, took notice of her as she approached. Laura stopped as soon as she could hear what they were saying.

"Oh Sam, you are just so adorable." Bella giggled. "You know, I find you very handsome." She traced her finger down his chest. "Maybe you and I can go inside and have a drink?"

"I don't think so. I've got work to do, Ms. Ormond."

"Oh, Sam, don't be like that. It's not like Michael even cares about the garden anymore. You can take a day off. We can entertain each other, if you take my meaning?" Bella inched her way even closer.

Sam put a hand forward, touching her shoulder to keep

her from moving any closer to him. "I do take your meaning, but I'm not interested, thanks."

Laura could see Bella huff from where she stood. She crossed her arms and jutted out her bottom lip. "It's because of Laura, isn't it? I mean, she's pretty and all, but you know she's screwing my brother, right?"

Laura shifted then, ready to storm forward, but Sam's eyes flicked to her, and he shook his head slightly, keeping her in place.

"Ms. Radcliffe is free to be with anyone she wants, though I have my doubts that what you say is true. Either way, I am sure she wouldn't want you spreading rumors about her, whether they are true or not."

"Sam," Bella whined, "come on, don't you want to have a good time? Look at me, look at this body... I promise I can make it worth your while."

Laura had heard enough. She wasn't going to let her continue to badger Sam, who seemed extremely uncomfortable. It was time to put a stop to Bella's flirtation.

26

Filled with a jealous rage that she attempted to keep under wraps, Laura moved around the tree and back to the path, making noise as she headed toward Bella and Sam. She felt her jaw tic as Bella tossed her a glance over her shoulder and smirked at her.

"Well, if it isn't *Laura.*"

"What are you doing here, Bella?"

"What are you doing here, Bella?" Bella mocked. "What does it look like, Laura? I'm here to be with Sam." She turned back and gave Sam a wink as she laid her hand on his chest.

Laura wanted to grab her by the hair and toss her down the front porch, but she reeled those feelings in and gritted her teeth hard. "I don't think Sam is interested in you."

"God, you are being such a prude, Laura. Of course he isn't going to act interested with his boss standing right here in front of him, but what we do on our own time is up to us. You have no say in it."

Laura was taken aback at her words. Was it possible that once again she was misreading the situation? But no, she'd distinctly heard her before she'd decided to walk up, and

Sam had been politely declining her attention. "I'm not a prude. Sam is welcome to enjoy being with whoever he wants, as are you. But at the moment, I'm pretty sure I'm paying you to be taking care of my dad, and with it being the middle of the day, I'm fairly certain that there are tasks that Sam needs to see to."

"You are being such a drag. You aren't even the one paying for anything!" Bella huffed, getting frustrated.

"Yes, well, maybe I am being a drag, but I can assure you that I am the one who takes care of my father's bills, so if you would..." Laura gestured toward the path, feeling like one more push and she was going to tackle the woman and physically move her away from Sam.

Bella turned back to Sam and winked. "Well, I guess your little girlfriend is here to spoil our fun, handsome. We'll have to meet up when she's not around." Bella winked at him again. "Ta!" She wiggled her fingers as she strode down the step, past Laura and onto the path.

Laura watched her go, wondering how she could have ever thought Bella could be a friend. Once she was well out of earshot, Laura turned back around to look at Sam. She couldn't hide the hurt she felt, but she tried. "I'm sorry I dropped by without letting you know first. I just wanted to check in, see if you found anything on the cameras—which, since you haven't called me, I guess I can assume you haven't. And I didn't mean to spoil anything you had going on with Bella." She turned and started to walk away. "Just do me a favor, Sam, don't eat anything or drink anything she gives you. I don't trust her." With that, she started to jog away.

"Laura!" Sam called after her.

Laura didn't want to hear it. Didn't want to hear him lie and tell her that she'd misinterpreted the situation. She didn't think he was in the wrong; she was pretty sure he had been turning Bella down. But her heart couldn't take it if he'd only been acting because he'd known she was right there.

She sped up her pace and decided she didn't want to go back to the estate house yet. So she continued jogging, an exercise she actually hated, to let go of some of the rage she felt. She wound her way all around the property before finally heading into the cabana by the pool. She still didn't want to go in the house. The cabana was attached to the gym and held a set of showers.

She'd explored the cabana on one of the early days she'd been here, since it was a new addition to the house. Inside the cabana, Laura had found that in addition to the showers, there were changing stalls that held cabinets filled with extra swimming attire for guests who needed them, towels, and robes, as well as two powder rooms so no one would track water through the main house.

She decided after her impromptu run that she actually did need a shower. She went into one of the changing rooms, grabbed a robe, then headed to the showers. She didn't want to have to put on her sweaty clothes after getting cleaned up.

Twenty minutes later, she felt better and crept into the estate house, up the back stairs and headed for her room before anyone noticed her.

27

L aura was sitting at her desk, writing up a new blog post, when her phone rang. She picked it up to see that it was Angela. "Hello?"

"Laura, hey, it's Angela Downey. I've got some information for you."

"Oh? That was fast!" Laura exclaimed.

"Well, I just began my dig into the two caregivers, and I found a few troubling things."

"Oh no, I was afraid of that."

"Yes, well, it seems neither Bella Ormond nor Andrei Ormond exist before five years ago."

"What? How is that possible?" she asked.

"Exactly. Now I'm looking into some of the references they gave you. I've got my computer doing some deep digs. I will have more information for you soon, but I wanted you to know that those two aren't who they say they are. You need to be careful and keep an eye on them when they're around your father."

"Okay, yeah. I will for sure. Thanks, Angela."

"I'll be in touch." Angela hung up.

Laura sat in her chair, nearly hyperventilating. Who the hell had she hired if they weren't actually who they said they were? Why had she just trusted them? She should have done thorough background checks prior to hiring anyone; it was stupid not to have done so, given the fact she'd asked these people to move into the house to care for her dad.

She fretted about it for hours, all afternoon and well into evening. At seven p.m., Laura found her stomach rumbling. She hadn't eaten hardly anything all day, not since Bella had tried to drug her again, and she was starving. She decided to chance going down to the kitchen to make herself something. She was quiet as she made her way down the hall to the back stairs, keeping her footfalls as silent as possible. She made it down to the kitchen only to find that she'd gone to all that trouble for nothing. Andrei was standing at the kitchen counter, eating a bag of chips. Laura paused at the bottom of the stairs and contemplated turning around and going back to her room, but he looked up at that moment, catching sight of her.

"Hey," he said, his gaze connecting with hers.

"Um, hi?"

"Can we talk a minute?" he asked as he set the bag down on the counter.

Laura felt slightly unsure about his motivation, but she didn't want to make him suspicious, so she agreed. She finished walking into the kitchen and stood about a foot away from him. "What's up?"

Andrei reached for her hand and drew her closer to him. "Well, it seems like we got off track somewhere. I mean, we were pretty hot and heavy for a minute there, and then you backed off." He pouted. "Did I do something to upset you?"

Laura sighed. She didn't want to tell him she no longer found him attractive because of his attitude. Plus, she knew from Angela that he and his sister were not exactly who they said they were. "I know; I'm sorry. You haven't done anything to upset me. I've just had a lot going on, but I didn't mean to push you away..." She let her words trail off, hoping he would assume she wanted to spend time with him still, and not think she was in any way onto him and his sister.

"That's good to hear, beautiful. How about we have a drink? I want to show you that I'm really into you."

"I know you are; you don't have to show me, Andrei—" She was actually curious about what he had in mind. Would he do something nice, or was he going to try something nefarious like Bella had done that morning? She'd have to keep her eyes open and make sure she didn't get caught up in him. "But I would like to spend time with you, so a drink sounds nice."

"Great. I already have everything ready. I was hoping you'd come down eventually."

Well, crap, Laura thought. If he'd already gotten everything ready, he could have done something without her seeing it. She'd have to figure out a way not to drink what he offered her. Still, she smiled at him and said, "I'm glad I did."

He took her hand and led her into the entertainment room, which he'd set up with a bottle of champagne chilling in ice, a platter of chocolate-covered strawberries, and candles on every surface. There was even romantic music playing from the stereo.

"Oh, this is... lovely." Laura felt her stomach tighten even more with dread. She didn't want to do this. Didn't want to have a romantic evening with him or whatever he thought this would lead to. However, she allowed him to draw her over to the couch so she could figure out what he was up to. Was this all just a way for him to get into her pants finally, or was she misreading the situation and he really was into her?

He picked up the bottle of champagne, popped the cork and then reached for a glass and poured some into it. He wasn't as slick as he thought he was, though, because Laura, having been on guard, noticed the tiny white pill that he dropped into it before he handed it to her.

Laura took the glass with a tight smile, not wanting to drink from it. Still, she lifted it to her lips and pretended to take a sip while he poured a second glass. "Mmm. This is good," she murmured. "Come sit next to me, Andrei." She patted the cushion next to her with the hand she wasn't holding the glass in. She needed to figure out a way to get rid of the drink. She turned sideways so her left hand, which was holding the glass, was close to the coffee table. It struck her that maybe she didn't have to get rid of the champagne, exactly. She figured if he was going to play games like attempting to drug her, she was going to do her damnedest to turn it around on him.

She smiled and reached for him with her right hand as she scooted closer to him. "This is all so unexpected and sweet of you. I don't know how to thank you for being so patient with me."

Andrei set his glass on the table and grinned. "I have a few ideas." He leaned forward and pulled her into his arms to kiss her.

Laura closed her eyes, pretending to be into it, but opened them a moment later to see he had closed his own. She softly set her glass down on the other side of his and allowed herself to kiss him. She tried to hide the fact that she now found him disgusting as he attempted to deepen the kiss, but she pulled back giggling. She grabbed the glass that had been his from the table and smiled up at him. "Wow, you really know how to woo a girl." She fanned her face and took a healthy gulp of her champagne.

He smiled, his eyes lighting up as he watched her swallow the drink. "Here, have a strawberry. They taste amazing with the champagne."

He lifted one to her lips, and she bit into it. She hesitated for a second before doing so, fearing those were drugged too, but she took the chance that he had only drugged the champagne, not the fruit. "Oh, it's so juicy. Mmmm. You have to try it." She reached for a strawberry as he picked up his glass and took a gulp. She held the strawberry to his lips, and he bit into it. She hoped it was quick enough that he hadn't realized he'd had a drink from the tainted glass.

"Delicious, but not as delicious as you," he murmured, leaning forward as if to kiss her again.

Laura quickly turned her face and took another drink, and he did the same. "This is so good," she murmured as she watched him.

"It is," he said, his words slightly slurring. "More?" he questioned.

"Oh, let me finish this glass first," Laura said, with a faked giggle. "I don't want to get too sloshed."

He grinned, but his eyes were a bit on the glassy side. "Have another berry," he commented, reaching for it.

It wasn't too much longer before he started to sway as though he couldn't sit up straight. Finally, his eyes closed, and he began to drop. She caught the glass he was holding and hopped up just as he fell face forward on the couch where she had been sitting.

"Asshole," she muttered glaring at him.

Setting both glasses down, she made sure to set the drugged one away from her on the other side of the strawberries so she wouldn't mix the two glasses up; then she started going through his pockets. In his front jeans pocket, she found a baggie full of little white pills. If she had to guess, it was one of those date-rape drugs, but she couldn't be sure. She set the baggie down on the table and then went for the wallet in his back pocket. She wanted to know if he was hiding anything else.

She pulled the wallet from his jeans, opened it, and began going through it. He had about three hundred dollars in cash, but then as she started pulling out credit cards, she noticed there were several different names on them. Not only that, but she was surprised to find that he had four different driver's licenses. She had her proof, not that he was an asshole who had tried to drug and probably rape her, but that he was a criminal, too!

Anger filled her as she dialed Sam's number. He was the only one she really trusted, and she knew he would have her back if things went sideways.

"Darlin', I'm so glad you called. I don't understand why you would ever think—"

"Sam, there's no time for that right now! I need your help! Andrei just tried to drug me; can you call the cops and get over here?"

"I'm on my way!"

Laura took a moment to text Angela shots of the licenses and explain what she'd found, then she headed upstairs. She needed to track down Bella and make sure she wasn't trying to steal anything. Or worse.

Laura headed for Bella's room first, but she wasn't there. She looked into Andrei's room, but she didn't happen to be in there either. She listened at her father's door, but at first, it was completely silent. A moment later, there was just the slightest noise. Laura decided she needed to check, even if she disturbed her dad's rest. She opened the door and saw Bella standing over him with a syringe.

"Hey! What are you doing?" Laura rushed into the room.

Bella smirked at her. "Don't come any closer or your dear father is going to become my latest victim."

28

L aura felt dread fill her even more than before. "What do you mean your latest?" she questioned.

Bella rolled her eyes. "You just couldn't play along for five minutes, could you? You could not just fall for Andrei like you were supposed to. It would have been so much easier, but no. You had to fall for the bumbling fool of a gardener."

Laura wanted to tell her that Sam wasn't a fool and that he was the estate manager, not just a gardener, but with Bella poised to inject her dad with who knew what, she didn't think that was the wisest move. Instead, she hesitated just for a moment before saying, "What are you talking about?"

Bella tossed her a frustrated glare. "What I'm talking about is how this was all supposed to play out. You were supposed to fall for Andrei, and he would have married you. In the meantime, your dear father would have taken a distinct turn for the worse and died just months after you wed him. Then, when the time was right and the will had gone through probate, you would have had a fatal accident. Then everything would have come to me and Andrei. But you just couldn't get on board!" Bella looked completely affronted by that fact.

"I hate to break it to you, but I was never going to marry Andrei. Even if I hadn't fallen for Sam, I wouldn't have. I mean, sure, I might have had a fling with him. After the marriage I had, I think I might have deserved one, don't you? And Andrei is pretty good looking; if he'd just kept his mouth shut, he'd have been the perfect man to have a summer fling with," Laura informed her.

Bella just stared at her, dumbfounded.

Laura continued, giving her a thoughtful look. "You're right about me falling for Sam, though. I've always had a thing for him, and after a while I started to realize he might feel the same, so whether you believe it or not, your plan wouldn't have worked anyway." Laura took a step closer.

With every word Laura said, she could see Bella growing angrier. By the time Laura finished, Bella was onto her. "Ah, ah, ah! Not another step, or this needle will go right in, and he'll be dead within seconds."

Laura put her hands on her hips, her eyes narrowed, watching Bella closely to make sure she didn't get that needle too close to her dad. "You realize I've already called the police, right? They'll be here any moment."

"You're bluffing." Bella looked a little uncertain now.

"I'm not."

There was a noise downstairs. A second later, Sam shouted, "Laura?"

"Up here, Sam!" she called, without taking her eyes off Bella.

"You really shouldn't have done that—" Bella started to say, moving back toward Laura's dad.

Laura could hear Sam on the stairs as he called out, "Police are on their way! Should be here right about—now."

At that moment, they could all hear the sirens.

Laura stared at Bella, who suddenly looked afraid. "You might want to drop that and run. You might actually even get away."

Bella took half a second to think about it, dropped the syringe and ran at Laura, shoving her violently out of the way as she headed for the door. She pushed past Sam, who rushed into the room to help Laura as she pushed herself up from the floor where she fell.

Laura started after her, racing out of the room as she called, "Thanks, Sam!" But Bella had a decent head start and had already made her way down the stairs.

A moment later, Bella flew through the open front door and into the darkening night.

29

"Laura!" Sam followed her and caught her as she stumbled on the last few steps of the stairs. "Are you okay?" he asked, pulling her up against his chest. Then he carried her down, to set her gently down at the bottom of the stairs.

"We have to go after her, Sam! She's getting away!" Laura struggled in his grasp as she looked at the flood of red and blue lights that were racing up the drive toward the house.

"The police are here. I'm going to bet that she's not gonna get far, darlin'." Sam held on to her. "Are you really okay? Did he hurt you? Did Bella?"

Laura stopped struggling and looked up at him. "No. No, I'm fine. Bella didn't hurt me. And neither did Andrei, really. I saw him drug the champagne; he wasn't very secretive about it." Laura grinned. "So I switched our glasses when he wasn't looking."

"Good girl." Sam pulled her close and held her tight. "I knew that guy was trouble. I think he's the one who sabotaged the mower, too. I have him on camera going through some things in the garage. The angle was off, but he was clearly being sneaky about something."

"What?" Laura exclaimed with a tinge of fear. "Don't use any of that stuff without checking it first, okay?"

"I won't. I will check it all before using anything, I promise," he said as the police entered the house.

"Get your hands up!"

Laura and Sam broke apart and put their hands up. "I'm Laura Radcliffe, and this is Sam Willoughby. We're the ones who called you!"

The police officer lowered his gun and then holstered it. "I'm sorry, ma'am, just have to be sure. What's going on here?"

"Come this way, Officer; the man who attempted to drug me is in here." Laura led the cop who seemed to be in charge as well as a handful of others to the entertainment room. She pointed to the couch. "He's over there. Told me his name was Andrei Ormond, but once I switched our glasses and he passed out, I looked in his wallet and found... well, that." She pointed to the table with all the false ID cards on it. "Not to mention, the private investigator I hired said he and his sister didn't exist before five years ago. She's still looking into who they really are."

One of the officers approached and used a glove to pick up the baggie of pills. "Looks like that date-rape drug, Rohypnol."

"That's what I thought." Laura nodded. "Oh, my fingerprints are on that too. I didn't think to use gloves or anything."

"That's all right, ma'am. We'll take your prints and rule them out."

Another officer picked up the five IDs on the table. "Andrei Ormond, Andrei Stevens, Steven Anderson, Andy

Mondor and Ormond Andretti." He looked at each one, then looked at Andrei's face. "All of them look like him, too."

Laura nodded again. "That's the glass he drugged." She pointed to the glass on the far side of the table. "My prints are on that, too."

"Seems you did most of our job for us. We'll cuff him and arrest him."

"Sir, his sister ran off right before you arrived. I hired them both as caregivers to take care of my dad. She was threatening to inject my dad with something, but she dropped the syringe when she heard the sirens and ran out the front door just before you pulled up."

"You should have mentioned that as soon as we arrived," the officer in charge said. He picked up the radio on his shoulder and began ordering, "Matthews, Harper, one of the suspects escaped; she's on foot—" He paused and looked at Laura. "What does she look like?"

"She's tall and has red hair."

"She's got blue eyes and a Sofia Vergara figure," Sam added.

Laura frowned; her eyes narrowed on him.

"What?" He smiled. "I wasn't interested in her, but I *did* notice she was attractive, darlin'."

Laura shook her head as she rolled her eyes. Sam pulled her closer, wrapping his arm around her. Laura took a moment to enjoy the feeling of being in Sam's arms.

The officer gave the description into the radio, then turned back to them. "We'll do what we can to find her. You said you hired her and her brother here to be caretakers?" He motioned to the still-passed-out Andrei.

Laura nodded and explained how she'd come to find them via a caregiver website and hired them. "I checked their references, and everything seemed legit about them. After a trial week, we thought everything was good, so they moved in."

"They were living here?" the officer exclaimed.

"Yes, my father needs twenty-four-hour care, and he wouldn't go into a nursing home. He wanted to stay here on the estate."

"Can you show us to their rooms?"

Laura led them upstairs and showed them where each of the Ormonds was staying. "This is the room Bella was in. Andrei was there, across the hall, next to my father's room."

One of the officers went into her father's room, retrieved the syringe, and checked on her father. The officer returned a few minutes later to announce, "He seems to be all right. Sleeping heavily, though. I think she may have drugged him."

Laura had feared that was the case since he hadn't woken up at all during all the chaos. "I'll call his doctor and have him come out in the morning."

"That would be a good idea," the officer agreed.

"Ms. Radcliffe, would you come in here, please?" the lead officer called into the hall.

Laura shifted between officers and went into the room that Bella had taken over. On the bed was another baggie of white pills, like the one Andrei had been carrying, several IDs, a stack of papers and a gun. "Oh my God." Laura paled as she looked at it all. "She had a gun?"

"I take it you were unaware she had a weapon?"

"Yes," Laura whispered, her eyes locked on the black firearm.

"It's probably unregistered," one of the other officers speculated.

"Sir, forensics has been going over the room and found what they believe is in the syringe. They found an empty bottle of potassium chloride on the floor just under the bed. Said what was in the syringe would be enough to stop the heart," the officer who had checked on her dad said from the hallway.

Laura's head was spinning. How could she have trusted these people with her father's life? She was shaking as she stood there listening to the conversations around her. Her eyes landed on the papers that the officer was gathering from Bella's things. "What's that?" Laura pointed at the stack of papers.

"Financial and medical records on you, your father, and Mr. Willoughby. Also, it seems, a Mr. William Radcliffe."

Feeling her heart racing as fear pooled in her stomach, she said, "My brother. She had information on all of us?"

"It looks that way, ma'am."

"Oh my God, I can't believe this," Laura muttered. She felt as though she was going to hyperventilate. Suddenly the air was too thin, and she couldn't get enough oxygen. She began gasping for air, and after a moment, she passed out.

30

"Darlin'?"

Laura felt a light tap on her cheek. She blinked her eyes open and looked up at the ceiling. From there, her gaze drifted downward. She was lying on the bed in her old room; she turned her head slightly to see Sam. "What happened?"

"You passed out. I caught you before you could hit the floor." Sam brushed the hair from her forehead. "How are you feeling?"

Laura took a moment to assess and murmured, "I'm okay, Sam. Thanks." She sat up and looked around the room. "Where did they go?"

"The police left a moment ago. They took all the evidence and Andrei with them, but they haven't found Bella yet."

"They didn't? Where could she be?"

"By now, who knows? They checked the house and all around the property, and she wasn't anywhere on it. But don't worry. They've put out an APB. They'll find her."

Laura nodded. "I was so scared for my dad—I'm *still*

scared. And to know she had a gun... I can't even... Oh God, and Billy! What if she's gone after him?"

"There would be no point in her doing that now, would there? She might have gone after him later, once her plan was further in motion, but I doubt she'd go to the trouble anymore."

"I hope you're right. Billy would never forgive me. He's already angry about me being here for Dad."

"He'll come around, sweetness. He just can't see past his own pain right now."

Sam held her hand as he sat next to her on the bed. It was very comforting to know that he was there for her. Laura gripped his hand tighter. "I don't know what I would do without you, Sam."

"You know I'm here for you, darlin', whatever you need." He gathered her close and held her.

"Will you stay? In the house, I mean. I don't want to be alone." She looked up at him, pleading for him to stay with her.

"If that's what you need, what you want, of course I'll stay," Sam assured her.

"Yes, please." Laura nodded. "Did the cops say what they are arresting Andrei for? Was he in on the attempted murder?"

"I know they're charging him with possession of a controlled substance, attempted assault, attempted rape, and they are holding him as an accessory to the attempted murder of your father. I'm sure after they interrogate him, they'll find other things that he's guilty of."

"I can't believe how fooled I was by them!" Laura shook her head.

"They fooled everyone, darlin', not just you. That's what con men and women do. They use your trust against you. You are a very trusting person, open and honest—their perfect target, unfortunately."

Laura crossed her arms over her chest. "It makes me feel vulnerable that they were able to take advantage like that. I feel like I should never trust people again," she whispered.

"I can understand that. But you can't allow the predators of the world to change who you are, because if you do, they win. This experience will make you stronger and wiser, and you'll put your trust in the people who have your back."

Laura smiled and glanced at him. Her hand went to his cheek. "People like you," she said softly. "I can trust you, Sam. I've always been able to trust you."

Sam nodded and leaned in closer. "You can always trust me. I will always be here for you, Laura." His eyes strayed to her lips, and he slightly licked his. "I want to kiss you."

"Please, Sam... please kiss me," Laura murmured. She was whisper-close to his lips, and she could feel his breath on hers.

Sam pressed his lips to hers and wrapped his arms around her, pulling her even closer until she was crushed against his chest. His tongue swept between her lips, and Laura felt like she was flying. It was like coming home. She felt comfortable and cared for and loved with that kiss, and she wanted more of it, but it ended all too soon. Sam drew back, breathing heavily, and Laura sighed at the pleasure she had just experienced.

"I've wanted to do that for a very long time."

Laura's gaze connected with his. "You have?"

He smiled. "Very much, darlin'."

"Why didn't you ever say so?" she asked.

He chuckled wryly. "You were with someone else."

She shook her head, not understanding. "You mean, before I moved back here?"

He nodded.

"You could have said something when I moved back in, though..." she added; her brow furrowed as she tried to figure out why he hadn't.

"I didn't want to push. You were just separated and hadn't said anything about divorcing Jim, so I was biding my time. Then you hired Andrei, and well..."

"That's when I finally realized that maybe you didn't just think of me as a friend," Laura said, blushing.

"I suppose, before, I was too subtle about my feelings."

Laura grinned. "Maybe just a little."

Sam leaned in and kissed her again, but it was a quick kiss. "So take this as me making my feelings known. I like you, Laura Radcliffe. A lot. And I have for a long time. I'd like to see you in a more personal fashion from this moment on. Are you okay with that?"

Laughing giddily, Laura nodded. "Yes, Sam. I am very, very okay with that."

"Good." He pulled her close again. "Now, I think I am going to head downstairs while you get some rest."

"What? No, Sam—" Laura shook her head, not wanting him to leave.

"I'll just be downstairs. You've been through a lot in the last twenty-four hours, and you'll have to get up and help your dad in the morning, so you need to rest."

Laura knew he was right. "Will you help me? With my dad, I mean?"

Sam smiled. "Of course, darlin'."

Looking around the room, she shuddered. "I can't stay in here, though. I want to go back to my suite. Will you walk me?"

Sam stood up and held out a hand to her, which Laura took. He walked her to her door and kissed her goodnight. "Get some sleep, sweetness. I promise I'll be downstairs, making sure you're safe."

"Thank you, Sam." She watched him saunter down the hall before she closed the door. She felt so much safer with him in the house with her. It made it easier for her to take a quick shower and get into her nightgown before falling into bed and into a deep sleep.

She woke as the sun started to rise and, after getting dressed, went to see her father. He seemed to be breathing fine, so she went down to start breakfast. She made simple egg sandwiches for them all, including Sam, who she found was dozing on the couch in the now-immaculate entertainment room.

"Did you clean up in here?" she asked.

Sam stretched and yawned. "Yup. Couldn't leave that mess for you, after everything." He smiled at her, still looking sleepy.

"Sam, that was so sweet of you." Laura felt her heart soar. "I made you breakfast." She offered him a plate.

"You didn't have to do that, darlin'."

Laura giggled. "It wasn't any trouble. Besides, I like doing it. I'm going to take this up to my dad and see how he's feeling before I call Dr. Temple."

Sam nodded. "Want me to come up and help?"

"That might be a good idea," Laura agreed.

They both took their plates, and Laura carried her father's as they went upstairs. Laura and Sam ate theirs as they waited for her father to wake. Ten minutes after they finished, he finally woke up.

"Dad, how are you feeling?"

He yawned and looked at her, confused. "Where's the other one?"

"Who? Bella?"

He nodded, still looking at her for a moment like he didn't know who she was, and then his expression cleared. "Laura? What are you doing here?"

Laura sighed. "Dad, there's been an incident."

"What do you mean?"

"The nurse and caregiver I hired... well, they weren't good people. The police have arrested Andrei, and Bella is on the run."

"She's trying to poison me! I told you!"

"I know, Dad. I am so sorry I didn't understand at first, but you were right. I'm going to call Dr. Temple out to see you this morning and have him re-evaluate you. I think Bella was giving you too much medicine and keeping you sedated."

Her dad mutinously folded his arms and glared at her. "He's in on it."

"I promise he's not. Like me, he trusted that Bella was a real nurse. He won't poison you, Dad."

"Hurumph." He blew a raspberry at her.

Sam chuckled. "Laura made you breakfast, sir. You should eat."

Her dad's eyes strayed to Sam, and he looked surprised to see him. "Sam? Did we have business to discuss this morning?"

"No, sir. I just came by to keep Laura company."

"Here, Dad." Laura handed him the sandwich, which, thankfully, he ate without a fuss.

While he ate, she got up and went through his meds, making sure to give him the minimum dosage so he wasn't sedated. She held them in her hand to show him that he wasn't being given too many. He counted them, then took them.

"I want to watch my business report."

"Why don't I help you dress while Laura takes our plates down to the kitchen; then we can head down to your study?" Sam suggested.

"Very well," he agreed.

Laura tossed him a grateful look and picked up the plates, heading down the stairs.

She cleaned up the kitchen and then placed an order for grocery delivery. Laura tossed out several of the things in the fridge and pantry that were open for fear that Bella had drugged them. She didn't trust that the woman hadn't vindictively added drugs to their food supply.

She started toward the door when a bell rang. It took her a moment to realize it was the front gate. She pulled out her phone and hit the app that let her speak to whoever was there. "May I help you?"

"Good morning, ma'am. My name is Special Agent Wanda Keene of the FBI. I'm here with my partner, Special Agent Oscar Milton. We need to speak with you about a pair of suspects in a few of our cases. I believe you know them as Bella and Andrei Ormond?"

31

S hock filled Laura as she listened to the agent at her gate. "Um, okay, yes, come on through." She hit the button to open the gate. "I'll meet you at the front door."

Laura hurried into her father's study and said, "Sam, can you join me for a bit? We have some FBI agents coming up the drive."

Sam looked surprised by her words but nodded. "Sir, are you all right, or would you like to head back upstairs?"

Her dad waved his hand at him. "Go. I'm watching my report." He never took his eyes from the television.

Sam joined her at the front door as she opened it for the agents.

"Hi, I'm Laura Radcliffe; this is Sam Willoughby, our estate manager. I would prefer you spoke with us and not my father. He's got dementia and is not really capable of answering your questions."

"That's fair," the female agent agreed. "I'm Agent Keene." She shook Laura's hand and then Sam's. "This is my partner, Agent Milton."

Agent Milton shook their hands as well. "Is there some place we can sit?"

"Yes, of course." Laura nodded and led them into the living room. "Can I get you anything? Coffee? Tea?"

"I'll take a bottled water if you've got one," Milton replied.

"I'll have the same."

Sam put a hand on Laura's shoulder, urging her to remain seated. "I've got it."

Laura patted his hand and smiled up at him. "Thank you." She turned back to the agents. "So, you said that the Ormonds are part of a couple of your cases?"

Agent Keene nodded. "Yes, as I believe you are now aware, the two have a few aliases, but we've been able to connect them to several murder-for-inheritance deaths. They seem to target wealthy dementia patients, usually those who are estranged from their children or childless. In one particular case—like your own—they targeted a patient who was close with their child, but then that child died under unusual circumstances shortly before the parent died, leaving their estate to one of the Ormond siblings."

Laura's jaw dropped. "So... so... you think that Bella and Andrei were planning to... to murder me and my brother and... and... my dad before we even met them?" It was one thing to be thinking about that in theory, but quite another to hear it as actual fact. Of course, Bella had told her as much, but at the time, Laura hadn't really considered that was actually what she'd been planning for real.

Sam returned with the bottled water and handed them around, then took the seat next to Laura without interrupting.

"I believe so. You see, you are their fourth victims that we are aware of. The first victim was a woman by the name of Nancy Maxson. She was a very wealthy widow of ninety-one. She and her husband had no living children or family. Two weeks before she died, of what was at first thought to be natural causes, she changed her will, leaving her entire estate to Lila Stevens, aka Bella Ormond."

"So... you said they thought it was natural causes?"

"Yes, well, her lawyer became suspicious after he passed out the inheritance. Something didn't sit right with him about the situation. He'd been a longtime friend of Nancy's, you see. So he had her body exhumed and an autopsy performed. Turns out she was given a lethal dose of potassium chloride, which stopped her heart."

"Potassium chloride?" Laura gasped.

"I understand that a syringe was found at your father's bedside filled with the same?"

"Y-yes, it was." Laura reached for Sam's hand, squeezing it.

"Their other victims each suffered the same."

Laura shuddered. The forensic report was still pending, but it wasn't hard to guess what had been in the syringe Bella had brandished at her father's bedside.

"It's taken us a bit of time to connect all the deaths to the Ormonds because of their aliases," Keene continued. "We also believe they may be working with additional partners who receive a cut of the money once the job is complete, but we aren't aware of who they are at this time."

"So... so what do you need from us?"

"Well, you're the first of their victims to have survived to speak to us. And because of you, Andrei Ormond is in custody. We're trying to get him to roll over on his sister so we can learn her whereabouts," Agent Keene said.

"Is there anything you can tell us about Bella Ormond?" Agent Milton asked.

Laura thought about it but shrugged. "I don't know that I really know anything. I have the phone numbers for the references they gave me, and I can show you the website that I got their names from. What else would you like to know?"

"Did she let anything slip about where they are from, or where they were before you hired them?"

"Well, Bella did say she had married her last patient. But after he died, she and Andrei were living in an apartment that they paid by the week."

"They do have a car in the garage. The police didn't move it," Sam added.

"We'll want to impound it."

Sam nodded. "Sure."

"The police went through their things, but you're welcome to as well."

"That would be great. They might have missed something."

"Do you think I'm still in danger from her?" Laura asked, feeling worried.

Keene and Milton looked at each other and then back to Laura.

Keene finally said, "Possibly. Since you are the first to have survived an encounter with them, we can't be sure what Bella will do."

Laura sighed. That was not the answer she had been hoping for. "I see."

"Can you show us to their rooms now?" Agent Keene asked.

Laura led them up the stairs to the two rooms that Bella and Andrei had been using, while Sam went and checked on her father. He returned to her side a few minutes later, to report that her dad was doing fine, still enthralled with the business report that he'd been missing for the past several weeks.

After going through the rooms, Agent Keene called in to their head office and set about placing an order for the car to be picked up. "Okay, I think that is all for now," she said.

"I think it might be best, given the circumstances, that you all evacuate and take up residence at a hotel. Somewhere Bella won't be able to find you easily," Agent Milton added.

Laura frowned. "I don't know if I can do that. My dad is pretty insistent about staying on the estate."

Sam put a hand on her back. "We'll talk him into it. It's for your and his safety."

"Okay, we can try. But even if we do get him to go along with it, I don't know how long he'll allow us to be away. I'm afraid he'll think we're taking him to a nursing home, and he's been adamant about not going to one."

"Hopefully, we'll have her in custody before the end of the day, but we can't guarantee it," Agent Keene said. "If you think of anything else, give me a call. Here's my card." She handed Laura a business card with her name and the number for her office at the FBI.

"Thank you for taking the time to speak with us. We appreciate your cooperation. We'll be in touch about the car," Agent Milton said as they stepped past the front door.

Laura saw them out, then turned back to Sam. "How are we supposed to convince my dad to leave?"

Sam ran a hand through his hair. "Would he believe we're going on vacation?"

"I have no idea. Before we do anything, I need to get Dr. Temple over to see him."

"Right. Maybe he'll have an idea on how to get your dad to vacate the estate for a bit."

"Maybe." Laura dialed Dr. Temple's number and spoke to him, informing him of what was going on.

"Oh my, yes, of course. I have a free hour at four. I'll come by then if that works for you?"

"Yes, thank you, Dr. Temple." She hung up. With that

finished, she made them all lunch from the groceries that arrived shortly after the FBI agents had left. Sam stayed with her every step of the way.

"You should probably call your brother as well," Sam suggested.

"He's going to be really upset. He didn't want me here, Sam, doesn't think I should be doing anything for Dad."

"That may be, but if Bella is as much of a psychopath as we think, she could target him as well. He needs to be aware."

Sighing, Laura nodded. "You're right. I know you're right. I'll call him after we get Dad upstairs for his nap."

"Good plan." Sam grinned as he kissed her temple.

Laura was truly enjoying how affectionate Sam had become. It was everything she'd ever imagined and written about. She just wished she had a moment to really enjoy the attention, without feeling as though she was under the threat of imminent death via Bella Ormond.

32

"Sleep well, Dad." Laura patted his arm and left his room, with Sam following her.

They headed back downstairs to the kitchen, and Laura pulled out her phone. She looked at the time and knew that Billy would be out of class soon. She set the phone on the table and stared at it.

"I don't think it works like that, darlin'."

Laura glanced at him and frowned. "What doesn't?"

"The phone. You have to actually dial the number and hit send."

Laura giggled. "I know. He's still in class for another five minutes, though."

"Ah, okay. You had me worried there." Sam chuckled. "How about I make us some tea while we wait?"

"Perfect."

Sam did his best to distract her for a few minutes by asking her about her upcoming novel, but Laura hadn't even had a chance to see if her editor had gotten back to her with second-round edits. She'd need to look into that to find out, but at the moment she was too stressed to worry about that.

"Okay, I'm going to call him," she said, picking up the phone.

Sam set her glass down on the table and sat next to her. "I'm right here if you need moral support." He smiled.

Laura bit her bottom lip as she waited for Billy to answer.

"Hey, sis, what's up?"

"Hey. Um... some things have happened..." Laura began.

"If it has anything to do with Dad, I'm hanging up. You know I don't care, and I want nothing to do with him."

"It does, but it doesn't. This is serious, Billy—"

"No. I told you, if you are going to talk about him, I'm hanging up, Laura! I'm not going to listen!"

"Wait! Billy, you don't understand! Please!"

"What? What don't I understand? Dad abandoned us to Mom's abuse! He always took her side! Well, now he can suffer the consequences! I. Do. Not. Care!"

"This has nothing to do with that! Please stop being a selfish idiot! This is about the people I hired; they're wanted by the FBI!"

"Wait—what are you talking about?"

Laura took a calming breath. "Okay, so I told you I hired a nurse and caregiver, a brother and sister, right?"

"And I told you that was all you should have done, and then left. But you didn't listen."

"I know! But it's a good thing I didn't. They are wanted for multiple murders, and they drugged me."

"What?" Billy roared.

"And I think they know who you are, and Bella may come after you, and I'm worried."

"What are you talking about? You told them where I am?"

"Well, not like that. I mean, I didn't know they were murderers. I mentioned you, and Bella asked where you were, and I told her UC Davis. It wasn't like I gave her your specific address or anything."

"Damn it, Laura! It's not enough that Mom abused us, and Dad ignored us, now you've got murderers after us? What the fuck?"

"I know! I know, I'm sorry! Okay? I didn't plan for this to happen. It's not like I went out looking for angel-of-death caregivers. Hell!" Laura tugged on her hair in frustration.

Sam captured her hand and squeezed it, encouraging her to calm down.

She said, "Look, I just want you to be aware that it is possible she may target you."

"What about the brother? Where is he?"

"The police have him in custody. He tried to drug me and rape me, but I knew what he was doing and switched the glasses, so he got the dose. The police arrested him. Bella escaped, though."

"Okay. That's good they've got him. But why would you think, after she escaped, that she'd come after me?"

"Well, I don't know. I just want you to be cautious because she could."

Billy growled into the phone, clearly frustrated. "Fine. So what is it I need to look for? What does she look like?"

"She's a tall, curvy redhead with big blue eyes. She acts all sweet and innocent, but can flirt like nobody's business, and can come on really strong. She's smart and very knowledgeable about medicine. Oh, and she's probably going by a different name. The police found numerous IDs with different names on them for both Bella and Andrei."

"Uh-oh..." Billy said.

Laura panicked. "What do you mean, *uh-oh?*"

"Well, she kind of sounds like a girl I met in an online chat about veterinary medicine. She sent me her picture, and she keeps messaging me privately, saying we should get together."

"What? Who is she?"

"I don't know. She's just some rando girl I met in a chat. I mean, I've been talking to her for a couple of weeks now."

"Billy! You know better than to hook up with a stranger via the internet!" Laura exclaimed.

"It wasn't like that. I mean, it wasn't just like Twitter or something. She joined the online community here on campus and was part of the discussion we were having about veterinary medicine, and we just started talking. She sent me a private message, saying she thought I was cute and that maybe we could study together."

"Did she give you her name?"

"Well, yeah, and it's not Bella, I can tell you that!"

"Of course she wouldn't give you the name Bella. Don't be stupid; she'd know that I told you I hired a 'Bella Ormond.' Besides, I told you the cops found multiple aliases for her. What name did she give you?"

"Fuck, I don't remember... Let me look it up. It's not like I am interested in her. I already have a girl I'm talking to who isn't this chick." He paused. "Okay, so her name is Lila S. That's all I got."

"Lila Stevens! That's Bella!"

"I can't believe this," Billy whined. "I can't believe I'm getting drawn into Dad's drama! I wanted to stay out of it! I didn't want this, Laura!"

"I know! I know you didn't." Laura sighed and took a steadying breath. A moment later, she said, "Please, please tell me you haven't given her any major information about you? Like your address or phone number?"

"Thank God, no, I haven't."

"Good, that's good."

"I can't believe you've dragged me into this," he muttered.

"Look, maybe she's not coming after you now that we've caught onto her scheme. You just need to keep yourself safe and be aware that she was targeting you. If you see anyone matching her description, get away as fast as you can, okay? She's really dangerous."

"Fine. Okay, I will," he grunted. "I hate this, you know?"

"I know. Please, promise me, Billy. Promise me you'll stay away from her. Don't look at her and think you can take her down, okay? She's a sneaky, desperate psychopath."

"Geez, I promise. I'll make sure I stay away from her. And if I see her, I'll call the cops. Happy?"

"Yes. Yes, I am, thank you."

"If we're done, I've got a ton of homework to do, and this doesn't help. I'm still really pissed off at you."

"Yeah, I know. Please stay safe. And Billy? I love you."

"Yeah. I have to go." Billy hung up.

Laura stared at her phone. She knew he was angry at her, but she hadn't thought he'd be so angry he wouldn't tell her he loved her back. They always did, for as long as she could remember. But he hadn't said it. He'd just hung up. Her heart squeezed at the thought that he'd pull away from her and never speak to her again.

"So I take it he's had a run-in with her?" Sam asked, pulling her from her thoughts.

Laura nodded. "Online apparently. She found him via some group chat thing at the university and sent him some private messages wanting to get together with him, but he hasn't done it," she said, continuing to stare at her phone.

"Well, that's good news at least."

Laura nodded again.

"Are you all right?"

"I don't know. I've never heard Billy so mad, and... and it's at me." She could feel tears burning the back of her eyes. "Sam, he's angry at me for dragging him into this."

Sam rubbed her back. "It'll be okay, darlin'. He'll come around after he has time to calm down."

"I wish this whole thing was over and behind us," she said softly, forcing the tears not to fall.

"Me too, but at least if we have to be in the middle of it, we're in the middle of it together." Sam smiled.

"True," Laura agreed, returning his smile.

AT FOUR, Dr. Temple arrived. Laura took him upstairs to her father while Sam went out to get a few things done for the estate, especially since they were all planning to leave for a while. Laura gave Dr. Temple a more detailed story about everything that had been going on as he evaluated her dad.

"Well, it looks as though he's okay. I don't think the disease has actually progressed from the last time I saw him in my office, before you hired the dastardly duo, thankfully. I'll get him set up on the proper dosage of meds again, and he should be back to his usual self fairly quickly."

"That's good to hear, Doctor." Laura gestured for him to follow her out to the hallway. "I wanted to ask... the FBI suggested we go stay at a hotel until they catch Bella, but I don't know how to go about getting Dad to agree. Do you have any suggestions?"

"Is there a favorite place your dad likes to visit? A favorite hotel or city? Maybe a vacation destination that he remembers?"

"Not that I know of. When he traveled for work, we never went with him or anything. And we never really went on vacation anywhere when I was a kid. He and Mom did, of course, but they never took me. And I know for a fact they never had Billy with them, either."

"Well, in that case, maybe tell him the house has to be fumigated?"

Laura sighed. That wasn't a very helpful solution, because her father would never believe it, and even if he did, that wouldn't last longer than a day, maybe two. She needed a reason that was going to be longer than that. "I'll think of something."

"Sorry I couldn't be more help." He shrugged. "I'll get those prescriptions in and make sure they are delivered this evening."

"Thank you, Doctor." Laura walked him out and waved as he drove away.

33

After Dr. Temple left, Laura felt the urgent need for them to get out of the house. She really didn't want Bella coming back and attacking them; she wanted to get her dad somewhere safe. She paced the kitchen as she waited for dinner to finish cooking and for Sam to rejoin her.

She turned back to the stove, where she had three burgers cooking. In the oven, she'd put a tray of fries. She figured that would be the easiest dinner she could make that her dad could eat on his own. As she cooked, her father's new prescriptions arrived and she called Sam, who went to retrieve them at the front gate.

"Smells good," Sam said when he entered the kitchen a bit later with her dad's prescriptions.

"Oh, thank God you're back."

Sam frowned and moved toward her, looking her over to see if she had somehow been hurt. "What? Did something happen since we spoke on the phone a few minutes ago?"

Laura sighed. "No, nothing's happened yet, thankfully. I'm just a nervous wreck. I keep hearing sounds and imagining it's Bella breaking in." She chewed the inside of her cheek nervously.

Sam wrapped his arms around her and held her for a moment. "Why don't you pack up a bag for you and your dad, and after we eat, we'll head to a hotel?"

"I can do that. I just don't know how to get Dad to agree to it."

"Dr. Temple didn't have any suggestions?"

"Nothing that would work with Dad, unfortunately."

"Okay, well, maybe we don't tell him that's where we're going until we get there."

Laura nodded. "Yeah, okay," she agreed. "Will you get him dressed? He's in his study."

Sam kissed her temple. "I'll be right back."

"Oh, before you go—did they get Bella's car?"

"Yeah, it's all taken care of. They had left about fifteen minutes before you called to tell me that your dad's prescriptions were here."

"Okay, good. I don't want Bella coming back for it."

Sam moved back to her and pulled her into his arms again. "Neither do I." He held her for another minute, then stepped back. "I'll go get your dad ready, and then after we eat, we'll lock up the house and get out of here."

"Okay." Laura smiled.

As Sam went to do as she asked, Laura pulled the fries out of the oven and split them between three plates. She scooped the burgers out of the pan and laid each one on a bun and added cheese. Sam and her dad came into the kitchen as she was setting the plates on the table.

"I've got ketchup, mustard, mayo, and pickles if you want any of those," she said quietly to Sam, so her dad didn't hear her.

"I'll take a pickle and some mustard." Sam brought his plate back over to the counter.

Laura pulled them out of the fridge for him and handed them to him to add to his burger. She returned them to the fridge before joining him and her dad at the table. She and Sam chatted a little quietly while her dad ate. He was still a bit out of it from being sedated for so long, so he wasn't really paying attention to their conversation.

"Do you have any idea where we should go?" she asked quietly.

"While you pack, I'll call and get us a reservation at the hotel in town. It's the closest one. It's probably best we don't go too far."

"That's a good idea. I don't want to have Dad in the car for too long."

After dinner, Laura cleaned up the kitchen as quickly as she could while Sam brought her dad back to the study. She rushed upstairs, grabbed a bag from her dad's closet and began packing up a few sets of pajamas, some clothes, his toiletries and medication. She set the bag in the hall by the stairs and then hurried to her room, grabbed her own suitcase and tossed in everything she thought she might need to wear and her own toiletries, as well as her laptop so she could work. It took her less than fifteen minutes, but she fretted that she was forgetting something.

At the top of the stairs, she picked up her dad's bag and brought both bags down to the garage, then tossed them in the trunk of her car. She hurried back in and joined her dad and Sam in the study. "Okay, ours are in the car. Do you want to go get yours?" she murmured.

"I'll be back as quickly as I can. I'm going to change the code for the gate, too. I should have already done it. I wasn't thinking."

"Thank you," Laura replied, placing a hand on his arm.

Sam kissed her cheek and hurried off.

Laura sank down in the chair next to her dad's and

focused on the TV. He was watching *Wheel of Fortune,* of all things, which wasn't his normal type of show. She couldn't recall him ever watching any kind of game show in the past. "Dad, do you want me to change the channel?"

"No." He continued to stare at the TV.

Laura shrugged and watched as well, making guesses in her head over what phrases the answer might be. She gave herself a point for each one she got correct. By the end of the show, she had eight points for ten boards. Sam still wasn't back, and she worried that maybe he was having trouble booking them a reservation at the local hotel.

Her dad picked up the controller, attempting to change the channel, but dropped it. He grunted in frustration and seemed to get slightly agitated.

"Oh, let me get that, Dad. I think it went under the chair." She hopped up and dug her hand under the chair, reaching for the control. "What channel did you want?"

He shook his head, looking confused.

"How about I put on the news for a few minutes. Sam is coming back, and we're going to take a drive. Won't that be nice?"

Her dad nodded, as if that were a normal thing for them to do.

Laura sighed in relief that he was going along with it for now. She put the news on for him, then slipped out of the study to the kitchen to peer outside and see if she could see Sam. She once again paced the kitchen, looking outside every time she moved past the windows and back door. Finally, she could see him in the garden area. She opened the door and rushed out.

"Do they have rooms available?" she asked.

"I got two rooms. Your dad and I can share one, and you can have the other, they adjoin, but that way you can have a bit of privacy." He smiled as he stepped up onto the deck. "Does he know we're leaving yet?"

"I told him we were going for a drive," Laura said. "I'm not sure what I will tell him when we get to the hotel."

"We'll deal with it when we get there, I guess. Let me put this in your car, and then I'll come help get him."

Laura handed him the keys as they entered the kitchen. She paused to lock the back door and check it, while Sam headed to the garage. She waited for him, and then they both made sure the front door was locked before going to the study.

"Hey, Dad, let's go for that drive."

He looked over at them, still a bit confused. "Drive?"

"You wanted to go for a drive," Laura assured him.

He slowly nodded and stood up.

Sam clicked the TV off, and the three of them headed for the garage, but when it came time to get into Laura's car, her dad refused. "I am not getting in there."

"Dad, we can't go for a drive if you don't get in the car."

"I want my own car."

Laura sighed and looked at Sam.

"I'll go get the keys." Sam went to the cabinet in the garage and pulled out a set of keys, then returned, clicking the button for the Rolls Royce, two spaces over. "Go ahead and help your dad in," he suggested.

"Come on, Dad. Sam will drive us." She walked with him over to the car and opened the door. Her father got in.

Sam moved the three bags from the trunk of Laura's car to the Rolls, and then slid into the driver's seat while Laura climbed into the front passenger seat. He hit the button to open the garage door and then backed the Rolls out.

"What's the new code?" Laura murmured, pulling out her phone to open the front gate.

"Four-three-seven-two-one."

Laura punched it in as they got closer to it, and the gate opened. When they were through, she closed it behind them. Sighing, she settled back in her seat and gazed out the window silently as Sam drove. After a few minutes, she peered over her shoulder at her dad to see that he was getting drowsy. She hoped that meant that he wouldn't fight her when they reached the hotel.

Fifteen minutes later, they pulled up outside the Lauren Oliver Hotel, which sounded fancy, but really wasn't. It was basically just a three-level modern building in the shape of an upper case U that had an outdoor pool in the middle. Sam pulled under the awning and ran inside to get them checked in, then returned to the Rolls to drive them around to the closest entrance to their rooms.

"We're on the first floor, rooms 104 and 105. Why don't you take your dad in, and I'll bring the bags."

"Thanks, Sam." Laura got out of the car and went around to the back driver's side to let her dad out. "Come on, Dad. We're here."

He climbed out and looked around. "Where?"

"We're going to be staying here for a little while." Laura took his arm and started walking.

Her father planted his feet and wouldn't move forward. "No."

"Dad, we already have rooms. You don't want to waste money, do you?" She hoped to play on his internal penny-pinching gene to get him to go along with her.

He stared at her, his jaw rigid. "Why are we here?"

"Just for a change, Dad. Something different..." She encouraged him to walk, nearly dragging him across the parking lot.

Finally he complied, but Laura was exhausted by the time she got him into the building. She used the key card Sam gave her to open the door, then led her dad inside. The room was nice with two queen beds, a desk, a table and chairs, a large dresser, with a closet and a big-screen TV. The bathroom was decent-sized with a bathtub and shower combo, two sinks and a toilet.

"Isn't this a nice room?" she said.

Sam entered then, set his and her dad's bags down, then opened the adjoining door and set Laura's bag on the other side. Laura smiled at him and mouthed, "Thank you."

"This is a nice room. We're going to sleep well here, won't we, sir?"

"You're staying here?" her dad replied, frowning. "Where is Laura staying?"

"I'll be right next door, Dad."

Laura dug through her father's bag, pulled out his pajamas and his nightly pills. She held the pajamas up for Sam and went to get her dad a glass of water to take the pills. She returned a moment later and handed them to him.

Her father took the pills, swallowing them with the glass of water. "I want to go home. I want to sleep in my own bed."

"Well, tonight we're sleeping here." Laura felt her patience slipping.

Sam drew her away toward the adjoining door and whispered, "Why don't you go relax in your room. I'll make sure your dad gets changed and into bed. He'll be asleep soon after taking those pills."

"I know. I'm just worried, Sam. And I hate fighting with him."

Sam touched her cheek and smiled at her. "I know you do. Go relax."

"Are you going to go to bed, too?"

"Hadn't really thought about it."

"Come over to my room after he goes to sleep. We can watch a movie or something."

Sam agreed.

Laura went into her room, closing the door behind her, but not locking it. She sat down on the queen bed closest to the door and pulled out her phone. She decided she needed to update Dr. Fischer about everything going on, so she called her on her emergency number.

"This is Dr. Fischer. Is everything alright?"

"Hi, Dr. Fischer, it's Laura Radcliffe. I... well, a lot has happened over the last twenty-four hours, and I needed to speak with you. I'm sorry about using your emergency line, but I don't know when I'll get a chance to see you—"

"That's all right, Laura; that is what this line is for. Now can you tell me what's going on?"

Laura explained what had happened with Andrei and Bella, and how the police were involved. She went on to explain that they were now staying in a hotel, and she was overwhelmed and stressed and worried about missing appointments.

"Let's not worry about that at the moment. I understand you're in a difficult situation. Why don't we put your sessions on hold until you are able to commit to them again. If you need me, you can use my after-hours cell number if it's an emergency; otherwise just call me at the office if you need a quick appointment."

"Thank you, Dr. Fischer; that is helpful."

They spoke for a little longer, and Laura felt better about everything going forward, even if she was still stressed over her dad and Bella. She put her phone away and picked up the remote from the side table, turned the TV on, and flipped channels.

Twenty-five minutes later, there came a soft tap on the door, and Sam entered. They chose a movie and kept the volume on low so it wouldn't disturb her father.

The next day, they dressed and headed out for breakfast. Her father was acting more agitated as they sat down in the restaurant and had to wait for their food. He was acting like a two-year-old, complaining that they were trying to starve him to death and waving his arms around. He even spilled two glasses of ice water, which luckily missed Laura's lap, but only just. When their food arrived, her father decided it wasn't what he wanted and flipped his plate onto the floor.

Laura groaned and closed her eyes. "Dad!" she muttered. "You can't do that here!"

"Go ahead and take him out to the car. I'll take care of this," Sam said, gesturing to the mess of their breakfast.

Laura was quite hungry; she'd gotten to eat hardly three bites of her meal. Still, she helped her dad up and walked him out to the car.

"I'm hungry!" he shouted.

"I know, Dad. We'll get you whatever you want to eat. What do you want?"

"I want an egg and sausage sandwich, like Bella makes me."

"I'll try to get you something like that, Dad, but Bella is gone. She tried to kill you."

"She did not! You're just jealous of her!"

Laura shook her head, not wanting to argue with him. "Get in the car." She opened the back door for him.

He climbed in and sat with his arms crossed, clearly pouting.

Laura got in the front and pulled her seat belt on. "Dad, put on the seat belt."

"No."

"Don't make me come back there!" She glared at him, like Mom used to glare at her when Laura didn't do what she asked.

He pulled the seat belt on but gave her a mutinous look.

Sam walked up to the car, handed Laura two to-go boxes

and slid in. "I saved our food, but I don't know what to do about your dad."

"Can we go through the drive-thru at Marcos? They have egg and sausage sandwiches."

"The coffee shop? Sure." Sam drove a couple of blocks, went through the drive-thru and ordered each of them a coffee, and an egg and sausage sandwich for her dad.

They headed back to the hotel and spent the next hour eating and trying to keep her dad from leaving the room. He was upset, though, and kept slamming the hotel room door. At lunchtime, Sam went out and got them sandwiches, which they once again ate in the room, but this time, her father took a nap afterwards.

Laura was so exhausted from the morning that she decided to take a nap herself. She didn't get to sleep long though, because her dad woke up earlier than normal and started carrying on like she and Sam were trying to murder him. Screaming and throwing things, he tried to leave the room several more times. Finally, the front desk called.

"Hello, this is the Lauren Oliver front desk—"

"No! I don't want to be here!" her father shouted.

"I'm sorry, what?" Laura said into the phone.

"I said this is the front desk. We need to ask you to leave. You are disturbing the other guests."

"But we can't!" Laura exclaimed.

"That isn't my problem, ma'am. We'll expect you to be at the front desk to check out within the next half an hour."

Laura hung up the phone in frustration. "Damn it!"

"What's wrong?" Sam asked as he ushered the struggling older man back toward his own bed.

"We have to leave. That was the front desk. We are disturbing the other guests."

"I want to go home!" her dad shouted.

"Now?" Sam asked.

Laura nodded. "Yes. Dad's being too loud."

"Okay, okay, go get your things. I'll try to get ours and keep him corralled."

"Thanks, Sam." It seemed she was constantly thanking him for things now. She didn't know what she would do without him. He was like her rock.

She hurried back to her room, grabbed her toiletries from the bathroom and shoved them in her bag. She hadn't bothered to unpack anything else. She returned to help with her dad while Sam gathered their things; then she headed for the car with her dad while Sam went to the front desk.

Her father smugly got into the backseat as though he'd gotten his way. "Take me home."

"Dad, we can't go home."

"I want to go home!"

"I know you do, but Bella is still out there somewhere, and the police haven't found her. We can't go back right now."

Sam got into the car and looked over the seat. "Mr. Radcliffe, you've just gotten us thrown out of the only hotel in the area. Our choices are to go stay at the only other nightly rental, the Comet Motel, or to drive forty-five more minutes away and try to find a safe place to stay."

"Sam, I'm not staying at the Comet," Laura said. "They just had a huge drug bust there, and wasn't a guy murdered?"

Sam nodded.

"I want to go home." Her dad was being extremely defiant. "Take me home, or you're just going to waste more money, because I'll get us thrown out of anywhere else that we go!"

Laura groaned. "Damn it, Dad." She tossed her head back against the seat and put her hands up to her eyes to keep herself from crying. She rolled her head over as she lowered her hands to look at Sam. "Let's just go home. At least he won't be causing us trouble if he's where he wants to be."

"Are you sure?"

"No. But what choice do we have?"

"We could still try driving east."

"No. I'm tired, Sam. I don't think I can handle any more tantrums."

Sam nodded. "Okay." He reached over and grabbed her hand, holding it for a moment. "I'll do what I can to keep you safe, darlin'. Both of you."

"Thanks, Sam." She let out a bemused chuckle.

"What's funny?" he asked as he put the Rolls in drive.

"Nothing really. I was just thinking earlier that the only thing I've done for the last several days is say, 'Thanks, Sam,' and that I owe you a huge debt of gratitude. I have no idea what I would ever do without you."

"Darlin', you don't owe me anything, I volunteered. And you'll never need to find out because I am always here for you." He smiled over at her.

34

Laura was so tired from their hotel experiment that she was struggling to keep her eyes open. On the way home, she'd had Sam stop at the grocery so she could pick up some things for dinner, because she didn't have anything thawed at the house.

She'd left her father in his study after they returned to the estate. He was watching an old movie that she was sure he'd seen a million times while she prepped dinner and did some of the regular household chores, like the laundry.

Sam had returned to his cottage to put his things away and then do a little yard work before he returned to the estate house to join them for dinner. Laura had told him that she'd make spaghetti and garlic bread with her homemade sauce. Of course, she couldn't serve that to her dad because he'd make a mess of it, so she was really going to be making two meals. For her dad, she was going to make a small meat loaf sandwich, some chopped sweet peppers and a salad.

She had already browned the ground beef for the spaghetti, chopped the tomatoes, onions, and sweet peppers, added the tomato paste and veggies to the pot with the beef, and now it was cooking on the stove. She then moved on to mix the remainder of the ground beef in a bowl with an egg, breadcrumbs, chopped onion, ketchup and Worcestershire sauce to make the meat loaf. She put it into a loaf pan and slid it into the already heated oven. Once that was done, she headed into the laundry room and sorted the clothes for the washer, tossing in the things she knew could go together.

"Where's Bella? I want Bella to make me dinner!" Laura's dad demanded as he stood in the kitchen. "Bella!"

"Dad, stop. Bella's not here," Laura replied as she set the washer in the laundry room to wash. She tossed what wouldn't fit in the washing machine back into the basket and poked her head out of the laundry room. "I've already got dinner in the oven for you."

He rounded on her, a look of mistrust on his face. He stormed forward, moving better than he had in a while. "I don't want *you* to make dinner! I want Bella!"

"Well, Bella is gone, and she's not coming back, Dad."

"I don't believe you! Why are you here?" He glared at her before turning away. "Bella! Where are you? You need to come make my dinner!" He was stomping through the house, purposely knocking things over.

Laura heard something in the living room crash to the floor and groaned. She wanted to sink to the floor and cry, but she couldn't. She needed to make sure her dad wasn't going to hurt himself in his agitated state. "Dad," she called after him, following him up the stairs as he stomped his way up them.

"Bella! Where is she?" he demanded, from the top of the stairs.

She couldn't believe he'd made it up them so quickly. She'd gotten so used to seeing him barely able to move when Bella had been dosing him with too many sedatives that his swift movements now were throwing her off.

Laura made it the rest of the way up and followed him to the room that Bella had been using. "She's gone, Dad! She ran away because she tried to poison you and got caught!" she yelled at him, trying to make him listen to reason.

"You're lying! Bella's a sweet girl! You ran her off! You did this! You're an ungrateful child! You are a hateful child! Always accusing people of doing terrible things that they never do! You did it to your poor mother, and now you've done it to Bella! You broke your mother's heart, and now you're breaking mine! I want Bella back! You fix this! Make her come back!" he screamed as he pushed past her and stomped his way to his room. He shoved the door open and stormed inside.

Laura followed him, feeling absolutely livid. She'd had enough of his accusations. Even if he didn't know what he was talking about, he seemed lucid at the moment, and she was going to give him some home truths, because she was tired of him acting like she was the bad guy, the terrible spoilt child in this scenario. She was tired of trying her best to keep him safe when he didn't want her there, didn't trust her and acted like she was the one trying to hurt him. It was all just too much for her to handle, and she gave in to her emotions, not just the ones from the past few months, but from her distant past. Calling him out on everything that had happened before with her mom and throughout her childhood.

"Listen here, you stupid, old, senile man! Mom was an abuser! She not only hurt me mentally and emotionally, but physically! She literally hit me with a poker! You can still see the scar!" She pointed to the scar on her temple. "She broke my wrist! She left bruises all over me! Mom was not the sweet woman you claim to believe she was! She didn't just beat the hell out of me, manipulate and gaslight me, she did it to you and Billy, too! I saw it happen! I heard it! Her giving you black eyes and busted lips! Accusing you of cheating! She even broke your nose!" Laura advanced on him, getting right up in his face as she declared everything that she'd had done to her by her mother and everything she'd witnessed.

"Lies! You're lying!" he screamed. He moved toward the bed, picking up a book from the night table and throwing it at her.

"I'm not lying!" Laura ducked the book flying at her face.

"You are!" He looked around for something else to throw, but thankfully the only thing he could get his hands on was a pillow. "Your mother was a saint!"

"Mom was an awful, terrible person and should never have been a mother! And you protected her! You stood up for her! You lied for her! And now you're doing the same for a woman you barely even know! Bella hasn't just tried to kill you, she tried to kill me and Sam, too, and she's gone after Billy! Is that what you want? You want her to kill me, Sam, and Billy and then steal your estate and kill you too? Is it? Is it!" she demanded he answer, feeling completely irrational at that point.

She knew she was handling this the wrong way, knew that she should not be yelling at him—or demanding anything, given his dementia. But she was past the point of caring at the moment. Between his tantrums and everything that had happened over the last few days, she had been driven to the brink of a mental breakdown. It was all just too much for her, mentally and emotionally.

"Stop it! Stop it! Stop lying! Bella wouldn't do that! It's you! You're the one who drove her off! You don't want me to be happy! You're an ungrateful, terrible child!" he screamed loudly at her as spittle hit her face.

Laura gasped as if he were physically attacking her. Her dad had never spoken to her in such a hateful way, and it hurt her heart to have him call her all these horrible things, even though the things she'd said to him were probably just as horrible. "Bella is a psychopathic murderer! She murdered all her other patients, Dad! She did it to steal their money! She was going to do it to you!"

"Get out! Just get out! I don't want you here! Get out!" he screamed, shoving her toward the door.

Laura bristled as she stumbled against the wall by the door. She stared at him for a full minute in utter shock and disbelief that he'd put his hands on her like that, before turning and fleeing from his room. Not once in her entire life had her father ever physically hurt her or tried to hurt her. He had always been the one parent she could count on to be somewhat loving and not actually physically hurt her, but that had suddenly changed in that moment. Tears raced down her cheeks as she burst into racking sobs. She couldn't deal with this, with him, anymore. She wished she'd never come back here. She wished she were back in her apartment and had her life back. She wished—she stopped there, because she didn't know what else she wished at that moment, only that she needed a break from all of this, from him, and from the stress of the situation they were in.

As she hit the bottom step, Sam caught her.

35

"Let me go!" Laura sobbed as she gripped his arms. "Let me go!" She didn't really want him to let her go, but she needed to get away from her dad. Being right there at the bottom of the steps, where her dad could probably still hear her, was making her panicky and desperate to flee.

"Shhh, darlin', I've got you," Sam murmured as he held her. "Come on, we'll go in the kitchen."

Laura allowed Sam to wrap his arm around her waist and help her to the kitchen while she continued to sob against his shoulder. A moment later, he was seated and she was in his lap, still weeping.

Sam rubbed her back as he murmured sweet, calming little sounds into her ear. "Sweetness, it's okay. It will all be all right. We'll get through this together," he whispered. "He doesn't mean it; he can't. It's the disease that affects his mind."

Sniffling, Laura nodded. In her head, she knew that. Knew that her dad was being taken over by the dementia that was affecting his thoughts and emotions. "I know, it just hurts so much, Sam," she said softly. "I'm trying so hard, and it just feels pointless."

"I know, baby." He rocked her in his arms.

Laura's racing heart calmed, and she sat upright. She used the back of her hand to wipe her tears and sniffled, hoping that her nose wasn't running too bad. She looked at his shirt and gave him a watery smile. "I've soaked your shirt. I'm sorry, Sam."

He chuckled. "I don't care," he murmured as he stroked her hair back from her face. "How are you feeling now?"

Laura sat still on his lap for a moment and thought about it. She was definitely tired, but the crying jag had actually been a bit freeing. Like it had relieved some of the stress she had been feeling. "Better, I think." She sniffled again.

"Good." His smile widened. "Now, why don't you go take a few minutes, and I'll finish up our dinner, then check on your dad."

"Oh, but I was supposed to—"

"And you did—you made the sauce; all that's left is the noodles and to heat up the bread, right?"

"Well, yes, but—"

"No buts." He stroked her cheek again and then gently kissed her lips. "Go on now, darlin'. I'll have it all on the table by the time you come back down."

"Okay," Laura said softly. She stood from his lap and blew out a breath before taking the back stairs up to her suite. She headed into the bathroom, where one look in the mirror told her she looked like she'd sunburnt her face and hadn't slept in a month, because her face was bright red and her eyes were all puffy. "Good golly, I'm a mess," she muttered.

She decided right then to jump in the shower and try to refresh herself so that she'd look halfway human when she went back down to dinner. She couldn't believe how good Sam was to her. He was so unlike Jim, unlike anyone she'd ever been with, but he was everything that she'd imagined he would be. He was the perfect but slightly flawed hero she'd written about in all of her romances. He was the man she'd always dreamed of being with but hadn't gotten. Until now.

Her shower lasted somewhat longer than she'd thought it would, but she'd needed it. She dressed in a cotton sundress and decided to go barefoot as she blew dry her hair. The image in the mirror told her she was looking much more like her normal self, and it was safe to go downstairs.

In the kitchen, she found that Sam had calmed her father down and managed to get him to come down to the kitchen for dinner. He was seated at the table with his meat loaf sandwich and veggies on a plate in front of him. Laura took a moment and then calmly said, "That looks good, Dad."

He glanced up at her and gave her a small smile as he picked up the sandwich. He didn't say anything, but he ate and remained calm. That was the best she could hope for at that point.

"What can I do to help, Sam?" she asked, approaching the stove.

"Not a thing, darlin'. I've got the pasta ready—your sauce tastes amazing by the way—and I'm about to pull the bread out of the oven. Go sit; I'll bring the plates over in a sec."

Dinner went by calmly, which Laura was grateful for, and then her dad actually claimed to be tired and asked to go to bed.

Sam put his hand on her shoulder and said, "Relax, I've got him."

Laura put her hand over his and looked up at him. "Are you sure? I can help—"

"Stay and relax. I won't be too long."

"Okay." She nodded.

As he took her dad upstairs, Laura decided to clean up the kitchen. She didn't feel like just sitting and thinking, and wanted to have it all done so she could just spend some time with Sam. She was putting the last pot in the dishwasher as Sam re-entered the kitchen.

"Darlin', I was going to do that."

"I know, but you've already done so much for me, and I... I just want to spend some time with you, if that's okay?" she murmured as she wrapped her arms around his neck.

Sam's hands went to her waist. "I'd like nothing better." He leaned down and kissed her lips, softly at first and then with more passion.

"Let's go upstairs," Laura whispered against his lips, not wanting to stop kissing him.

He pulled back a little and looked at her. "We don't have to... you don't owe me any—"

Laura put her finger to his lips. "I want to, Sam. Please?"

Sam scooped her up in his arms and carried her up the back stairs. Laura pressed kisses to his neck as they moved down the hallway, tucking her feet so they wouldn't hit the wall. She giggled as he opened her door and laid her on the bed.

"You're sure?" he asked, standing at the edge of the bed, watching her.

Laura reached for him. "Absolutely, Sam. I've never been more sure about anything in my life."

Sam knelt on the bed and hovered over her, leaning down and kissing her. He moved slowly, as though he was savoring every kiss, every touch, every moment they were together and imprinting it on his brain.

Laura knew she was doing the same. She wanted to feel his hands everywhere, wanted his kisses to cover her body. She'd imagined this moment for ten years and had written scenes with him in mind during that time, as well. She couldn't believe that it was actually happening, and she never wanted it to end. Sam was her everything.

He drew her up and reached for the bottom of her sundress, lifting it over her head and tossing it to the floor. Laura went to remove her bra, but he stalled her hands.

"I want to," he whispered.

Laura felt a shiver of pleasure race through her as he pulled her to him and kissed her as he unhooked her bra. When he broke the kiss, he drew the bra slowly down her arms, revealing minute bits of skin until she was fully uncovered.

"God, you're beautiful," he said huskily.

Laura felt her cheeks heat at the look he was giving her. She reached for him, pulling his lips to hers. He pressed kisses to her lips, her neck, her collarbone and then down her chest, leaving nowhere untouched. His fingers were rough from his physical labor as an estate manager, but his touch was as gentle as could be and left a fire in its wake.

Her entire body was alive for him. She watched him through a hooded gaze as he too stripped and then took something from his jeans pocket. She watched him open his wallet and remove a condom. She hadn't even had to ask; he just did it without any prompting from her. It made her heart swell that he was thinking of her protection even in the heat of the moment and wasn't leaving it up to her.

Laura took it from him and opened it as he slid his underwear down his muscular legs. She glanced up and felt the anticipation of the moment fill her as she gazed at him. He was everything she could have ever asked for. She reached for him and rolled the condom over him.

Sam took her into his arms again, wrapping himself around her. He gazed into her eyes lovingly and murmured, "You're sure?"

"Yes, Sam, please make love to me," Laura answered, nibbling at his lips.

"God, I've waited to do this for ten years, darlin'." He

centered himself at her entrance and slowly slid himself into her.

Laura gasped at the feelings that filled her. She glanced up at him with surprise at his words. "You have?" A wave of emotion hit her in that moment, an overwhelming feeling of love and passion and attraction.

Sam chuckled against her neck. "Darlin', you have been the only one in my thoughts and dreams for the last ten years."

After that, not much talk was had because emotions took over, and the two of them were too caught up in them to speak.

Later, as they lay blissfully satisfied in each other's arms, Laura returned to the subject. "Why didn't you ever ask me out?"

Sam kissed her temple. "I didn't think you noticed me. After all, I was just your parents' estate manager. And you were always seeing someone anyway."

"Of course I noticed you! I always made excuses to come talk to you, but I didn't think you were interested in me like that. I can't believe we've wasted so much time."

"Well, let's not waste any more." Sam pulled her tighter against him and kissed her passionately.

They made love again several more times before the sun came up.

36

"Ugh. It's too early," Laura groaned as the sun peeked through her curtains. She pressed her face into Sam's shoulder and snuggled into his side.

Sam chuckled. "Come on, darlin'. We've got your dad to get up and dressed and breakfast to make, and a million other things."

"Don't wanna," she murmured, trying to press herself into him.

Sam tickled her, and she giggled. "As much as I would rather stay here snuggled in bed with you, we need to get up."

Laura rolled over flat on her back and dramatically sighed. "Fine." She pushed herself up on her elbows. "But we are doing this again. Soon."

Sam grinned at her, put his hand behind her head and drew her closer to kiss her. "Definitely."

They got up and started the day, with Sam helping her dad dress while she got breakfast going. She was in a really good mood despite the fact that she hadn't really done a whole lot of sleeping the night before.

When Sam and her dad entered the kitchen, she cheerily said, "Good morning, Dad, did you sleep well?"

"Where's my paper?" he asked instead of answering.

Laura rolled her eyes. "I'll get it in a moment. I'm making the eggs right now."

"Don't worry, sir, I'll get it." Sam patted his shoulder, sent Laura a wink and headed to the front of the house.

"Sam will be back in a couple of minutes with your paper. Would you like some coffee?" She glanced at him as she spoke.

Her dad nodded and sat down. "Sam staying here now too?"

"Sam has been very helpful. Don't you think so?" she said instead of answering his question directly. She poured his coffee into his mug and brought it over to him.

He grunted but didn't really answer. Laura was okay with that for the moment.

Sam returned and set the paper down next to her dad. "Here you are, sir. I already turned it to the business section for you."

Her dad picked it up and immediately began reading.

Sam approached her and pulled another section of the paper from behind his back. He held it up so Laura could read the headline. Her eyes widened at the words 'FBI fugitive Bella Ormond on the run'. Her eyes flew to Sam's, and she bit her lip with worry.

"We'll talk after breakfast," he whispered.

Laura nodded and turned back to the stove. She split the eggs up into three and made them each a sandwich with eggs and sausage patties. She and Sam joined her dad at the table. "Dad, here's your breakfast."

He folded up the paper and set it aside, then picked up half of his sandwich. "Just like Bella's," he murmured.

Laura felt herself tense up at his words, but Sam laid a

calming hand on her knee. She nodded at him and then ate her own breakfast. She didn't want to get worked up just because her dad didn't understand that Bella was a killer. It was like he was a little kid who could only focus on one or maybe two things. It was very frustrating, but she needed to remember it wasn't his fault. Besides, it was probably better that he didn't remember Bella attempting to kill him anyway.

Later, once her dad was settled in his study, watching his business report, Sam helped her with the dishes, and they talked about the newspaper headlines. "What should I do, Sam? What if she comes back here?"

"Maybe you should call Agent Keene and find out what they are doing to catch her. Maybe she'll have some suggestions for us."

"That's a good idea," Laura agreed. "Can you hang out with my dad for a while so I can call?"

"Whatever you need, darlin'." He smiled and kissed her cheek.

Laura reached for him and gave him a proper kiss, then went upstairs for her phone. She dialed the number on the card that Agent Keene had given her shortly before she'd left when they'd visited the first time.

"Special Agent Keene, how may I help you?"

"Agent Keene, this is Laura Radcliffe."

"Yes, I know, Ms. Radcliffe. What can I do for you?"

"Oh, well, we tried to take my father to a hotel, but... well, we were asked to leave because he was disturbing the other guests with his tantrums. And I'm worried about Bella coming back here, and I just read the paper, and it says she's still on the run, and I just... I'm scared and at my wit's end. I need some help."

"There isn't much that I can tell you. We've had a few sightings of her, but nothing that's panned out. We've got the local PD watching for her; we've got agents at the airport, bus station, and a couple of people in place at the taxi company. We're stretched thin. I can try to see if the locals can station someone at your estate, but I can't promise."

"I see. Well, anything you can do, I'd appreciate it."

"You're sure you can't get him to go to a different hotel? Maybe take a vacation and leave the area entirely?"

Laura shook her head. "No, I can't even get him to leave the house now."

"All right, we'll do our best to catch her, but you might consider getting a permit for a weapon to keep there at the house."

"Okay. I will look into that." Laura had never fired a gun in her life. She didn't know the first thing about getting a gun permit, but she was determined to keep her dad, Sam and herself safe.

"I will be in touch. Goodbye, Ms. Radcliffe."

Laura hung up and returned downstairs to talk to Sam. She gestured for him to join her in the kitchen, and when he did, she said, "She's going to see if they can get a cop stationed here, but she suggested I look into getting a gun permit."

Sam gave her a considering look. "That's not a bad idea. Do you know how to shoot?"

"No, not really."

"I can teach you."

Laura smiled. "How do I go about getting the permit?"

"We'll have to go to a sporting goods store. They'll have all the paperwork and run the background checks. Might take a day or two. Mine did."

"You have a gun?"

"Just a hunting rifle, but I know how to use a handgun too."

Laura frowned. "Sam, we can't both leave my dad here, and we can't take him with us."

"No, you're right." He thought about it a minute, then said, "I don't like it, but you'll have to go on your own."

Sighing, Laura nodded. Just then, her phone buzzed, and she looked at it. "It's a text from Agent Keene." She pulled it up and looked at it. "She says the cops can only do a drive-by every hour or so, because they don't have enough staff to have an officer stationed here." She dropped her hand with her phone to her side.

"I'm sorry, darlin'." Sam hugged her.

"Me too." Laura wrapped her arms around his middle and just held on. "I guess I could go look at the sporting goods store. What do I even look for?"

Sam said, "How about this: Go get your laptop, and we'll look to see what they have in stock. I can guide you through."

"Okay." Laura ran up the back stairs to her room, grabbed her laptop and returned to the kitchen.

She and Sam sat at the table until lunch, going through various weapons and everything Laura would need to know to purchase the handgun that would work the best for her. After lunch, she headed out to the store, followed Sam's directions and filled out all of the necessary paperwork to purchase the Glock 19 that they'd decided on. Once that was finished, she returned home to start dinner.

It felt as though her entire day, and all her future days, revolved around protecting and caring for her dad and Sam. Not that she regretted that, but she was putting her writing on hold because of it. She needed to let her editor, personal assistant, and publicist know she was going to be on hiatus until Bella was caught. She just hoped her fans understood.

"Sam?" she called as she entered the house through the garage.

"In here," Sam replied, from the kitchen. "How did it go?"

"Okay, I guess. They said they'd call when the paperwork

is ready." Laura looked at him and realized he was marinating steaks. "What are you doing?"

"Prepping dinner so you can get some work done."

"Ah, Sam. You are too good to me." She pushed up on her toes and kissed him.

"I don't know what you're talkin' about, darlin'. I'm just making sure I get to read that next book of yours." He winked at her.

Laura laughed. "I guess I'd better finish up those edits, then. It's the second round, so it shouldn't take too long."

She sat down at the computer and pulled up the file her editor had sent back a few days earlier. She spent the next hour and a half going through it, meticulously making sure everything was as perfect as she could get it. When she was done, she returned it to her editor for her final say.

Here you go, Erin. I've done everything I can to it. Please just go ahead and fix any errors you find and send it to Tori for formatting and upload. Things are hectic here, and I'm going to have to go on hiatus for a bit. Everything is okay at the moment, but we've had a bit of a shock. It seems the woman I hired to take care of my dad is a psychopath. We've had to have the police in, and now the FBI are trying to track her down. I'll explain more in depth at a later time. However, until things settle down, I just can't work. Thank you for all you do! Talk soon!
Xoxoxo Laura

Laura hit send and then went on to write emails to both Tori, her personal assistant, and Jacklyn, her publicist, giving them the same information. All three wrote back with understanding words, and telling her not to worry, that they would take care of everything. Tori even said she would write up a quick blog and explain to Laura's fans about what was going on without giving too many details. Laura was so grateful to have them in her life.

She shut the computer and looked up to find Sam leaning against the kitchen counter, looking at something on his phone. She smiled at the sight. "I'm finished."

He set his phone down and wrapped his arms around her. "I've been thinking."

"Oh?"

"Maybe we should talk about getting your dad into a care home until Bella is caught?"

"I wish he would go for that," Laura said, with a sigh. "Besides, what if Bella is working there under another alias? I mean, she has to be lying low somewhere."

"Hmmm, I hadn't thought of that. You're right, if she wants to stay in the area, she could very well be at one of the care homes in town." He rested his chin on her head as she put her cheek against his chest.

"I'm worried about her, Sam. What if she really does come back here?"

"I'm worried about that, too. Maybe we should sleep in shifts. If she's going to come back, she'll do it under the cover of darkness. She won't want to be seen."

"I hate that, but you're probably right."

He kissed her forehead. "I'll take the first shift tonight and wake you around two; then I'll get back up at six and help with your dad. You can take a nap after breakfast. Will that work?"

"I guess. I just don't like the fact that I won't get to cuddle up to you tonight."

"Me too, darlin', me too."

37

T he sleeping shifts were taking a toll on Laura. It had been three days, and she was already tired of it. She wanted her life back. Or at the very least, she wanted her life as it had been before Bella came into it back. Of course, that didn't mean she wanted to go back to the way things had been before with Sam. She wanted to keep that part exactly as it was at that moment.

In all this time since the incident with Bella and Andrei, she'd only had one contact with Dr. Fischer, and the one via phone at the hotel, since she didn't want to leave Sam or her dad. Dr. Fischer had agreed to suspend her appointments until she could come into the office again, with the under-standing that Laura would get in touch if she felt herself getting overwhelmed again.

Laura had immediately agreed but hadn't called her when she had the fight with her dad after the hotel experi-ment. Instead, Sam had soothed her. Still, she knew she was going to need to get in touch with her soon and let her know what was going on. She wasn't looking forward to it, though.

She and Sam had just finished helping her dad to bed

and were going to watch a movie before she headed up to bed herself for her sleeping shift. "I wish you could come up to bed with me," she said as she snuggled into his side.

"I know, darlin'. I wish I could too. I like holding you in my arms at night."

They sat together on the couch, watching an old Johnny Depp movie and making out. Too soon it ended, and it was time for Laura to head upstairs. She was tired, but she didn't want to go to bed.

"Nothing's happening. Maybe we're wrong. Maybe she's not coming back here?"

Sam arched a brow. "Do you really want to take that chance?"

Laura sighed. "No." She pressed her forehead into his chest. "I hate this."

"I do too, but until we know she's been caught, I don't want to chance it."

"Walk me up?" she asked.

Sam smiled and took her hand, pulling her up from the couch. He walked her up to her room, kissed her goodnight and then headed back downstairs to patrol the house.

Laura felt safe knowing he was down there, but it didn't stop her from wishing that he didn't have to be down there and could be up in bed with her.

She climbed into bed and plugged her phone in to charge. As she turned out the light, her phone rang. It was just after nine; she didn't know who could be calling her. Picking up her phone, she saw *Unknown Number*.

Feeling a bit of trepidation, she answered. "Hello?"

"Silly little Laura, guess who?"

Laura sat up in bed, chilled. "Bella."

"Got it in one, you sniveling little brat! I hope you're enjoying yourself, because you won't be alive much longer. I'm going to kill you, and then I'm going to murder that little brother of yours, and then when I'm done with him, I'm going to seduce Sam. I might slit his throat while I have my way with him. I haven't decided yet..."

"Shut up! You stay away from us! The police are looking for you! The FBI is all over the place, Bella! They are hunting you down!"

Bella laughed. "You are a riot! No wonder your mommy tried to beat sense into you every chance she got! She must have known how pathetic and weak you would turn out to be! Too bad she failed; she might have saved me the trouble! Still, what would be the fun in that?"

"I'm warning you, Bella, don't come here! You'll just add time to your sentence!"

Bella's cackling increased. "They'll have to catch me first! And I bet I can get to you and your precious Sam, not to mention your dear old dad—who is *so* pathetic, more pathetic than you even, I might add, and make him willingly swallow poison because he's so weak and wimpy."

"They will catch you; they will! You aren't going to get away with this, Bella. They know everything! They know about the other people you murdered! They know about your aliases; they have your brother in custody! He's being charged, too! You're going to make this worse for him! Turn yourself in!"

Bella growled into the phone. "You keep my brother out of your filthy mouth! You are a slut and a whore who was ready to jump his bones the first chance you got! You disgust me! And Andrei won't be in jail for long. I'll see to that!"

"You're delusional, Bella! You need help! Turn yourself in! Maybe they won't give you a lethal injection if you do. Just stay away from me and my family!"

"You know, after everything I did for you, the least you could do is be grateful," Bella commented.

"What?"

"I had to sit and listen to your pathetic ass whine and cry and carry on about your stupid philandering husband, and even gave you advice, but do you thank me? No. Now it's 'stay away, Bella; don't come here, Bella; don't kill me, Bella!' You are nothing but a whiny, pitiful, sad little brat who can't have her way. Oh, and Laura, you might want to find a flashlight."

At that, Bella hung up. A moment later, the entire house went dark.

38

"Sam!" Laura screamed, scared to death that Bella had somehow gotten into the house.

She sprinted from her room, using her phone as a flashlight as she ran. She hit the back stairs at a sprint, taking them three at a time as she called for Sam.

"What's happening?" Sam asked, meeting her at the bottom of the back stairs.

"Bella! She called," Laura gasped out as she held onto his arm for a moment. "I think she's cut the power!"

"Head up to your dad. I'll check the downstairs and see if I can stop her from getting in." Sam kissed her and headed to the kitchen counter.

As Laura headed toward the front stairs, she saw him grab a large knife from the block on the counter. It was a good idea to have a weapon, she thought, so on her way through the living room, she grabbed the iron poker that her mother had hit her with. She supposed if it had worked to knock her unconscious as a kid, it would work on Bella, too.

Laura raced up the stairs and straight to her father's room. She closed and locked the door behind her, and then stood guard over her dad. Every second that went by felt like an hour. She was terrified that every creak, every groan of the house, was Bella coming closer.

She heard Sam downstairs yell, "Stop, Bella! I'm not going to let you hurt them!"

Then Bella cackled that deranged laugh of hers. "As if you could stop me, you fucking busybody. We could have had some fun, but you just had to go stick your dick in my brother's leftovers. Well, I guess the party's over for you, huh?"

Laura stormed toward the door. How dare she imply to Sam that she'd slept with Andrei! She was irate that she would insinuate such a thing when she knew damn well that Laura had turned him down.

A loud crack sounded, and Laura stopped cold. She knew that sound from a million movies. It was the sound of a gun firing. "Sam!" she gasped. Her heart filled with dread as she backed up. She wanted to run to him, wanted to go and make sure he was okay, but she couldn't leave her dad if Bella was still out there.

"Oh Laura... pathetic, pitiful, Laura... looks like your sweetie Sam has an ouchy-wouchy! Aren't you going to come and save him?" Bella's voice sounded from the top of the stairs.

"Stay away from him, Bella!"

"Oh, don't you worry your dreary little heart about him. You should be worrying about what I'm going to do to you and Daddy Dearest. Sammie won't be with us too much longer anyway, he's taking a little nap at the bottom of the stairs, and I don't think he'll wake up anymore."

"You bitch!" Laura seethed.

"Knock, knock, knock... are you in there, poor, pitiful Laura? Don't you want to see your sweetie one last time before he bites the big one?"

Tears slipped from Laura's eyes. Sam couldn't be dead. She wouldn't believe it. "Fuck you!" she cried out.

"Tut, tut, tut, is that anyway to talk to the woman with the gun?" Bella asked, through the door.

"Fuck you and go to hell, Bella!"

Bella's answer was to shoot at the door handle and push the door open. "There you are! I have been looking everywhere for you! Now come here, you sniveling little bitch!" Bella raised the gun.

Laura swung the fire poker and hit Bella's wrist as she fired, knocking the gun from her hand. The gun flew to the side of the room, near the dresser.

Bella screamed and raced toward the bed. At that moment, a flash of silver in the moonlight glinted in Bella's hand as she grabbed Laura's father.

"Dad!" Laura cried out.

"Wakey, wakey, Michael," Bella whispered in his ear as she pressed the knife to his throat.

"Leave him alone! He's done nothing to you."

"Oh, but I can't do that. You all are the reason my brother is rotting away in jail, and you need to be punished for that. Don't worry, though, I'll be your judge, jury and executioner. Of course, it will be a torturous death, which is what you deserve."

"Bella? What... what? I don't understand," he muttered groggily.

"You're insane!" Laura shrieked, scared to death that Bella would nick the artery in her dad's neck and she'd have to watch him bleed out.

"I'm not the one seeing a shrink, am I?" Bella smirked. "I'm pretty sure you've got the market covered on the crazy department." She dragged Laura's dad out of bed and over toward the doorway.

Laura ignored that comment as she tried to figure out

how to save her dad. She couldn't let Bella hurt him. "Let him go, Bella; he can't hurt you."

"Bella, what's going on? Why do you have a knife?" her dad asked.

"Don't you worry about it, Michael dear, Bella is going to make sure you sleep really well. You won't ever have to worry about anything ever again by the time I'm done with you." Bella giggled like she was enjoying herself.

"You're hurting me," he muttered as he struggled in her arms.

A shadow passed behind Bella, and before she could answer him, her hand holding the knife was yanked forward and away from Michael's throat. "What the fuck?" Bella screeched as she turned around, letting Laura's dad drop to the floor in the process. "You! Why can't you just die?"

Laura ran to her father, shifting him out of the way as Bella struggled with Sam, who must have crawled his way up the stairs to get to them. Laura worried that Bella was going to kill Sam, and knew she had to do something. She just didn't know what that something was. She'd dropped the fire poker somewhere in the room, but in the darkness, she couldn't see it and wasn't sure where it was that she'd dropped it.

As Laura searched the floor, Sam screamed in pain, and Laura spun back around to see what was going on. Bella had her fingers dug into the wound on Sam's shoulder.

"Hmmm, looks like I missed your heart... maybe I can get to it through here," Bella commented as she dug her finger in deeper. "I've always heard the way to a man's heart is through his stomach, but maybe it's through the shoulder instead."

Laura suddenly remembered the gun, which had landed by the dresser. She scrambled to it, picked it up and aimed at Bella. "Sam! Move!" As soon as he was clear, Laura fired the gun, and Bella dropped.

"Sam!" Laura shouted, dropping the weapon to the ground. "Sam!" She raced across the room, hurdled over Bella's dead body into the hall to find Sam.

He was lying on the hallway floor, panting hard. "Darlin', are you okay?"

Laura knelt by him. "I'm okay, are you?"

"Other than being shot?" he said weakly.

"Right, shit! I'll call 9-1-1!"

Sam laid his head on the floor. "I'm o—" he started as Laura raced for her phone.

Laura returned a minute later, dialing as she ran back to him. "Hang on, Sam. I'm getting help."

"Your dad?" he murmured.

"Crap! Dad!" Laura hopped back up with the phone to her ear. "Hello?"

"9-1-1, what is your emergency?"

"Yes, hello, there's been a shooting! I need an ambulance!"

"Calm down, ma'am, I need the address, and I need to know if the shooter is still active."

Laura gave her the address and said, "No, no, the shooter is dead. I shot her. Please hurry! He needs an ambulance."

"The ambulance and officers are on their way."

"Thank you." Laura dropped her phone and went to check on her dad. "Dad, are you okay?"

"What's wrong with Bella?" He was staring at Bella's body in the doorway.

Laura sighed. "Bella tried to kill us. She's dead, Dad."

He nodded groggily. "I'm tired."

Laura helped him up and over to his bed. "Just rest here, Dad. I've got to see to Sam."

She hurried back into the hallway, picked up her phone and opened the front gate so the ambulance and police could enter. "Sam?"

"Mmm?"

"Sam, I need to go open the door; the ambulance is on its way, okay? I'll be right back." She put a hand to his cheek.

"M'kay," he said, but his voice was weak.

Panic filled Laura's heart as she raced down the stairs to let the coming paramedics and police officers into the house.

39

"Police! Put your hands on your head!" the officer entering the house said upon seeing Laura.

"But—" Laura started.

"Do as I said, or I'll shoot!"

Laura immediately complied. "Please! Sam's been shot! He's upstairs bleeding, and my dad is ill. He's got dementia—"

One of the officers gripped her wrists and twisted her arms behind her back, locking cuffs on her. "You have the right to remain silent, anything you say can be used against you in a court of law—" He went on telling her what her rights were.

Laura was confused. She couldn't figure out why she was being cuffed and read her Miranda rights. "Wait... what's going on?" she asked as she was patted down and her phone was taken.

"Ma'am, just sit here while we investigate the scene."

"But—" Laura started again.

"Ma'am, not another word or I will load you into the police car."

Tears slipped from her eyes. She sat down as she watched the cops go through the house.

"We've recovered the gun. There's a deceased woman up here, plus an elderly male, and another male with a shoulder wound. He appears to have passed out. Call in the medics."

The officer standing guard over Laura pressed the radio on his shoulder and called out to the ambulance that it was safe for them to enter. She watched as they came in with a gurney and followed the officer's directions to the top of the stairs.

A few minutes later, as they came back down with Sam strapped in, Laura cried out, "Sam!"

The officer restrained her, keeping her from going to Sam. "Ma'am, you are to remain here."

"Sam!" Laura cried out again. "Where are they taking him? Is he going to be okay?"

The officer ignored her.

"Load her into the car. We're taking her in for questioning. She admitted to killing this person up here in the 9-1-1 call," one of the officers upstairs called down the stairs.

"What? No! I didn't, I mean I did, but she was trying to kill us!"

"Ma'am, come with me." The officer next to her gripped her arm, pulling her to her feet.

"But my dad! He can't be left alone, he's got dementia, and he needs someone here to look after him!"

"We'll make sure someone is here to take care of your dad. Do you have a number for his primary care physician?"

"Yes, it's in my phone. Dr. Temple, but—"

"We'll make sure he's called," the officer said as he put a hand on her head and guided her into the squad car.

Laura sat in the back of the car, terrified that she would be going to jail for murder when she'd only acted in self-defense. She couldn't understand how they were arresting her when it was Bella who had been trying to kill them.

A few minutes later, the officer climbed into the driver's seat and explained that they were taking her in for questioning.

Laura silently cried, wishing she could be with Sam at the hospital. She was worried about her dad. She was worried about herself, too. She imagined all kinds of horrible things happening to her if she was charged with murder.

They pulled up to the precinct, and the officer helped her out of the car. She was fingerprinted and taken to a holding cell, where she sat with a couple of other women until an officer came to get her. She was nervous and scared, and anytime one of the other women in the cell tried to talk to her, she just shook her head and tried to make herself as small as possible.

Finally, an officer came to get her and escorted her to an interrogation room. A detective came in a moment later.

"Hello, Ms. Radcliffe, I'm Detective Robins. Would you like a coffee?"

"No, thank you."

"Very well. Can you give me your version of the events that took place earlier this evening?"

Laura nodded. "It started well before tonight, though. Can I start there?"

"If you must."

"I hired Bella and Andrei Ormond to care for my father, who has dementia. At first, everything was fine. But things started happening. Our estate manager Sam was injured; his mower was sabotaged. Then Bella claimed my dad had taken a turn for the worse, and she had his medication increased. I was suspicious and called his doctor and found out that it was only supposed to be increased if he was agitated, not daily like Bella was doing—"

"Ma'am, that has nothing to do with this evening's activities, does it? Unless you are saying you murdered her for revenge?"

"What? No! That's not what happened!" Laura exclaimed. "Please, let me tell you everything."

"Fine, go on." He was clearly annoyed, as he looked down at his watch and sighed.

"Well, I confronted her, and she made me believe that Dad was worse than I thought. Then she drugged me, and I woke up to find her going through my things."

"She drugged you?" he asked, sounding as though he didn't believe her.

"Yes! I couldn't prove it, but she did. She tried to do it again, but I knew the minute I put the food in my mouth it wasn't right, so I spit it out and got rid of it."

"So there's no proof she tried to drug you."

"Well, no—but then later, Andrei tried to drug me, and you guys came and arrested him, and Bella got away. She was going to murder my dad, but I disturbed her. You all even found the syringe she was going to use."

"I'll check on that. None of that explains what happened tonight."

"I was getting to that. I had just gone to bed when my phone rang; it was Bella. She was... well, she was telling me she was going to kill me and everyone I love. I tried to convince her to turn herself in, but she laughed and hung up, then the lights went out. I have no idea how she got back onto the property. We have a locked gate, and the property is surrounded by stone fencing. Anyway, I went to find Sam, and he said he was going to make sure she wasn't in the house, and I took a poker upstairs to defend my dad."

"We'll figure out how she got onto the property, I'm sure." He looked over his notes, then asked, "So where did you get the gun?"

"I didn't. Bella had the gun. She shot Sam, and then she shot the door to get into my dad's room. I hit her with the poker and got the gun away from her."

"Where did she shoot Mr. Willoughby?"

"In the shoulder."

"No, where in the house?"

"Oh, I'm not sure. I was upstairs in my dad's room with the door locked. I could hear them, though, so I think maybe in the front hall at the bottom of the front stairs."

"Okay, stay here. I'm going to check on your story. Can I get you that coffee while you wait?"

"No, thank you."

"Well, there will be an officer outside the door if you change your mind."

Laura sighed. She sat there for another hour, waiting for them to confirm her story.

Finally Detective Robins returned. "It looks like everything checks out and this was a case of self-defense. It seems Ms. Ormond hacked your computer gate code to get onto the property. You're free to go, Ms. Radcliffe." He handed her back her house keys and her phone.

Laura breathed a sigh of relief. "Thank you." She stood up and then realized she had no way to leave. "Can someone give me a ride home?"

"Yes, I'll have an officer drive you home," the detective agreed. "By the way, your father's doctor said to let you know that he had your dad admitted to the hospital for the night."

"What? Why?"

"He didn't say, ma'am."

As soon as Laura reached the estate, she headed into the house, went to the garage and hopped in her car. She headed straight to the hospital, speeding the whole way. She didn't care if the cops were watching, after the shit she'd just been through. She had to get to Sam and her dad. She pulled into the parking lot, parked and ran through the emergency room entrance and straight to the information desk.

"Hi, I'm here to see Sam Willoughby and my dad, Michael Radcliffe. They were both brought in, like, three hours ago."

The receptionist gave her their room numbers, and she quickly made her way to her father's room first. She needed to see that he was well. "Dad," she murmured as she entered the room.

He turned his head and looked at her. "Laura, you're here."

"Hi, Dad. Are you okay?"

He nodded. "Dr. Temple is changing my medicine." He frowned. "I'm sorry, Laura. I should have trusted you. You were right about Bella."

Laura was surprised by his words and by the fact that he remembered enough about the evening to even say that. "It's okay, Dad. I love you. I'm always going to look out for you."

He gave her a little smile. "I love you too, button. I know you will."

Button. She hadn't heard that nickname in a very long time. He used to call her that when she was a little girl. Smiling, Laura hugged him, happy that he was lucid for the moment, and that he'd told her he loved her and understood that she was trying to protect him. He probably wouldn't remember, but she would.

She stayed with him for a while, until he went to sleep. Just as she was about to leave his room, Dr. Temple entered.

"Laura, I'm glad you are okay after your ordeal. Did you get a chance to talk to your dad before he fell asleep?"

"I did. Thank you, Dr. Temple. Dad mentioned you're changing his medicine?"

"It's a new trial drug, but I thought it might help. We'll try it for a bit and see if it works. If it does, he hopefully will remain lucid for longer periods of time."

"That's good to hear."

"I'm not going to wake him, but I wanted to check his vitals. As long as he is still lucid and doing well later this morning, I'll have him released, and you can take him home."

"Thank you, Doctor."

Laura waited for him to finish with her dad, and then she hurried down the hall to Sam's room. She crept in to check on him and found him asleep. He had his shirt off, a large bandage over his left shoulder, and his arm in a sling across his chest. He looked peaceful as he slept, and she didn't want to wake him, so she quietly moved to his good side, sat down in the chair, slid her hand into his and put her head on the bed.

Laura woke a few hours later to Sam stroking her hair. She sat up and looked at him with a smile. "Sam."

"Darlin', that chair doesn't look too comfortable."

She giggled. "After the night I've had, I guess I can sleep anywhere." She stood up and kissed him. "How are you feeling?"

"I'm okay. A bit sore. The doctor said they're going to keep me another night. How's your dad? Where is he?"

"Dad's down the hall. Dr. Temple had him admitted for the night. I'm going to take him home later this morning."

"Good. Probably be best he was back in his own bed before he starts throwing a tantrum."

"True," Laura agreed. "Though, he told me Dr. Temple is changing his medicine, which I confirmed with Dr. Temple, and he told me he loves me and understands what happened with Bella."

"Wow, I'm glad to hear that. Does he think the new medicine will help?"

"It was good to hear, and yeah. Dr. Temple said it's a new trial drug that should help Dad stay lucid for longer periods of time."

"If it works, that will be great." He smiled at her but looked tired still. "Are you okay, darlin'? The cop who came in to interview me said you were at the station being questioned."

She nodded. "Yes, but after they confirmed what I was saying, they let me go. I got here as fast as I could, Sam. I was so worried." Laura felt her eyes welling up with tears. "Oh God, Sam, I thought I lost you!"

Sam pulled her down toward him and held her with his good arm. "Shhh. I'm okay, sweetness. She only winged me. She wasn't as good a shot as you are."

"That's not funny, Sam." But she gave him a watery smile anyway as she shook her head at him.

"No, you're right; still, I'm grateful that you were able to remember my directions on how to handle a gun." He kissed her. "You saved my life, darlin'. You saved all of our lives."

Laura gave him a brighter smile, but it quickly faded. "I did what I had to. I was so scared, Sam."

"I know, but you acted anyway, and I'm proud of you."

Laura curled up on the side of the bed close to him. "I wish you were coming home today too."

"Me too. Will you be able to pick me up tomorrow morning?"

"Try to stop me." Laura grinned.

"Who is going to stay with your dad?"

"I don't know yet, but if I have to call a local babysitter, I will. Nothing is going to stop me from being here to pick you up."

True to her word, the next morning at ten a.m., Laura arrived at his hospital room ready to walk out with him. She was carrying a big bouquet of flowers and a balloon that said

'Get Well Soon' on it and another that said 'I love you' and was shaped like a heart.

Sam eyed the balloons. "Is that true?" he asked, pulling her into his arms as he sat on the side of the bed, waiting for the nurse to bring the wheelchair that they were making him use to get out of the hospital.

Laura nodded. "It is absolutely true. I love you, Sam."

"I love you too, darlin'."

She walked with him down to the front entrance and then went to get the car. The nurse opened the passenger door, and Sam waved her off before she attempted to help him in. Laura had to swallow a smile as the tiny woman tried to manhandle him into the seat.

"Thank you, Nurse Cara, I think I can take it from here," Sam grumbled.

"Take care now," she said and waved.

Laura drove Sam back to the estate and told him he was staying in her suite while he recovered. When they reached the house, Laura said, "Oh, I want to introduce you to someone."

"Who?" Sam asked, following her in and capturing her hand.

"My best friend. I called her last night, and she drove up this morning to stay with my dad so I could come get you." Laura held Sam's hand as they walked out to the back deck, where her dad and Kelly were sitting enjoying the nice weather.

"Hey, how's the hero?" Kelly asked.

"Who? Me or Laura?" Sam asked with a grin.

"If you're Sam—which I'm guessing, by the look of you and the fact that Laura has a death grip on your hand, you are—then I meant you," Kelly replied with a laugh.

Laura shook her head as she grinned at her best friend.

"Kelly, this is Sam. Sam, this is Kelly, my best friend in the entire world."

Kelly eyed him and then leaned in toward Laura. "You're right. He's a hottie!"

Sam laughed. "It's nice to meet you, Kelly."

"It's nice to meet you too, Sam." Kelly shook his hand. "Laura has told me a lot about you."

"Is that why my ears have been burning over the years?" Sam asked, laughing.

Laura blushed and squeezed his fingers in hers.

Laura's dad looked between her and Sam and noticed their clasped hands as he stood to hold a hand out for Sam to shake. "Sam, thank you for helping protect me and Laura," he said, still as lucid as he had been the day before.

The new pills that Dr. Temple had him on seemed to be working pretty well, which made Laura very happy. Things had been much easier around the house because of it.

After shaking her dad's hand, Sam leaned in and kissed Laura's temple. "Anytime, sir. I would do anything to protect her and you."

Her dad sat back down, grumbling about public displays of affection.

Laura didn't care what he thought. She turned in Sam's arm, wrapped her arms around his neck and kissed him. He was her hero, and she loved him more than anything. There wasn't a thing in the world her dad could say that would destroy her happiness now that she'd found it.

40

FOUR MONTHS LATER...

"Quiet, Billy, we can't let Mom know we're outside; she'll be mad at us." *Laura hushed her brother as they snuck out the kitchen door to the deck. She needed to get them clear of the house so her mother wouldn't see them.*

"But I wanna watch cartoons, Laurie! Blue is coming on!"

"I know you do, but Mom is in one of her moods, and she's yelling at Dad. If she sees us, it will be us she comes after. Do you want her to beat you with the wooden spoon again?"

Billy immediately shut down and started crying.

Laura picked him up and hurried down the deck steps out to the yard. She ran with him as quickly as she could past the caretaker cottage where old man Freemont lived. The place looked like it had seen better years. Ivy crawled up the side, there were spots on the roof that were in disrepair, and the steps to the porch were broken. Laura didn't stop, though, even when Mr. Freemont tried to call them over. She just kept going while Billy wailed.

She was lucky that he was still small enough to carry and wasn't too heavy. Otherwise, she was sure that their mother would have caught them. Once they were past the cottage, Laura stopped.

She had built a little fort back here at the edge of the property years ago, well before Billy was born. It had always been her refuge when her mother was on the attack and she needed to get out of the way.

Mr. Freemont never told on her, and her mother never ventured this far back on the property, so it was the perfect place to hide out. He'd even helped her build a roof over the little fort so that she could be out there when it rained if she had to be. In the fort she kept some books, a few little toys, a deck of cards and a blanket. Sometimes Mr. Freemont would bring his portable radio out and set it up for her so she could listen to music.

Laura set Billy down. "Hush now, Billy. Mom won't find us here. It's okay."

Billy sniffled.

"Do you want to play a game with me?"

He nodded.

Laura pulled out the deck of cards and set up a game of Go Fish. They played for much longer than they should have, and Laura now feared running into her mom when they made their way back to the house.

"Billy, we need to go..."

Billy helped her put everything away in the wooden box where she kept everything, and then, as the sun was setting, they hurried down the path.

"You'd better run for it," Mr. Freemont suggested. "She's looking for you."

Laura felt a shiver of fear pass through her. "Come on, Billy. We have to get back to the house and upstairs without Mom catching us," she urged.

It didn't matter though. As they passed the pond, she could see their mother standing at the edge of the deck, her arms folded, the heavy rolling pin in her hand. Laura was terrified she would hit Billy with it.

"I'll distract Mom, you run, okay? Find Mrs. Shepard, she'll get you upstairs away from Mom," Laura whispered.

Billy looked up at her and nodded.

Laura let go of Billy's hand just before they reached the deck. "Wait till I get her to come for me," she murmured, "then run as fast as you can."

Laura knew that they were both faster than her mom. She'd put on a lot more weight since having Billy. Still, she'd take a beating to keep him safe. Laura put a brave face on and tried to smile. "I was just taking Billy f-for a... a walk, Mom. Did... did you need me?"

Her mother dropped her arms, the rolling pin swinging from her hand as she moved forward, her face filled with wrath. "You are nothing but a filthy little liar!" she yelled.

Laura swallowed hard but stayed where she was, about three feet from her mom. "Go, Billy," she murmured, barely moving her lips.

"You think I don't know you've been gone for hours? Sneaking out of the house like some little harlot! And in that!" She came toward Laura.

"Mom, it's just shorts and a tee shirt, and I stayed on our prop—"

"Lies!" Mom screamed, swinging the rolling pin at her.

Laura put her arm up to block the blow as Billy ran past their mom and into the house. She shrieked in pain as the wooden pin connected with her wrist. "Fuck!" she cried out and then regretted it as her mother swung the pin again with one hand and slapped her with her other.

"Shut your filthy mouth! You will not use foul words in my house!"

Laura screamed again as the rolling pin connected with her side.

Her mom grabbed her by her hair and dragged her into the

house. "Get inside, you little slut! I will not have you out whoring yourself to the neighbors!"

Laura whimpered.

"Sweetness, shhhh, it's just a nightmare," a voice murmured as a soothing hand stroked her hair.

Laura blinked, coming awake. "Sam?" she asked, trying to calm her racing heart.

"It's me, baby. You're okay..." he replied.

Laura went through her steps, grounding herself in reality with things she could see, hear and feel. Things that were real. After a moment she sat up and then snuggled into Sam's waiting arms. "Thank you."

"Want to talk about it?"

She sighed. "It was another nightmare from when I was kid. Billy was maybe two or three... I think he was just about to turn three, actually. Mom broke my wrist." She shook her head. "She was an awful woman. I hated her so much. I still do."

"After hearing some of your stories, I don't blame you, darlin'." Sam held her.

Laura smiled and looked at the clock. It was just a little after midnight. "I'm sorry I woke you."

"You don't have to apologize; I don't like knowing you're suffering. I'd rather you did wake me up so I can help you through it."

Laura lifted a hand to his cheek and looked him in the eyes. "I love you, Sam."

"I love you too, baby. You ready to try sleeping again, or do you want to pass some time in another activity?" He wiggled his eyebrows at her.

Laura giggled and then kissed him.

They spent the next hour making love, and by the time they were finished, Laura was well and truly exhausted. She fell into a restful sleep and didn't have another nightmare.

Hours later, Laura yawned and stretched as she woke up in Sam's arms. She'd slept much more peacefully this time around. The nightmares overall were getting fewer and farther between, though, now that she had Sam in her life, and she was grateful for it.

She snuggled closer to him, nuzzling his neck. When he didn't stir, she began nibbling at his ear, then planting kisses along his jaw and up to his lips. Sam grinned as she kissed him.

"Good morning, darlin'," he mumbled against her lips and pulled her close.

"Good morning, Sam." Laura kissed him again.

"How did you sleep?" he asked.

She knew that he was asking if she'd had any more troubling dreams. "Really well. No more traumatic nightmares." She smiled at him.

"Good. I hate that you have them."

Laura thought about it. "It wasn't all bad. I did recall something that I'd forgotten. Something good, well, not good exactly, but something that wasn't bad."

"What's that?" Sam asked, clearly curious.

"When I was little and wanted to hide from my mother for a while, I had a fort. It was just behind this cottage. Did you ever meet Mr. Freemont?"

"The estate manager who was here before me?"

Laura nodded. "Yes, him."

"Once. He was pretty old and decided to retire in Florida near his daughter, didn't he?"

Laura shrugged. "I don't know about that part. Anyway, he helped me build it and usually tried to keep watch for me so I would have a warning if Mom was on the warpath. He and Mrs. Shepard both did."

"Why did they never do something about your mom?"

"I think they were just as afraid of her as Dad was, and they didn't want to lose their positions."

"Hmmm. I wouldn't have kept quiet if I'd known she was beating you or Billy."

And that was another thing she loved about Sam. She knew he wouldn't have. "I know. She stopped hitting Billy, though, once he made it through puberty. He was much bigger than she was, so Dad was her only punching bag left."

"I did hear some doozies of a fight, though, between them. Yelling, shouting... Billy stayed out a lot in his teen years. My guess it was to keep away from her."

Laura nodded. "Yeah. I tried to have him come stay with me, but the dorms weren't great for that."

"I guess they weren't," Sam agreed. "So tell me about this fort?"

"Oh, right." Laura smiled. "It was just back there, a little ways into the trees. Mr. Freemont put a roof on it for me. Mom never came back here, so she didn't know about it. I had a wooden box with a few things in it, a little wooden chair, a blanket. Anything I could bring without Mom noticing, it made its way back there to the fort."

"Wait, I remember seeing something like that when I moved in. It was falling down, and I thought Mr. Freemont had just used that area to store extra firewood or something for the cottage. I didn't know it was your safe space."

Laura smiled. "Kind of the point," she said, lying in his arms. "If anyone knew that's what it was, it wouldn't have been a safe space for long."

"True," he agreed. "Well, I'm sorry you had to have that."

Laura patted his chest and smiled. Sam was a good man. The best. "How about some breakfast?" she asked.

"Mmmm, sounds delicious, but how about dessert first?" He quirked an eyebrow at her.

An hour later, after they'd both had their fair share of

'dessert', Laura climbed out of bed. She scurried to the bathroom, showering and getting dressed while Sam got the coffee started. She headed to the kitchen down the hall from their room in his cottage. She wrapped her arms around his back and kissed his shoulder.

Sam turned in her arms and gathered her close before kissing her properly. "I'm going to go shower while you fix food."

"Good plan," Laura said with a grin. "Don't take too long."

Sam winked and headed back to the bathroom.

Laura made them pancakes and bacon and had them on the table by the time he returned. "What's on the agenda for today?" she asked as he sat down.

"The usual: I've got the front lawn to mow, the garden to weed..." He grinned as he picked up his fork. "Are you staying here or headed up to your dad's?"

"I'm going to go up there and check on the staff and Dad. I might sit out on the deck and do some writing while I watch my muse in the garden." She leered at him.

Sam laughed. "So you think this group is working out?"

"I do. I like them, they're professional, and I had Angela do every kind of background check she could think of on each of them." Laura laughed.

She'd hired an entire staff of people to care for and protect her dad, but not without making one hundred percent sure that each of them were who they said they were. She wasn't about to hire another Bella and Andrei by accident. Because of that, she met with all the caregivers' references in person, since they were all people from the surrounding area. Unlike the references Bella and Andrei had used, who'd turned out to be other con artists.

"I'm glad. Now, what is it you'll be working on today? The new book or something else?"

"Probably the new book..." Laura paused and then gave

him a shy look. "You didn't say what you thought of the one you were reading before bed last night. What did you think?"

"Well, I have to admit, I didn't really care for the Andrew character."

Laura snickered. "Obviously. Neither did I or Lydia, considering how the story ended."

Sam chuckled. "True. It's funny, in all the books I've read that you've written, the hero is always very similar."

Laura blushed. "Well, they are always modeled after the same muse."

"Oh, really?" Sam grinned. "And who might that be?" he asked as he nuzzled her neck.

"You really don't know?" She laughed.

"I'd rather you tell me yourself."

"You, Sam. My hero is always you. He goes by many different names, but it is and always will be you." Laura leaned in and kissed him.

"You never used Jim?" Sam pulled back slightly. He had a curious look in his eye.

"Nope." Laura shook her head. "I settled when I shouldn't have. I'm just glad he finally signed the papers, and we didn't have to go to court."

"I think he figured out you've learned how to stand up for yourself, and he wouldn't be weaseling his way back into your life by not signing." Sam grinned.

"Now, if I could just get Billy to talk to me, everything would be perfect." Laura sighed as she thought about her brother.

After telling him about Bella, Billy had started to ghost her, claiming he needed time to decide if he wanted Laura in his life. It hurt her that he was being so distant, but she understood his feelings and didn't push the issue.

"He still hasn't called?" Sam asked gently.

Laura shrugged. "No. But I promised him I'm give him his space and let him work through it without me bugging him."

Sam drew her close and kissed her. "It will all work out, sweetness. I promise. He'll come around."

"I hope so, Sam." Laura snuggled into his shoulder. "I hope so."

A FEW DAYS LATER, Laura's phone rang. She reached for it with her heart in her throat. "Billy?"

"Hi, sis."

"Billy, I'm so glad you called. How are you?"

"I'm doing okay. I'm... I'm sorry I didn't call sooner, it's just been—I'm seeing a therapist. He's helping me work through my anger issues and the fact that Mom abused us."

"That's great, Billy. I don't know if I told you, but I've been seeing a therapist of my own for a while now. It helps to talk to a professional."

"It does. I need to tell you I'm sorry. I'm sorry I wasn't there to help with Dad when you needed me to. And I'm sorry I blamed you for the whole 'Bella and Andrei being murderers and coming after me' thing."

"It's okay. I understood."

He gave a wry laugh. "You always say that. Are you doing okay? I mean, I know you had to defend yourself, and well... are you okay, sis?"

"I'm good, for the most part. No nightmares about that, at least."

"That's good to hear," Billy said. "I read in the paper that Andrei got a life sentence for two of the murders he and his sister committed."

"Yeah, he'll be in jail for the rest of his life. We don't have to worry about him anymore."

"I'm glad." Billy paused for a moment and then said, "So I've been thinking I might come for a visit."

"Really? That would be great. Can you do that with school?"

"I have a break coming up, so yeah."

"Do you want me to have a room at the house ready for you?"

"No, no, I'm not going to stay there. I don't think I can stomach that. I'll get a hotel room."

"If you're sure."

"I'm sure."

They chatted for a bit longer, and then Laura hung up and went to find Sam. "Guess what!" she exclaimed.

Sam pulled her into his arms. "What?"

"You were right. Billy called. He's coming to visit on his next school break!"

Sam swung her up into his arms and kissed her passionately. "I'm glad to hear it, sweetness."

Laura wrapped her arms around his neck and kissed him back.

With everything that she had been through, the abuse from her mother, the disaster of her marriage, the events with Bella and Andrei, and then Bella's death at her hands, Laura knew that she'd had to go through all of it to come out the other side stronger for it. She was so grateful to have made it through alive and even more grateful that her dad and Sam had as well.

She promised herself that she would always cherish every second of every day that she got to spend with them. Especially Sam. The man who loved her. He was her muse and her one true love, and she would do everything in the world to make him as happy as he made her.

THANK YOU FOR READING

Did you enjoy reading *The Night Nurse*? Please consider leaving a review on Amazon. Your review will help other readers to discover the novel.

ABOUT THE AUTHOR

Cole Baxter loves writing psychological suspense thrillers. It's all about that last reveal that he loves shocking readers with.

He grew up in New York, where there was crime all around. He decided to turn that into something positive with his fiction.

His stories will have you reading through the night—they are very addictive!

ALSO BY COLE BAXTER

Inkubator Books Titles

The Perfect Suitor

The Betrayal

I Won't Let You Go

The Night Nurse

Other Titles

Prime Suspect

What She Witnessed

Deadly Truth

Finding The Other Woman

Trust A Stranger

Follow You

Did He Do It

What Happened Last Night

Perfect Obsession

Going Insane

She's Missing

The Perfect Nanny

What She Forgot

Stolen Son

Before She's Gone

Printed in Poland
by Amazon Fulfillment
Poland Sp. z o.o., Wrocław
09 December 2022

fce37fd5-96a2-4786-8ba6-e40608d894d9R01